HEROES OF AFGHANISTAN
GHOSTS OF TORA BORA

ERIC MEYER

HEROES OF AFGHANISTAN

GHOSTS OF TORA BORA

ERIC MEYER

PROLOGUE

The village stank worse than the last. That one was Deh Bala, in Southern Afghanistan, near the border with Pakistan, nestling in the foothills of the mountain range that divided the two countries, known as the Hindu Kush. This village didn't even have a name. As if they hadn't considered it worth the effort. It stank of decay, of filth, of neglect, and of despair. Second Lieutenant Sara Carver glanced at the part ruined dwellings, at the men sitting outside, their faces reflecting a dull acceptance of the hardship of their lives, an absence of any hope, sometimes, an absence of any emotion. Their sole bulwark against the hopelessness of their existence. The production of the opium was Afghanistan's wealth and its poverty, for the crop brought in huge sums of money, courtesy of the illegal drugs trade. Money used to fill the coffers of the offshore bank accounts, or to buy weapons and munitions for the insurgents. Little found its way to those most in need.

"We'll call a halt here and search the houses," her platoon commander First Lieutenant Tony Arnaz called over the radio, "We'll cover the track at either end. Sergeant Becker, position the SAWs."

Carver indicated her approval. There was little sign of any threat, and the Squad Automatic Weapons, M249 light machine guns, would be more than enough to guard against any unwelcome surprises.

"Lieutenant Carver, start checking out the houses. You know what you're looking for. Guns, explosives, anything the Talibs could use against us."

"Drugs, Lt?"

"Nope, forget the drugs. I reckon if I was in this place, I'd need some compensation."

"Copy that."

She stretched out a hand and reached up to open the hatch of the Stryker AFV. She climbed down to the muddy track that comprised the main street and looked around. It all looked peaceful, so there was no need to worry too much. Since she'd been in Afghanistan, she'd searched a dozen places like this. Wretched, poverty stricken, and the inhabitants had enough problems without joining the insurgency. A quick check and they could move on. The stench was fearful. The rain had been and gone, leaving in its place a sticky, humid heat. She went inside the first hut, a single room. Four children stared back at her, their faces covered in sores. A bundle of rags moved, and she swung her M-16 around, but she recognized a woman. She looked ancient, but this was Afghanistan, so she would be half the age she looked.

Besides the sores, her eyes were half closed, covered in mucous so she looked almost blind. A simple infection, all this family needed was antibiotic cream, and it would clear up in days. She may as well tell them they needed a shipment of gold bars, they had about as much chance of getting hold of them. Except she had the antiseptic, and she could at least help these people. Private DeJesus was covering the door, and he looked alarmed as she tumbled out.

"Something wrong, Lt?"

"No, we're good. I need the medical kit from the Stryker, would you bring it for me."

"Sure, give me a minute."

While she waited, she looked up and down the street. The soldiers were going from house to house, and from the expression on their faces most felt as sickened as she did.

What are we fighting for? How can we tell these people we're winning? That when we finally leave the country, their government will keep them safe and secure. It won't. Their government will continue to treat them worse than dogs. I know it, and they know it.

DeJesus brought the medical bag. She went back inside and spent time cleaning the worst of their sores with swabs and applying the ointment. Whether they would remember the American largesse was moot. The next day could bring the Taliban, Al Qaeda, ISIS, or some other jumped up warlord. Hand out a few loaves of bread, and they'd have bought the souls of these villagers forever. Although it wasn't why she did what she did. People didn't deserve to live like this. Period.

As she finished up, she thought for the hundredth time of her motives for being here. She'd planned to be a lawyer, and after graduating law school, elected to join the military branch, the JAG. The love of her life, Kevin Fallon, had been a line infantry officer with the First Infantry Division, the Big Red One. She had a golden future mapped out. Her mind wandered back to the previous year, when it had all seemed perfect.

* * *

"Sara, I'll do a few years in the military, see some service overseas, and when I get back, I'm going into politics. My father is a Senator, and I know my way around Washington, the way the system works. I can make a difference, my darling. I know I can. Not like the usual yes-men. I'll work to give ordinary people a chance to have good, prosperous lives. Create jobs, work to reduce our dependence on crude oil for energy. Clean up the environment."

She'd laughed. "You need to get elected first, Kevin. One step at a time before you become a clean energy crusader, first things first."

His look was serious. "First things first, every politician needs a wife. Sara, will you marry me?"

Two months later, they tied the knot. Six weeks after that, he shipped out for Afghanistan, as a military adviser. He was in country for five weeks before a long-range sniper bullet killed him with a shot to the head. The day after the funeral, she applied for transfer to the Infantry Branch. This was her first assignment, Afghanistan, just like Kevin, and over the protestations of her family. She was determined to make a difference, continue what her deceased husband had started. Besides, she was a first-rate shot, had learned the art of shooting at her father's ranch in Oregon. All she needed was a chance to prove it. Now she was here, and there were other priorities, like antiseptic ointment.

* * *

She still had time. The engines hadn't started, and no one was shouting the recall. She rummaged in the pockets of her camos and came up with two Hershey bars. She kept them for emergencies, although so far she hadn't needed them. This was an emergency. The kids looked half-starved. Broke them into two each, and shared them out. Dull, brutalized faces lit up, and they munched the candy. It felt good. Real good. They needed the ointment, but they needed the sweet treat more, a reminder that humanity hadn't deserted them. Now it was time to leave.

"Private DeJesus, I'm coming out."

She walked toward the door and felt uneasy. No answering shout, and no noise from outside. Come to think of it, she'd heard nothing for some time. She emerged into the open, and she was staring into the barrel of a gun, an American weapon, an M-16 like the one she carried. However, the man holding the weapon wasn't an American. Tribal robes, black turban, and beard.

Oh, shit. Oh, no!

He gestured for her to drop the weapon. When she obeyed, he held out his hand for the pistol she carried in the holster on her belt. The other members of her platoon were already disarmed, with their hands held high the air. The man holding the gun swung it around and clubbed her on the side of the head. She went down into the mud, half-conscious. As she lay there, she watched them tie the hands of the soldiers behind their backs and force them to kneel. What happened next made her feel sick and shake with fear. An insurgent went to each man and executed him with a bullet to the back of the head.

Finally, he got to her and raised the pistol. Part of her was terrified, and part elated. She'd be reunited with Kevin, in a better place. She felt the steel muzzle placed against her head. The elation went away, to be replaced with terror.

It can't end here, in this stinking shithole. It can't.

Someone shouted. He'd found the medical kit she'd used inside the hut. The man standing behind her came around to face her. A big man, heavily muscled, and taller than his companions. His brutal face showed the scars of countless conflicts. No mustache, just a long beard below his chin.

"You are a doctor?"

He spoke English, but the accent was strange. Not American. She couldn't contain her surprise. "You're what, Russian, Uzbek, something like that?"

The next blow from the butt of the M-16 hurled her back into the mud. "I asked you a question."

Consumed with fury, she screamed up at him, "Fuck you, asshole. No, I'm not a doctor. Shoot me, you worthless piece of shit!"

She expected the bullet to come, welcomed it, and wanted an end to this. It didn't come.

"You know how to use these things?" He gestured to the medical kit.

"Of course I know."

A pause. "Very well, you may live. We have need of someone to nurse those who are sick and wounded, and who know how to use our captured American medical supplies. If you do as I tell you, perhaps I won't kill you."

His eyes flicked to a man standing behind her, and she felt her arms twisted behind her back and tied together. The man pushed her, and she looked back at the man who'd spoken to her.

"Where are you taking me?"

He smiled. "Where? To my home, our local headquarters."

"And where would that be? Pakistan?" She needed to know, it could be to her advantage, if she got to escape. Knowing which country she was in would be a start.

"Pakistan? No, it is quite close to here. A cave complex, you may have heard of it. The name is Spin Ghar. Local people know it as the Black Cave."

"I've never heard of it."

His smile was ruthless and cruel. "You will have heard of it. You Americans call it Tora Bora."

CHAPTER ONE

Rafe Stoner glanced out the window of his apartment and surveyed the street below. Everything was quiet, and why shouldn't it be? The insurgency was a long way away, in Helmand, and in the regions bordering the Pakistan frontier. Jalalabad was peaceful. Well, almost peaceful, if you excluded the guy trying to kill him. Twice in the past ten days. The first time, he was driving his black Jeep Wrangler along the highway when a bullet whined past the open window, missed his head by two inches, and exited through the passenger window; which was also open, so he didn't need to replace the glass.

He put it down to a stray shot, not unusual in Afghanistan, until the second time. He'd stepped outside the door to his building and stopped to check he hadn't forgotten his billfold. A bullet spat toward him, past where he would have been if he'd kept on going, and buried itself far behind. It was enough to make him take notice, yet when he went looking for the shooter, he'd gone. This time he put it down to enemy action. He'd made more than a few enemies during his time in country, both during his service in the U.S. Navy SEALs and since, when he earned his living in ways that didn't meet with universal approval. Officially, he ran a surplus machinery business that rarely seemed to sell anything. Off the record, he part-owned Ma Kelly's, the brothel that was also his home in the apartment on the third floor.

Less well known was his major source of cash. Stoner was a gun for hire, a man who would take on the more difficult jobs, where the target was both wary and well defended. They were also the jobs that paid best, large sums of money. He was good at what he did and had no shortage of clients. Life was good, as long as he stayed alive to enjoy it. He made a mental note to take a good, long look for whoever was trying to fill his body full of holes. He took it seriously when people tried to kill him. So much so he'd even cut down on the booze. It wasn't easy, but neither was dying. That's what he'd do if he staggered out through the front door with half his brain still drowned in last night's alcohol.

He shrugged on the harness that held the holsters for his guns, the two .50 caliber Desert Eagles. Despite their weight, he never felt dressed without them. Pulled on the long, black leather coat and prepared to go out. Someone wrapped their arms around him. His nose twitched as he sensed the familiar fragrance of the eager young woman who often shared his bed, Anahita, one of the whores from downstairs. In her early twenties, she still looked fresh and young, despite the rigors of the life she led.

"Stoner, you're going out. Will you be back soon?" She meant would it be before she started her shift in the brothel.

He turned and regarded her face, her makeup renewed after the frenzied night they'd spent together. "I'll be a while, Anahita. You'd best get to work."

She pulled a face. "You should marry me, and then I wouldn't need to go with other men. You'd have me all for yourself."

She waited for an answer, her face anxious as always. She asked that question at least once a week.

"I told you, I'm not the marrying kind."

Her face fell. "You don't know what you're missing."

He didn't argue, but he knew what he was missing. He'd had plenty of girls, and most ended up the same way. Dead. His was a violent business.

"I'll see you tomorrow, if I'm around."

"You're a cold-hearted bastard, Stoner, you know that?"

"Sure do."

"What about giving me a key for the front door?" she shouted as he was leaving.

"Pick the lock like you always do. I'll be seeing you."

He made it out the front door before his cellphone rang. When he answered, it was his longtime friend. He had a single friend. Greg Blum. Half Russian, half Afghan, and married to the Afghan girl Stoner had once fallen in love with.

"I thought you might care to come out here for dinner tonight, if you're not doing anything. Faria and the kids would like to see you."

He thought with pleasure of the family he'd come to regard as his own, and loved as his own. He'd even become godfather to the three children. "Sure, sure, I'd love to. Everything okay?"

A pause. "Not exactly, no."

He felt concern. Anything that threatened the Blum family he took seriously. "Tell me about it."

"I'll talk to you tonight. Faria's cooking up something good, and we can enjoy it first with the kids. When they've gone to bed, we can have a chat."

"It's nothing urgent, is it? I mean, you don't have a problem out at the farm?"

"Nothing like that. We'll see you later."

He ended the call and walked down the staircase to the first floor, through the door into the bar, AKA Ma Kelly's brothel. Lots of brass, tasteful paintings on the wall, woodwork, plush furnishings, and thick carpet; to Western eyes, a tacky collection, put together with more money than sense. To Afghan eyes, the very height of good taste and opulence, the punters were primarily Afghan, as was their money.

The odors were the same as ever, despite a thorough daily clean; stale booze, tobacco smoke, and the charged, indefinable smell of sexual tension. He waved a hello to Ma Kelly, the busty Western peroxide blonde who owned the other half of the premises. She ran a good business, and girls clamored to work in the brothel. The pay was a fortune for most Afghans. Besides, each girl knew she'd enjoy security and protection during her employment. She would also receive every penny of the money she earned, cash on the nail, every week.

He walked through to the street door and peered out. He sensed something, and he couldn't figure it out. A feeling of being watched, and hard as he looked, he saw no one. No sign of eyes watching from inside a darkened room across the street. No parked cars with occupants carefully doing nothing as they averted their eyes. Yet he couldn't shake the feeling.

A last look around, he loosened the Desert Eagles in their holsters, and stepped out into the bustle of Jalalabad. He had business to attend to, and it would take him most of the day. Provided he stayed alive. Nothing had changed from the day before, and the day before that, lots of four-story buildings, street markets, motor scooters, and a few Tuk Tuks. SUVS everywhere, and on the sidewalks, men with guns, most were AKs. Carrying a gun in Afghanistan was a mark of adulthood, although some children carried AKs. But none were shooting at him.

He relaxed and went to the lock up where he kept the Wrangler these days. Unlocked the doors, and there was his Jeep, in all its shining, gloss black and chrome glory. The engine fired up first time, and he drove out through the city to Jalalabad International Airport, five klicks away. Parked outside a dilapidated looking office building close to the main runway and went inside. The obese Afghan who looked up didn't seem pleased to see him. He was sweating, despite the temperature being cool, and beads of perspiration dripped down his cheeks.

"Stoner."

"Yeah, it's me. How you doing, Shafiq?"

"Good, good. What can I do for you?"

"You can pay me for starters. You owe me ten thousand dollars."

He closed his eyes for a second. "I thought it was ten thousand."

"Twenty, ten on account and ten when the job was done. Payment is overdue."

"Stoner, business has been very bad, very bad. I need more time."

He nodded. "Yeah, I guess you do. I'll give you two minutes to come up with the cash."

He pretended not to notice the man push a button under his desk. Knew why he was going it, and prepared himself for what was about to happen. Shafiq Mohammed was an import/export merchant. That's what it said on his letterhead. It didn't say what he exported, opium to eager buyers around Asia. Neither did he say how he dealt with those who tried to muscle in on his operations. Stoner was fine with legitimate competition. But when Shafiq had a contender who also dabbled in the insurgency, killed soldiers and cops, and traded in drugged up female slaves for Asian brothels, he drew the line. The last contract was one such target. A man who enjoyed inflicting vicious cruelty on the women he traded. Stoner was happy to kill him. He'd be even happier when Shafiq paid him.

The door opened, and two men stepped into the office. One was big, with a face that told of a lifelong drug habit, and a long history of street fighting. A thug. He carried an assault rifle. Russian made, or Chinese copy. Crude wooden stocks and enclosed front sights, so it would be a Type 56. Chinese 7.62mm made by Norinco. The other man was shorter and younger than the merchant, although on his way to a similar problem with obesity. He carried a pistol tucked into the waistband of his pants.

The merchant smiled. "These men will escort you out through the door, Stoner. I'm sorry, but I paid you the money. Ten thousand, what we agreed."

He glanced at the two men, and his eyes should have warned them. "I don't want to hurt them, Shafiq. Why don't you pay me what you owe?"

"Goodbye, Stoner."

"I'll see you in hell, Shafiq."

He heard a chuckle behind him. "Probably."

He'd have warned them about the Desert Eagles, so he left them in their holsters, walked between the two men, and struck. Slammed a finger strike into the eyes of the big man, swept a leg around to bring down the smaller man on his right, and as he went down, slid out the Desert Eagles. Cocked and aimed them at the two men. The big man was struggling to get up.

"No, don't kill them. Please!"

He wasn't fixing to kill them, but if he wanted to believe it, that was no problem.

"Why shouldn't I kill them?"

"He is my son." He meant the shorter man, "I will pay you what I owe you."

He unlocked a drawer in his desk, took out a bundle of cash, and passed it to Stoner with trembling hands. "Now we are square."

"Good to do business with you, Shafiq. Call me any time."

He started again for the door and again stopped. The shorter man, the son, had drawn his pistol, a Colt .45 automatic. Aimed it at Stoner's belly, and his hand was shaking like he had the palsy. "I...I c-can't let you l-leave. Give my father back the m-money."

"No."

"No!" His eyes widened, and he tried, without success, to hold the gun steady, "I'll shoot."

Stoner walked toward the door and stared at the young man. "No, you won't shoot."

"W-why is that?"

"Because you left the safety catch on. That gun won't fire until you take it off."

His eyes looked down, and Stoner hit him. Smashed a fist into his face, and as he fell, knocked the gun out of his hand and kicked it away. He lay on the floor, blood streaming from a broken nose. He looked up in despair. "You're going to kill me."

Stoner sighed. "Not this time, but I'd watch yourself. Next time, the man you point a gun at may not be so friendly and forgiving as me. Got it?"

"Y-yes."

"Good."

He walked from the office and climbed into his Wrangler. They were all the same, amateurs. Thought a gun in their hands made them God. It didn't. It just made them an amateur with a gun, a fatal combination.

Later that day, he drove the thirty klicks to the Blum farm, two klicks outside the village of Mehtar Lam. Greg and Faria farmed a few acres, and lived with their adopted children seventeen-year-old Ahmed, and two younger girls, Kaawa and Rahima. And their dog, no ordinary dog, Archer was a former Marine dog. Trained to sniff out explosives, he had a much wider range of talents, like tracking an enemy, sometimes at incredible distances. No matter where they went, or how far they traveled, Archer would find them. When he found them, he was every bit as ferocious as the Marines who'd trained him. When he wasn't tracking, he was a pussycat.

Stoner parked the Wrangler, and the kids came tumbling out. He handed out presents for each of them. He always kept a stock of goodies in the glove box of the Wrangler. This time it was boxes of candy, almost unobtainable in Afghanistan. He left them squealing and greeted Greg and Faria, simultaneously smoothing Archer's coat.

"Good to see you both. You're looking well."

"Which is more than I can say for you," Faria admonished him, "You should cut down on the booze, and find yourself a good woman."

"I did cut down, and the woman I found told me to take a hike."

They swapped glances. He'd never got over her, yet they both knew it had ended long ago. All that remained in his heart were memories, and he wished them both all the best.

"I don't blame her," Greg chuckled, "Especially since she found a better-looking guy."

She'd found Greg, and they'd been happy ever since, more so since the kids joined them after the death of their parents. They settled around the table. Faria and the girls served up heaps of delicious food, spicy, Afghan delicacies, although in deference to Stoner, an American, there was always a plate of fries. When they'd finished, they watched the kids play for a while, and then they went to bed. Night had fallen, and they sat on the stoop, watching the stars. The night was cold and crisp, but also fine and dry, too good to end by going inside. Besides, they didn't want the kids to overhear.

He waited as Faria told him how Ahmed still wasn't sure when to make another stab at medical training. He already knew about his doubts, and he listened and waited. Eventually, Greg came to the point.

"It's Faria's cousin. Her name is Shahay, and she needs help. The girl lives in Achin, in the Nangarhar Province that borders on Pakistan. The locals are all Pashtun, all Muslim. Tribal, you know what I mean."

"I know."

He knew more, but he didn't want to say. He had fought a bloody battle in that region and left more than a few men behind when they finally pulled out.

"Achin is home to the Shinwari tribe, one of the largest of the Pashtun tribes.

A while back she fell in love with a man from the Tajik region of Northern Afghanistan. He came there on a contracting job for a local utility company. They met, and they fell in love, you know how it goes."

He darted Faria a surreptitious glance.

"Her family went crazy, forbid her to see him. Yet despite everything, she said she plans to marry this man."

"I assume they weren't impressed."

"They're going to kill her. It's a matter of family honor. They're just waiting for the local Mullah to return from the Haj, and they want his approval. Which he'll give, of course.

Then she dies."

The story was familiar, medieval attitude, and medieval butchery. "Is there no one in her family who'll help her?"

"They're Muslims."

End of the story!

"There's something else," Greg went on, "She's a covert Christian. She converted in secret, like me and Faria did."

"Oh, fuck."

"Oh, fuck indeed. They must suspect, and if she did have a slight chance before, it's gone. I want you to help me get her out, Stoner. They're holding her in the village jail, pending the sentence of death."

"What about the local cops, what do they say?"

"The police chief is her father."

"Okay, so we do it the hard way. Count me in."

He smiled to himself. He'd just been reflecting how peaceful it all was, apart from the guy trying to put a bullet in him, that is.

Thing is, I'm bored and need some action to get the adrenaline moving again.

"Thank you, Stoner," Faria said, in that soft, sultry voice that even now turned his knees to putty. Archer gave a soft growl of approval.

"No sweat. I'll need some gear from home. Greg, why don't we make a start right now? We can drive through the night. Call at my place at Jbad first and pick up some gear, and go straight down there. She may not have long. You may need the rifle. We don't know what we're up against."

"Give me a minute."

When he emerged, he was carrying a soft canvas rifle bag. He opened it and removed the contents, a Dragunov sniper rifle.

The Dragunov, officially designated, 'Sniper Rifle, System of Dragunov, Model of the Year 1963,' was a semi-automatic marksman rifle chambered in 7.62mm and developed in Russia. Designed as a squad support weapon, the Dragunov became the standard squad support weapon in several countries, including those of the former Warsaw Pact. Unsurprisingly, the Chinese, always ready to latch onto a good thing, produced a licensed version, the Type 79. Popular with the men who did the shooting, the rifle was rugged, quick to load and fire, and accurate to within a hair's breadth. Greg Blum had never served in any army, but he'd trained himself to the rough level of a military sniper. When he pulled the trigger of the Dragunov, the target went down.

Stoner watched him check the weapon carefully. Greg ensured the detachable box magazine carried a full load of ten rounds and packed it back in the bag. He gave a nod.

"I'm ready. We'll take the GAZ."

He closed his eyes for a second, recalling the uncomfortable, bouncing, and bumpy ride in the Soviet era relic. "No, not this time. We take the Wrangler."

Greg grimaced. "That shiny black piece of pimped-up tin, they'll see us coming before we even get close. The GAZ is perfect, because it blends in with the local landscape."

First produced in the early fifties, dating back almost to Stalin's grip on the Soviet Union, the chunky SUV was ugly and tough. Painted in drab, Russian-military green, the two-liter engine could reach almost sixty mph, on a good day. On a bad day, fifty mph was more realistic, although it was rugged and reliable, with nothing else good to say about it.

"Shitty, you mean."

"She's a tough little workhorse, the GAZ. Never lets me down."

He gave in, and they left the farm. Archer watched them go, his tail hanging down, dejected. They were going back into action, just like the Marines trained him to do, except they were leaving him behind.

The track to Mehtar Lam was rutted and a foretaste of things to come. The GAZ bumped and rattled over every pothole, until they reached the slightly smoother highway that would take them to Jalalabad. Around thirty klicks, and they made the first twenty without any problems. Then they stopped. The vehicles slewed across the road gave them no choice, a chunky Nissan Patrol, and a slightly less chunky Land Cruiser. Five men were standing in front of the roadblock, four armed with automatic rifles, and the fifth apparently unarmed.

A lean, hard-looking man, and he wore a brown leather aviator's jacket and beige chinos tucked into polished jump boots. As they drew nearer, they could make out the hard, cold face reflected in the light of the headlamps. Greg braked to a halt, and Stoner said, "Stay there. I'll handle this."

"Is that who I think it is?"

He nodded. "It is. We've got trouble."

He climbed out and walked to meet him. "Ivan."

The other man gave him a cold grin. "Good to see you again, Stoner."

The accent was Russian, which was no surprise. Ivan 'The Terrible' Vasilyevich roamed Afghanistan in search of profit for his various criminal enterprises. Tall, slim, and hard as steel, he looked more like an American than a Russian, which his name and accent would imply. The name and the accent were both fake. An American, Ivan was a long-time CIA agent in place, with the perfect cover. Who would suspect a smuggler, gunrunner, and all-time bad boy of being a spy? The result was he fed a steady stream of intel back to Langley. He also grew rich on his profitable enterprises.

Two men with him Stoner recognized, Gorgy Bukharin, a Russian, and Akram Latif, an Afghan, hard fighting men who acted as his bodyguards.

"I wish I could say the same. What do you want, Ivan? We're in a hurry."

He adopted a hurt expression. "I just want to help you, that's all."

"We don't need your help to drive back to Jbad, but thanks for the offer. All I need is for you to move those vehicles so we can pass."

Ivan didn't reply at first, glanced around at his SUVs, grinned at the GAZ, and then his eyes swung back to Stoner. "You won't find her in Achin."

He was rocked, but he kept his expression neutral. "Who said anything about Achin?"

The warlord ignored the question. "Thing is, they moved her. That's why I wanted a friendly chat, so you'd know where to find her." A pause, "Before they kill her, that is. I don't know what they have planned. Stoning, a bullet to the head, sometimes they use gasoline, set the victim on fire. It's not pretty."

He sighed. "Okay, how much?"

Ivan's main product was information. He never, ever let slip anything without demanding a price. And his prices were high. Astronomical.

"All I'm asking is for you to do a little favor for me. Nothing too arduous, but it's something that would make a lot of people happy."

"The United States government, you mean."

He winced. "Ouch. Here's the thing, local insurgents, Talibs, took a soldier. They wiped out an entire platoon, except for this officer, Lieutenant Sara Carver. Took her prisoner, and people are making loud noises about getting her back."

"You mean Langley, or the Pentagon?"

"Something like that."

"Who is this Lieutenant Carver?"

He shrugged. "They tell me she's just a regular infantry officer, second lieutenant on her first patrol in country. Thing is, if they send in regular troops, even Special Forces, you know what security is like in this country. They see a helo fly out of Bagram with men in black, and they'll be on alert. No one would suspect a couple of civilians in a rusty old heap your friend's driving to be serious. Chances are they'll kill her before they can get her out. Soon as you've done the job, I'll give you the exact location of this Shahay as soon as I have it."

It sounded like the worse deal he'd ever heard of. "So why don't you get her out?"

He shrugged. "It's complicated. See, we're up to our necks with a problem that's come up. Bunch of guys threatening my entire organization, and I know only one way to deal with them. We're staging a raid to hit them before they hit us. There's no time to attend to this other thing, which is why I thought of you guys. Favor for a favor."

"Can't it wait until you get back?"

He shook his head. "Negative, it doesn't work like that."

"Like what?"

He lowered his voice. "Like we may not make it back. In which case Lieutenant Carver is toast."

"That bad, uh?"

"Yeah, that bad. This one's make or break, and if we don't destroy these guys, I'm finished in this part of the world." He looked thoughtful, "Maybe fatally. Besides, there's another problem. These guys holding Lieutenant Carver, I do business

26

with them on occasion. They supply me with intel about insurgent activity in Southeast Afghanistan." He grinned. "Although I doubt they know who benefits from it. Stupid bastards think I even sympathize with the Taliban."

"Which is what you tell everyone."

"Yeah, I do. So how about it, can you do this little thing for me? Get this girl out before they do anything nasty to her?"

Stoner's thoughts raced through the possibilities.

How did Ivan know what we're up to? Then again, with the massive resources of NSA, they'd intercept every cellphone and landline call in Afghanistan. A simple algorithm would listen for names they're interested in. There's something Ivan isn't telling me. He made it sound simple, but if it were that simple, they'd send in Special Forces, men trained to deal with that kind of operation. Even better, if worried about security, use his own men.

"Where are they holding this Lieutenant Carver?"

The pseudo Russian smiled. "It's a place you know pretty well, so you shouldn't have any trouble finding it."

"Go on."

"Tora Bora."

He didn't need to give it any thought. "No."

Stoner felt a stab of fear though his belly. Tora Bora, where he'd been part of a bloody battle, part of the effort to locate and kill Osama bin Laden, amongst others, and to destroy the terrorists responsible for 911, and those harboring them. They didn't get Osama, not then, but they took the objective. The cave system was deep and complex, and easy to defend. Ironically, CIA funded the effort to enlarge and secure the caves, to aid the mujahideen during the Soviet invasion.

Enemy casualties after the operation numbered around two hundred, but no Coalition troops lost their lives. Although one man, a Special Forces vet, was unaccounted after the shooting stopped. They never found him even though they looked hard. It was assumed he'd fallen inside a cave when they dynamited them, and his body buried for all time under thousands of tons of rock.

There were many friendly casualties. Many tribesmen allied to the Coalition either died or were severely wounded. Stoner recalled the area of the caves once the action had died down. Hundreds of bodies littered the ground and inside the caves, and he counted himself lucky not to have joined them.

"It's not such a tough one," Ivan said, "Not like it used to be. You can be in and out of there before they even realize you've called."

"The answer is no, Ivan. Not Tora Bora. Not now, not ever."

He sighed. "Okay, well, don't say I didn't warn you. Pity about Faria's cousin, I saw a photo, lovely girl. Stoning is a bastard. She won't look like that when they bury her."

He looked back to the GAZ. Greg couldn't overhear the conversation, and he wasn't certain he wanted him to. Tora Bora was a deathtrap to anyone who ventured inside. And a deathtrap to a prisoner held in the caves, who they'd execute the moment they suspected an attack was under way.

"Ivan, why don't you tell me now where they're holding Shahay?"

"I will, of course. Only, I do need that favor. Like I said, the U.S. government would be forever grateful."

"Which means she must be important. Who is she?"

"No idea. They just asked me to get her out. Alive. Just in case you happen to be in the area, here's a photo so you can identify her."

He took a six by four image from the pocket of his leather jacket and handed it across. Stoner felt a lurch in his guts. It was her, or as near to her as dammit.

Many years before, he'd been engaged to a young UN aid worker. A French girl named Madeleine Charpentier. The officer in the photo was her spitting image, slim and lithe, with dark hair cropped in a bob. Milky skin, and a curvy body a man could die for. Madeleine bled to death after an explosion caused by an IED, a roadside bomb. He looked at the other man, waiting with a slight smile on his face.

"You bastard, Ivan. You knew I'd have to agree."

"I guessed you might, sure. So how about it?"

He was trapped, and both men knew it. "Okay, but you'd better keep your part of the bargain. If you don't come across with the location of Shahay, I'll come looking for you."

"Sure you will, but don't worry, I always keep a promise. I guess we're finished here. I'll get them to clear the road."

"How long?"

"Excuse me?"

"Shahay, how long before they pronounce sentence of death and kill her? How long does she have?"

He pursed his lips, lost in thought. "They have to have the approval of the local Mullah, and he's on a Haj to Mecca, so she has a little time. My guess is around ten days, maximum. That's how long you have to get Sara Carver out. Good luck with it."

"I'll pay you to give me her location. Name the price."

"I already did, and besides, I don't know for sure, not yet. See you around, Stoner."

Ivan knew he was desperate, and knew he'd take it. Besides, there was that resemblance to Madeleine. What choice did he have? "I'll do it."

"I kind of thought you would. There's something you'll need."

He went to the Land Cruiser and took out a satphone.

"This device is encrypted, and no matter where you are, you'll get through to me at any time of night or day. I must know how you're progressing, so keep me posted. My people in Washington will start to get itchy if we don't keep them in the loop."

"She's not just any second lieutenant, is she? She has to be someone special."

He gave an airy wave to deflect the question. "They just want her back. That's all there is to it."

You're a liar, Ivan. Behind that fake Russian name and accent, you wouldn't know the truth if it bounced up and smacked you in the teeth.

He took the phone. "I'll call you when I can. Not every day, you know how it goes."

"Every day, make sure you do. We're under the cosh on this one. Anything you need before you go?"

"How about a squad of Navy SEALs, and a fleet of gunships flying top cover."

"Funnee. Let me know how it goes."

He waved a hand, engines started, and the two vehicles backed up to allow them to get through. He climbed back into the GAZ, and Greg drove away. They were going to the last place in the world he'd want to visit. Last time, as a raw recruit, he experienced his baptism of hell in that place. Since then, he knew the Talibs had retaken it, and it would take something special to get in there and get out. All they had going for them was they were civilian. Any military unit going into that cauldron would be up against a formidable enemy. Would two men be enough to slip inside the defenses and get her out? They'd soon find out. He had an overwhelming motive to succeed. That picture of Sara Carver was like looking at a ghost from the past. That's what he was doing, going to find a ghost, and pluck her from the jaws of hell.

ERIC MEYER

CHAPTER TWO

Ivan returned to the Nissan Patrol, and gave Akram Latif the okay to drive away. He had confidence in Rafe Stoner. The guy always came across. Besides, he had the clinchers. The location of the girl related to Greg's wife. He'd never met Madeleine Charpentier, but he'd seen photos of her. A nurse working with UNHCR, she was a beautiful girl, murdered by a Taliban IED. She was also the spitting image of Sara Carver, and he'd seen his expression when he showed him the photo. Stoner was hooked, no question.

He had his own problems. Several shipments had been hit over the past weeks, and he'd found out who was doing the hitting. A warlord once an active member of the Taliban, and who'd fled the country. Now he operated from Chitral, in Northeast Pakistan. A convenient location for cross border raids, and when the going got too hot, he could slip across into Tajikistan, or even China, and wait until the heat died down.

He'd hit Ivan badly, and his reputation was going down the tubes, as well as his business. He relied on a well-financed trade between the various parties inside and outside the country to pay his contacts and his people. So far, he'd lost several shipments of drugs and guns, and almost twenty of his men had failed to return to his base. He didn't speculate on what happened to them. The sole reason for a man not turning up to collect his pay was because he was dead.

It couldn't go on. He needed to restore equilibrium to his business, and restore the vital flow of information. Without which he may as well give up and find somewhere remote to live out the rest of his life. Far from the legions of enemies he'd made along the way. It wasn't in his nature. He was a fighter, a brawler. When the chips were down, his instinct was to fight back, and that's what he was doing right now. He glanced at Gorgy Bukharin. "We need a helicopter."

"Sure we do, Boss. You want to steal a helicopter, tell me what sort. Troop carrier, cargo, or what?"

"A gunship. We're going into Chitral."

Bukharin stared back at him. "Yeah, I guessed that was on the cards. You want to fly a gunship into Chitral and take out the Mongol."

"That's about it. Batu, that slant-eyed bastard. I don't know why he couldn't have stayed in his own country."

Ivan's enemy, Batu Amar, was a formidable man because he owed allegiance to no one. He operated secretly and struck where the target least expected it. A professional soldier from his native Mongolia, he'd been one of the youngest colonels in the Mongolian Army. That was before he decided his colonel's salary was too miserly, and he moved to Afghanistan, where the rich pickings from the drug and arms trades would make him rich.

"Because there's no money to be made in Mongolia."

"No, I guess not. How many men do you reckon he has in Chitral?"

"Fifty, sixty maybe. He won't be an easy target. It could be messy, taking him out. We'll need a lot more men."

Ivan's smile was sly. "Or a gunship."

"Ah, that's different. You're planning on a low-level ground attack, hose them down with a chain gun, is that it?"

"You got it in one, Gorgy. No fuss, no muss. Do it all in a single operation. Now where can we find that gunship? It'll be just us, the less the better. After it's done, the shit's gonna hit the fan, so we make sure no one knows who's behind it."

"They'll suspect it was you. Everyone knows Batu is gunning for your operation."

"They can suspect all they want. As long as no one knows, it'll be a clean operation. Cross the border into Pakland, take out Batu's place, and fly back. We can ditch the gunship somewhere it won't be found for a long time."

Bukharin looked dubious. "My suggestion is we drive over the border into Pakistan and grab a PAF helicopter; less chance of problems if we don't need to fly over the border. The easiest way would be to buy one."

"Buy one? You know someone?"

"There's a guy who works in the training base outside Peshawar. Air Force officer, a captain."

"He's short of money? Enough to risk his career?"

"You know the recent clampdown on homosexuality inside Pakistan? He lives in fear of discovery, has to pay out a fortune in bribes to keep his secret, poor bastard. He'd do it, if we paid him enough. I doubt he'd fly it for us, though. If they found out, they'd sentence him to death."

"As a traitor, or as a homosexual?"

Bukharin's reply was smooth. "Both. Shoot him as a traitor, and hang him as a sexual pervert."

"Okay, we don't need a pilot. Call him, and fix it up."

"When do we cross the border?"

"Tonight. Make the arrangements, and we fly out after dark tomorrow. And tell him I want a full load of ordnance. I don't want to be lobbing stones at Batu."

"I'll tell him."

* * *

Greg shot him a curious glance as he drove. "What was all that about?"

He explained the deal he'd just made with Ivan, a deal with the devil. Blum jammed on the brakes and stared at him in astonishment.

"Hold on there. Did you just say get this officer out of Tora Bora before he'll tell us where they're holding Shahay?"

"Yep. Ivan said we have the perfect cover. No one would suspect two civilians in a rusty old heap like the GAZ."

Greg ignored the insult. "How many insurgents are hiding out in there, do we know?"

"He didn't say, but my best guess is around fifty to a hundred."

"Fifty to a hundred. And there's two of us."

"Right."

"But Shahay doesn't have any other chances?"

"Right."

He started the engine and drove on. "We'll do it, because we don't have an alternative. But when we get back, I'd like to pay Ivan a visit."

Stoner grinned. "You'd have to join a long queue, but I'd forget it. He's too well protected, and more cunning than a barrel of monkeys. Besides, he's not all bad. Helped us out on occasion."

"After he'd got us into a heap of trouble."

It was true. Ivan was a cold, calculating machine. Personable, even likeable, until you stepped away and found he's stolen the watch off your wrist. Greg put the pedal to the metal, and they arrived in Jbad an hour after midnight. The lights were blazing inside Ma Kelly's, and business was in full swing. They used the rear entrance, and Stoner hastily changed into working fear. Well-worn dark green camo pants tucked into leather jump boots, and a thick jacket with multiple pockets under his leather coat. He strapped the harness back on with the Desert Eagles, grabbed a bag of food and bottles of water, and passed it to Greg to carry. He left the apartment, and they started back down the stairs to visit the next destination, his basement storage unit underneath the building. Converted into a high security store for the tools of his trade, guns, explosives, and ammunition; even Claymore mines, useful for dissuading an enemy from following too close.

He opened the door to exit the building and stepped out into the street. Greg was still coming down the staircase, when he slipped and dropped the bottles of water. They cascaded down the stairs, and Stoner turned back to help him gather them up. The bullet smacked into the doorframe next to where his head would have been if he hadn't turned back.

His hand shot to the light switch, and darkness overwhelmed them. A second bullet splintered wood from the doorframe, and he dove outside, rolled, and came up running. Pulling out the Desert Eagles, he'd pinpointed the shooter's position. Across the street, the single open window in the four-story building was at the top. The place was commercial premises. Closed at night, and there should have been no one there.

When the second shot came, he'd been looking upward, and he saw the muzzle flash. It was enough to go on, and he sprinted through the main door, which was unlocked, tore up the staircase, taking them two at a time, and made the top floor in seconds. Unless he moved with the speed of greased lighting, the shooter had to be close. He cautioned himself to be careful. This was a man trying to kill him. He checked the office from where he'd seen the shots but saw no one. Checked again, poked around, and saw nothing. Stepped out into the hallway, and a movement caused him to swing around, and he almost fired.

"Can I help you?"

He froze. An old man was walking toward him. He recognized him and holstered the guns. The janitor, he'd seen him around occasionally, an old guy who shuffled around the building most days, pushing a broom and taking out the garbage. Harmless.

"Someone tried to take a shot at me. It came from in here. Have you seen anyone?"

The janitor thought long and hard. "A shot? Was that what you said?"

He was almost deaf, and Stoner stifled his frustration. "Yes, a shot. Did you see anyone?"

"See? Of course I can see."

"No, no, the man who fired the shot. Is he still here, or did he escape?"

The old man raised a shaking hand and pointed to the end of the hallway. "Fire escape, yes, at the end."

"Did you see him go that way?"

"If you like, yes."

He thanked him. Suspecting he was wasting his time, raced to the fire exit door, and opened it. An iron staircase led to the ground floor.

Empty. The bastard's gone. Next time, I'll be ready for him, and I'll nail his ass.

He returned to the street level where Greg waited with a pistol in his hand, a Makarov. A big, heavy Russian-made 9mm. Covering his back, should anyone try to come in behind him. He nodded his thanks.

"He's gone. Next time he won't be so lucky."

"Who is it?"

He shrugged. "No idea. All I do know is he wants me dead. There's no time to deal with him now. I'll sort it out when we get back. We'll grab some hardware and go looking for this Second Lieutenant Sara Carver. Find out what all the fuss is about."

* * *

Through the darkness, he watched the American go and hated him even more. He'd missed him this time, like before, but he couldn't get lucky every time. He'd be patient and wait for the moment. Then he'd strike, and his sole regret was he'd have to kill the man. He was too dangerous to wound, to leave alive. He had to pay for his crimes, for the things he'd done, crimes against his family, crimes against God. What he'd done was unforgivable, and he had no right to strut around like some wealthy bigshot from Kabul.

So far, Stoner didn't know who was trying to kill him. He wouldn't know until the last moment, when he pulled the trigger and the American was dead. He would descend into hell for what he'd done, and suffer for a thousand years. He smiled as he crept from the darkness. It was the Afghan way. Seek justice, no matter how long it took. Was it not a Chinese philosopher who'd said 'Revenge is a dish best tasted cold?' The waiting was frustrating, but it would taste all the better when it happened, when his mortal enemy was dead.

* * *

He unlocked the basement, and they went inside to a room filled with enough weaponry to start a small war. The assault rifles were not American. He handed Greg a Kalashnikov AK47S. The shorter, folding stock weapon carried by many airborne troops and Russian Spetsnaz.

"Where we're going, there won't be room for a regular assault rifle. And besides, the insurgents love the AK, so we'll find plenty of ammo if we run low."

"You think we may need more!" Greg was looking at the four boxes of 7.62mm loose rounds, and the canvas webbing belts each loaded with eight full mags.

Stoner frowned. "If we get her away, and they come after us, we'll burn up ammo like it's gone out of fashion. So, yeah, it's possible. That's why we're taking the Claymores."

He put four lethal land mines on the stack, each with the words 'Front Toward Enemy' embossed on the metal front, and on top of the mines, an M57 firing device. When they detonated, seven hundred steel balls would cascade outward. Anyone coming after them, any pursuers would be torn to shreds. That was the theory, and unlike many theories, this one worked in practice. He added a box of C4 plastic explosive, with an electric detonator and a long, thin cable.

"We may need to bring the roof of the cave system down, and this little baby'll do the trick. That should do us. We'll carry it up to the street and load it all into the GAZ. If we travel through the night, we should find somewhere to hole up before dawn. We'll wait out the day, and go in tonight. Hopefully, catch them all sleeping."

Greg drove the laden jeep and pointed the hood toward

the east, following the highway for Torkham, the town that straddled the Afghan Pakistan border. Stoner contented himself with checking the crude but reliable AKs, and double-checking the wiring connections for the mines and explosives. Twenty klicks further, he pointed to a left turn, and Greg swung the wheel over. The GAZ lurched and bumped, and once again, he cursed himself for allowing Greg to use the Soviet-era relic.

They were headed toward Deh Bala, scene of fierce fighting during the Coalition hunt for Osama bin Laden. Close to Deh Bala lay the cave system known as The Black Cave. Tora Bora.

His mind returned to all those years ago, driving along this same road in a fleet of Humvees, with a Bradley leading the charge. He'd been a new U.S. Navy recruit, yet already he had designs on becoming a SEAL. They'd asked for volunteers for the operation to locate and kill bin Laden. In the early days of the Afghan War, he'd been keen to get in on the kill before it was all over, and to gain combat experience. He got the combat experience. They didn't get bin Laden. Not then.

The action flashed through his mind, as if they were replaying a filmstrip. Soldiers of many nations fighting their way through ambush after ambush, bearded, screaming Taliban and al-Qaeda fighters coming at them in waves. Their fury was intense, that the infidels had dared to attack the hideout of their revered leader, Osama bin Laden.

Coalition troops of every nation advanced with grim determination. Twenty CIA National Clandestine Service operators and elements of 5th Special Forces Group spearheaded them. Code-named Jawbreaker, the operators were inserted by helicopter close to Jalalabad. Afghans, Northern Alliance fighters, fought their way through to the low ground below Tora Bora, forcing the al-Qaeda fighters to retreat to their holes in the ground.

Several days later, seventy Special Forces operators from the Delta Force, U.S. Navy SEALs, and Air Force arrived to support the campaign.

Meanwhile, Northern Alliance fighters advanced toward their objective, backed by Coalition air strikes, until they finally reached the caves. Their bird had flown. Bin Laden had gone, and the operation ended in bitter recrimination. Plenty of al-Qaeda bodies littered the ground, with those of loyal Afghan fighters, but the big bad wolf was still on the loose; still able to foment trouble and mischief, and to encourage men to sell their lives cheaply for a lost cause.

He'd come out of that nightmare hell without a scratch, but it was close. The image of screaming fanatics charging down their guns was not an easy one to forget. Now he was going back. Back to where it all started, and this time, the beasts had captured a female soldier. An infantry officer who was a chilling reminder to him of the girl he'd lost all those years ago. He vowed to get her out, no matter what. The Islamic animals would not treat her well. They didn't treat their own women as anything more than dirt beneath their feet. Chattels, to be used, abused, bought and sold. The captivity of Second Lieutenant Sara Carver would not be comfortable.

Greg fought the wheel of the GAZ, and the track became progressively worse. He spoke without looking around.

"How far to this place now, Stoner? This isn't getting any easier."

"I estimate about ten klicks. Soon, we'll need to find somewhere to hide the jeep and go in on foot. Otherwise, they'll hear us coming, and they'll be waiting for us."

"Right. There's a bend coming up. As soon as we're on the next stretch, I'll start looking."

He maneuvered through a hairpin bend and jammed on the

brakes. In front, a mere one hundred meters away, an armored fighting vehicle blocked the road.

"Jesus Christ, not again! This time it's a tank!" he shouted, "What the hell is going on here?"

"It's not a tank. It's an M3 Bradley. Armored fighting vehicle, infantry support. It looks like the U.S. Army beat us to it."

He regarded the other vehicles, half a dozen Humvees, a Stryker, and another couple of Bradleys at the opposite end of the column. A soldier on sentry duty came toward them, his M-16 pointed in their direction.

"Folks, you can't come this way. You'll have to turn back."

Greg tried to reason with him. "We don't plan to interfere with Army operations. We're just passing this way. Why don't you let us get through? It'll take a minute, no more."

The soldier looked doubtful. "You know where this track goes? It's the main route into Tora Bora. Lot of nasty people in these parts, I'd advise you to turn around and head back."

"It's also the route to the village of Deh Bala, and that's where we're headed. We're visiting a relative."

"I hear you, buddy, but I don't think the Colonel will allow it. One moment."

He spoke into his headset, and half a minute later, an engine started and a Humvee reversed down the track at speed. It stopped two meters from them, spraying gravel over the sentry and the GAZ. The passenger door flew open, and a man leapt out, his face red with anger. He wore a colonel's tabs on his shoulders.

"What the fuck do you think you're doing, interfering with my operation? I want you to clear the area, now!"

"We're heading for Deh Bala," Stoner offered, "Just two klicks further along the track. We won't interfere with anything."

"Damn right you won't, because you're not going there.

Turn back."

"Colonel, it's…"

He glared back at Stoner. "Who are you, Mister?"

He gave him their names, seeing no reason not to. Why make the vinegary bastard even worse, although Stoner had taken an instant dislike to the snotty senior officer.

"What's it all about, Colonel? What are you guys doing here?"

"One moment." He addressed his driver, who'd stepped out to watch, "Make a note, Corporal."

The man gave him a weary nod, took out a notebook and pen, and started writing.

The Colonel looked back at them. "My name is Lieutenant-Colonel Harold H. Brewer, and I'm in command of this outfit. One of our officers from the 18th Infantry Regt, 1st Infantry Brigade, 1st Infantry Division was captured by insurgents hiding out in Tora Bora. What it's all about is this. We're about to launch an operation to get her out." He checked his watch, "In twenty-eight minutes, American aircraft are gonna plaster the approaches to the caves, and anyone caught out in the open between here and Tora Bora is gonna become Afghan stew. After they've unloaded their ordnance, we're going in, and we're going to kick ass. You're not going this way, so forget it. Come back in a few days when it's all over, apart from burying the dead bodies."

Stoner thought of that photo of Sara Carver and the resemblance to Madeleine Charpentier. Thought of how she'd fare when the bombers struck. As soon as the last bomb had fallen, the infantry would move in, to find a hacked-up corpse.

"They'll kill her, you know that."

His red face darkened even more. "Are you telling me my job, Mister? That's one of my officers in there, and we're going to hit the enemy so hard they'll regret the day they ever laid hands on her. They won't kill her. She's a valuable hostage. Not that it's any of your business. If I look around in the next couple of minutes and see you still here, my men will arrest you. Savvy?"

He gave them a final glare, returned to the Humvee, and they watched it drive away. The sentry gestured to them with his rifle. "I reckon that's it, boys. I'd do what he says if I were you. Lieutenant-Colonel Brewer isn't the kind of man I'd want to cross."

Stoner thanked him for the advice. "I hear you, buddy. Good luck with the operation. You'll need it."

The man shot him a quizzical glance. "Have you been here before? You know there was some kind of a battle, back in the early days."

"I heard about it, yeah. Be seeing you."

Greg was waiting, and he turned the GAZ around. "What do we do now? It looks like we'll have to head back."

"They'll kill Sara Carver the moment they see the infantry move in. SOP for these sadistic bastards. That's assuming a bomb doesn't fall on the place they're hiding her. We don't get her out, Ivan won't come across, and Faria's cousin is toast. That's two dead girls on our consciences, and it's not going to happen. It's time to go to Plan B."

"What's Plan B?"

"We go in the back way."

"Which way is that?"

"The hard way."

* * *

Lieutenant-Colonel Harold H. Brewer jumped from the

Humvee as he reached the head of his column. He glanced back to see if the interfering civilians had gone and saw no rear lights, so he assumed they'd hightailed it in a hurry. The threat of a few bombs and bullets flying around usually did the trick. These people didn't understand what soldiering was all about. He didn't buy the reason those men were in the area.

Visiting relations in some shit-stinking Afghan village, no way! If I were a betting man, which I'm not, I'd say they're journalists. Probably from some pinko liberal news organization that paints every man in uniform as a brutal baby killer. And the enemy they go after, the insurgents, are always poor, hard done-by peasants. Just carrying AK-47s and RPG missile launchers to hunt wild pigs, or whatever game they hunt in their godforsaken country.

"Colonel, Sir, I've had word from the Air Force liaison officer. He says the bombing raid is coming in. They'll start unloading in around ten minutes."

Brewer looked at his watch and felt a twinge of irritation. "They're early, Captain. How come?"

Captain Oliver Stevens, a Connecticut native, flinched under Brewer's glare. The man was a stickler for punctuality, and somehow he didn't appreciate the difficulties of marshaling fleets of fighter-bombers from different locations. Of putting refueling tankers aloft, reconnaissance aircraft to overfly the target and confirm the enemy hadn't moved away; dealing with the unforeseen, breakdowns, foul-ups, and the hundreds of things that could go wrong when men and machines come together. He insisted on perfection. Punctuality.

"According to the Air Force, they had a weather warning. A storm coming in that could make it difficult to recover the aircraft after the raid."

"They should have told us sooner," he snapped, "It's sloppy, Captain, very sloppy."

"Yes, Sir. They got warning of the weather a few minutes ago, a tropical storm that came out of nowhere."

"Sloppy," he repeated, "Still, we can't do anything about it. Give the order to prepare to advance. We'll push up to the outer perimeter, so we're ready to move the moment they're gone."

Stevens regarded him for a few moments, not sure whether to contradict him or not. The safety of the men under his command came first. "Sir, our orders are to stand off until the bombers have done their work. If we go now, it'll put us inside the danger zone. A stray bomb could hit one of our vehicles, and we could lose men. It's an unnecessary risk."

Brewer reddened once more. "Captain, I gave you an order. Of course it's a risk, but it's called soldiering, Mister. Taking risks, that's what it's all about. We must be in position so we can hit them the second the bombers start to leave. See to it."

"Yes, Sir."

Stevens ran to his command vehicle, the M3 Bradley, and swung inside to his command seat in the turret. Clipped on his headset and spoke to the crew.

"We're moving off early. They advanced the time of the raid. We're moving into a Taliban and al Qaeda controlled area, so heads up, and make sure we don't drive into an ambush."

As they were acknowledging, he switched to the command net. "This is Captain Stevens, prepare to move out. We're moving up the schedule. There's been a change of plan. Some shit to do with a weather warning. The bombers are on their way in, but they're early, so stay tight behind me. I don't want any strays. They see a vehicle on its own, and they might see it as an enemy."

He gave the order. "Driver, advance."

The driver sounded nervous. "Cap, you sure about this? I

mean, we were supposed to wait until the aircraft had gone home. What if someone forgets to tell them we've changed position?"

"That won't happen, Private Powell. Air Force liaison takes care of those things."

"Like they did that weather warning?"

He sighed. The guy had a point, but Brewer gave the order to move, so move is what they'd do. "It's taken care of. Get her rolling, Powell. Right now, that's an order."

The Bradley lurched forward, less gently than was necessary, and Stevens cursed as his helmet banged on the steel of the turret. Not that he blamed Powell. He'd told him Air Force liaison was responsible for these things, but the truth was, sometimes things went wrong. Shit happened. What else could he do, but hope and pray this wasn't one of those times.

* * *

He pointed to a narrow goat track off to the north of the trail. Greg swung the GAZ over and fought to keep the wheels from going over the edge of a steep incline.

"If this gets any worse, there'll be no need for the enemy to kill us. We'll be lying dead at the bottom of a three-hundred-meter drop."

Stoner was watching the terrain, looking around and peering through the gloom, searching; searching for the players in the unfolding drama. Brewer's infantry, and he could hear them on the move, heading away from them, toward the caves, could see them, too. The fool bringing up the rear in the M3 had a red light illuminated. Just like he was on the main highway, making sure no half-asleep trucker didn't pile into the back.

The aircraft were overhead. He could hear the drone of

engines. The raid Brewer mentioned was under way, earlier than he'd stated, and the fireworks would start soon, an interesting exercise in coordination between the infantry and the Air Force; difficult at night, but effective for throwing the enemy into terrified confusion, if it worked.

He pointed to another trail about fifty meters ahead of their position. "Take that turning, and we can follow it to the other side of the caves. With luck, they won't see us coming."

"Who won't see us coming?"

"Any of 'em."

They were an unknown. An unmarked civilian vehicle, and any of the combatants would open fire if they saw them enter the battle zone. The trick was to make sure they didn't see them. They were driving across a long ridge, several meters below the crest and almost invisible. In the shallow valley, the column was moving at a steady pace, faintly visible in the moonlight. Then they disappeared as the valley snaked away from them.

They drove another five kilometers, and every sense was on alert. He held the AK-47S in his hands ready to cut loose the moment he saw any sign of hostiles. Then the first aircraft came in, a low, screaming dive from the west. It dropped its ordnance on a target around three klicks ahead of them. The area of the caves, and no doubt they'd catch plenty of the insurgents out in the open. They had to know about the impending attack, so they'd be preparing to hit back with missiles and rockets when they got close enough. Now they would ambush no one, and the flames lit up the sky as the bombs detonated.

He made out the dark shadow of an F/A 18 as it banked away, and then another came in low and fast. Too low, they wouldn't have a grandstand view of the surrounding countryside, and he knew they couldn't have a man on the ground with a laser target designator. Pity, it meant they had to leave so much to chance, to the vagaries of GPS satellite navigation. All fine and dandy until the target moved. Then the coordinates meant diddlysquat, and they'd be bombing empty rock.

Aircraft after aircraft came in until the ground was a flaming inferno. A few missiles soared into the sky, but none found a target, although it caused some bombers to veer off course. A short pause, and then the second wave came in. More bombs fell, and the area of smoke and flames became one giant conflagration. It was spreading. One problem with night bombing is mission creep. Aircraft observe the target lit up by flames, ignore the mission coordinates, and put their ordnance plumb center. Aircrews didn't want to miss the fun.

Problem was, the center of the target was no longer the ground surrounding the caves. The circle of flames was widening to the east, toward where the infantry were making slow, careful progress to the target area. Their gung-ho colonel wanted them close. Close enough to leap into the attack moment the last aircraft went away. However, it was a fine judgment. In the heat of the action, not every aircrew got it right.

"Jesus Christ, no!" Stoner shouted, as if they could hear him. He didn't need night vision or any other artificial aid. The area was lit up like a sports ground under arc lamps, and the vehicles came into sharp focus. The Bradley in the lead halted, seeing the danger, but the flames didn't halt. Instead, they crawled toward the armored vehicle as more bombs fell until the inevitable happened, and a Mark 80 GP bomb scored a direct hit on the M3. It disappeared. One moment it was intact, and the next all that remained was a flaming heap of wreckage. No one emerged, and as both men watched in stunned silence, the surviving vehicles backed away.

"What do we do?" Greg asked; his face lit up by the flames

even though they were at least two klicks away.

"Do?" Stoner looked at him, his face showing the horror he was reliving. Except this time, it was Americans down there, burning and dying. "We keep going. That's what we do."

"But those men," he said, "They're trapped in that thing."

He recalled Greg hadn't seen an AFV hit by a bomb or missile during a battle. "Those men are dead. The others are doing the sensible thing and getting out of there. All we can do is keep going, and use this raid as cover. With any luck, they'll be looking the other way when we make entry to the caves. Get the wheels rolling. Follow the track ahead."

"Uh, right."

He pressed the starter switch, and...nothing. Pressed it again, still nothing.

"What is it, what's wrong?"

He gave Stoner a guilty look. "The engine won't start. We've broken down."

"So fix it."

"I'll try, but we can't show a light, so I won't be able to see a thing. We'll have to wait until dawn."

"They'll see us and know we're here. It has to be now."

He nodded. "Okay, I'll try."

He spent an hour struggling under the hood, and still the engine wouldn't start. He looked up as Stoner reappeared from the darkness.

"There's nothing. I can't fix it until I can see what I'm doing."

"We can't wait until then. As soon as the infantry go in, that girl is dead. I found a cave about fifty meters further along the track, so we can stash the GAZ in there. We'll have to push it inside. Leave it out of sight, and we'll continue on foot."

"A cave?"

He grinned. "That's what this area is famous for. Could be

a tourist attraction if they stopped shooting at each other. Let's do it."

It took them a half hour to push the GAZ fifty meters along the rough, uneven track. Dripping with sweat, they got it into the mouth of the cave and prepared the supplies they'd need. The AKs, a Claymore mine apiece, and a few sticks of C4 and detonators in canvas packs. They rammed food into their mouths, washed it down with bottled water, and Stoner led the way, heading west toward Deh Bala, toward Tora Bora.

* * *

He emerged into the open and sniffed the air. The stink of burned explosives and scorched bodies. The flames had almost died down, and night had returned. Darkness they could use to prepare. In the distance, the sound of engines was loud. Rumi Khan waved them forward, and they came behind him. Khan wasn't his real name, and he wasn't an Afghan. Born a Chechen Muslim, he'd deserted and stayed in Afghanistan when his army left in 1989. He'd had good reason to drop out of sight.

A murder charge awaited him, and a trial for killing three men in his unit. They called it a robbery gone wrong, but what did they know? The bastards he'd killed had tried to cheat him after they robbed a rich Kabul merchant. The victim had just collected a large sum in gold from the bank to pay for a shipment of machinery. The split was planned to be four ways, but they'd dealt him out.

He killed them, deserted his unit, and found a bunch of former insurgents turned common bandits. His real name was Arbu Achmadov, and he came from Chechnya. As well as the name change, he'd learned to speak fluent Pashto and had earned the trust of his Afghan Muslim brothers. It was that or they'd kill him, and he'd murdered many Coalition troops and Western aid workers to earn his way up through the ranks.

"They've gone, thank be to Allah," he said, giving the obligatory nod to the Islamic deity. A deity whose existence he privately doubted. His face was ghastly, with one empty eye socket and ragged scars on one cheek he wore like badges of pride. One hand was missing and he walked with a pronounced limp, after his own bomb, an IED, exploded prematurely.

"Now their ground forces will advance, and we will be ready for them."

His second-in-command, Mohammed Abdullah, was trying to keep the doubts from his face. Unusually for the Taliban unit that held the caves at Tora Bora, he was another foreigner. Like his boss, his name was not the one he was born with. Unlike his boss, he never admitted his origins, although many assumed him to be a Turk, or even a Syrian. Inside the complex hierarchy of the warband, men recognized him as the military brains, a man who'd helped plan many victories. It was enough. Rumi Khan was the ferocious warlord, and Abdullah the cool planner. Both were sociopaths, and the men who served under them were wary of making mistakes, lest they fall victim to a vengeful bullet. Their leaders were not forgiving men.

Khan had sent most of their fighters out into the open to meet the coming American advance, a big mistake. He hadn't counted on the air strike, which was almost an act of madness. Who didn't understand the awesome intensity of American bombers, especially at night, when they could strike at targets that should have been invisible?

"What are your orders, Rumi?" Abdullah spoke with his peculiar mangled Pashto, enough for them to understand, but no more, "You wish to deploy more men out in the open? There is always a chance they could come back."

"They will not come back," he said firmly, "How could they risk dropping munitions on their own troops. Now we have a chance to fight them on even terms. Their armored vehicles must be dealt with, so ensure every man has rockets and missiles. How many Malyutkas do we have left?"

"Five," he replied promptly, anticipating the question, "The men caught in the open carried the rest, and now they are destroyed."

"Five will be enough. Along with the RPG-7s, we can hit them from the flanks as they approach the caves. Then we'll finish them off while they are still reeling from our assault. Use the Malyutkas on the Bradleys. Hit them first. That will box them in. Then the Stryker, that one is dangerous. The RPG-7s will be adequate for the Humvees. I want machine guns in position ready to mow down the survivors." He stared at Abdullah. "They think they have us boxed in, and are coming in to finish us off. Soon, they will realize their mistake. See to it. We don't have much time."

"At once, Rumi. And the prisoner, what about her?"

He'd been mulling over that problem ever since they'd spotted the American column a long distance away.

Would they take all that trouble over a single prisoner, a junior officer? It doesn't make sense, unless she's important to them. Who is she? An intelligence specialist, does she have secrets she could reveal that would hurt the American military? Or is she highly connected? In which case, a valuable hostage we could use to our advantage.

"We keep her alive for the time being, unless there is a possibility of them freeing her. You will station a man with her at all times. His orders are to kill her if a rescue operation looks as if it is coming close. Any sign of an enemy soldier inside the caves, and she dies. Clear?"

"I will pass on your order, yes."

"Five minutes, Abdullah. Get them in position now. Today, we will score a great victory, one that will force the Americans to understand the futility of fighting the soldiers of God."

"As you say, Rumi. But if Allah turns his back on us this day, and we lose the caves, where will we go to escape the Americans?"

He answered him with a glare. "He will not desert us. I promise you."

"But if there was something, something we haven't thought of?"

He sighed. "We have a truck fueled and waiting just over the border. As a last resort, we will travel to join our Muslim brothers in Pakistan, and there we will rest and regroup. When we come back, we will be stronger than ever, and we will seek vengeance. In time, we will sweep the invaders from our land forever."

"The same place as last time?"

"In Peshawar, yes, the walled villa by the Qissa Khwani Bazaar. But it will not be necessary. We will achieve victory this day."

Abdullah sniffed the air, and the scent of burning bodies was strong.

How can we achieve victory after we've lost so many men? Without any doubt, we will be in Peshawar by this time tomorrow.

* * *

She crouched in the darkness, listening to the terrible noise outside. One part of her cheered on the aircraft bombing the crap out of her captors, the other part terrified lest they scored a direct hit on the cave where they were holding her. The bombing eased, and she heard shouts and screams.

Wounded men and shouted arguments. Her people had hurt the insurgents badly. She felt better until the door to her cell opened, and a man walked inside. He aimed the muzzle of the AK at her head.

"Your aircraft have gone, and now we will see your American friends die."

She wanted to wipe the sneer off his face, but she also needed to escape, which meant no antagonizing him.

"Did the bombers kill many of your men? I can hear the wounded screaming out there. Perhaps I can help. I have a good knowledge of first aid."

And a good knowledge of weaponry. I don't like to hear them screaming in pain, but if I have a chance to grab a weapon, I could be out of here.

The sneer deepened. "You think these men would want an infidel to touch them! They are devout Muslims, and their beliefs are stronger than a little pain. Besides, my orders are to keep you in here. If the Americans get close, I am to kill you."

It always came to that with Muslims. Kill. Never any alternative, and forget the men crying in agony she could help. Just kill, the answer to everything. She tried a different tack.

"You speak good English, where did you learn?"

He nodded. "I worked for the Americans on their base at Bagram. I learned English and made a good living. I even bought a small house for my wife. She lives in Peshawar, in Pakistan."

"Not Afghanistan?"

A chuckle. "This country is too violent. She is safer in Peshawar."

Too violent because shitheads like you make it that way.

She couldn't think of anything to say, and she had no idea how she could get close enough to disarm and somehow incapacitate him. It was him who gave her the opening. He put down his AK next to the door and removed his coat, tugging at the leather belt supporting his baggy Afghan pants. He came toward her with a grin on his face that sent a chill of fear through her.

"What are you doing?"

"What do you think? Take off your clothes, woman. We don't have much time."

'No!"

His brow darkened. "You will remove your clothes, unless you want a good beating. Perhaps I should beat you anyway. Western women are too pampered, too soft."

Anger overcame her fear.

This motherfucker wants to rape me. I'll put up a damn good fight before he lays a finger on me. Then again, maybe it's the opportunity I wanted. He'll come close, and that will be my chance. If I see an opening, I'll take it.

She'd learned some unarmed combat skills during basic training. Before that she'd attended women's self-defense classes in Washington. A violent city, and she'd wanted to be ready. She figured she'd get one chance, and she needed to make it good.

He was coming nearer, and his rank stench appalled her. The thought of that animal touching her body, raping her, his foul hands groping at her. The anger grew, and she decided. The self-defense classes gave her the idea, how to ruin the day of a man overcome with lust. He was almost there, and then he made a swift grab for her jacket. Pulled her toward him, and she struck. Brought up her knee into his groin, and every ounce of her strength, determination, and anger went into the blow.

It was perfectly timed and perfectly delivered. The knee sunk into the soft flesh, and his reaction was immediate. A cry of agony every bit as loud as the screams of the wounded men outside in the caves, and he sunk to his knees, his hands grabbing at his damaged groin. The target was perfect, and she couldn't miss. The bearded face was directly in front of her, and she bunched a fist and swung.

It wasn't enough. He teetered lower, but didn't go down. He was still howling in agony, his hands trying to favor the damage to his groin. His eyes were closed in disbelief at what she, a mere woman, was doing to a solider of Allah. She looked around for a weapon. She didn't have the weight or strength to finish him, and her eyes lit on the AK. She grabbed it by the barrel, lined up the shot like she was hitting a baseball, and swung. The wooden butt slammed against the side of his head. The shock almost made her drop the rifle, but it was enough, and he went down.

His breathing was a hoarse rasp, and she knew he was still alive, but he'd be out for a while, enough for her to escape. She kept hold of the rifle and darted a look outside the cell. There was nobody in sight. She slipped out, stepped into a side tunnel, and almost tripped over a man. A swift examination showed he was dead, and she ignored him and carried on. She'd no idea where she was going, or which way she was headed. Only that she needed to get out. More bodies lay along the tunnel, and she came to a staircase cut into the stone.

Without thinking, she started to climb. All she needed was to escape her captors, and the sounds she'd heard came from lower down. She came to a second staircase, ducking aside as voices called out, and men ran down the steps toward where she'd been about to climb. She waited until they ran past and climbed again, reaching a long tunnel that seemed deserted and ran along the rough floor. When she came to the end, she appreciated a new sensation. Wind. Air was circulating inside the tunnel. She was near an exit. A chance to get out, and she began to jog. Tripped on the rough floor, got up, and continued jogging until she saw the night sky ahead of her.

Stars in the sky, and she eased out through a narrow entrance, past a straggly bush, and she was on the mountainside. The stink of explosives was powerful, an odor that overhung everything, along with the smoke blowing to the north. A few fires still blazed, but lower down. She was free, and she looked around for some way to get her bearings. Above her loomed the huge mountain range, and the snow on the slopes looked close. The temperature felt cold, bitterly cold, and she was about to climb down the slope, away from the snowline, when she heard voices calling out from below, and then she saw dark shapes of men moving out from a lower cave opening.

They were going out to do battle with the oncoming infantry. She fervently hoped her old buddies would kick the living shit out of them. But it was no place for her to go, the middle of a battlefield. Armed with a single rifle, an enemy rifle, and she'd be a target for both sides. She had no choice, and she headed on the nearest path that led away from the battle. The path sloped gently upward, and she knew she was heading toward the snowline, but she'd detour when she was far enough away from the caves and try to link up with friendly troops.

They were near. She could hear the familiar sounding engines of Bradleys, Humvees, and at least one Stryker.

They're coming for me, thank god. I have to remain free until I can reach them.

She began to run.

* * *

"Target, up on the mountain. You see him?"

59

Captain Stevens grinned at the shout of his driver and stared through the lenses of his night vision sight. Sure enough, someone was moving up there. Powell was the most gung-ho of his crew, always looking for an enemy to kill. It was what they paid them for, so he couldn't fault him.

"I can't identify him as a hostile, Private. What do you think?"

"Check out the rifle, Cap. The magazine, that sure as hell isn't one of ours. It's an AK, no question."

He looked again, and Private Powell was right. The dark figure was carrying an AK-47, or one of its derivatives. They were about to engage in a major battle. It was enough.

"Gunner, use the 25mm cannon. Send 'em to hell."

"Copy that, Cap."

Corporal Wojinski squeezed the firing lever of the M242 Bushmaster 25mm cannon mounted in the turret. The cannon fired up to two hundred rounds per minute, and was accurate up to three thousand meters. If Corporal Wojinski has been firing across level ground, the burst would have torn his victim to shreds, but all he managed was to hose down the area around the target. Even the sophisticated sighting mechanism was challenged in the icy terrain, an uphill shot in temperature and winds that were anything but conducive to accuracy. The massive shells tore into the rocks, dissolving the area into a tornado of chips and stone fragments.

"Did you hit it?" Stevens shouted, trying to make sense of the target that was just a cloud of dust and smoke.

Something flew into the air, and Wojinski shouted in triumph. "Fuckin' A, Cap. Look at that. I reckon we can chalk that one up as a hit. He's gone to join his boss Osama."

"Well done, Corporal. Driver, advance. It's time to find the rest of these bastards and finish them off. Stay sharp, men. The

Air Force gave them a good pasting, but there's sure to be a few left, and they could have missiles."

Powell hit the gas pedal, and the Armored Fighting Vehicle jerked forward. Even Captain Stevens felt the thrill of anticipation. They were going in to kill the Islamic scum, and they'd get Second Lieutenant Sara Carver out, "Hold on, Lieutenant, the 18th Infantry is on the way, and we're gonna give them hell. We're coming to save you."

CHAPTER THREE

"Someone's up there, Stoner. Look, up on the slope. An insurgent, what're they doing up there?"

He looked where Blum was pointing, but found it difficult to make anything out. A shaft of moonlight lit up the night, and it had to be an insurgent, holding an AK-47 what else could it be? Then the figure turned to the side and turned back. A gust of wind ruffled their clothes, and they didn't look like anything an insurgent would wear. Tresses of long hair streamed out in the wind. He knew Afghans wore their hair long, but not like that. When he looked lower, perceived the body shape, it was no man.

The person holding the rifle was a woman. And she was wearing what looked very much like an army uniform. He gulped in astonishment. Unless he was wrong, and he didn't think he was, he was staring at Sara Carver, high on the slope. Somehow, she'd slipped away and grabbed a rifle.

"Greg, it's her. Either we get to her, or we alert the infantry she's up there. They could miss her if..."

He stopped as the first of the armored vehicles nosed

into view and edged past the wreckage of the Bradley. He felt in his guts something was wrong, something else terrible was about to happen. He couldn't put his finger on it when something exploded down there, closer to the caves. Probably some ammunition or a delayed action bomb, and flames lit up the night. And he saw them. Men, hostiles, scores of them. The survivors of the bombing had waited until the raid was over, and some had sheltered inside the caves. They'd come out to meet the infantry attack, and the APCs were driving into disaster. The aircraft had done them a favor and destroyed one armored vehicle, free of charge. Now they wanted to finish the rest.

The enemy wasn't just armed with rifles and machine guns. In that brief flare of light, he'd seen more, much more. Down below, the Americans couldn't see what awaited them. Missiles, the usual RPG-7s, which may have done them some harm, although they should have been safe, buttoned up inside the steel hulls. It wasn't the RPG-7s that worried him. They had other, more sophisticated missiles, anti-armor systems. The friendlies were walking, or rather driving, into a trap.

Greg tapped him on the shoulder. "We can't leave her up there. She could…Jesus Christ, they're shooting at her!" The lead Bradley opened fire and hosed down the slope with heavy caliber cannon shells. The ground where the cannon fire hit was empty of life, just shattered chunks of rock, torn about by the heavy shells, and dust still settling, "Stoner, we need to get her out of there."

He frowned. "She's dead, Greg. There's no way anyone could survive that burst. The right thing to do now is to warn the crews of those vehicles. You know they have Malyutkas. They'll rip those Bradleys apart like cans of beans. The Stryker I don't know, it may survive, but somehow I doubt it. We're looking at a massacre."

Greg looked at him in astonishment. "We go down there, and they'll chew us up and spit us out. There's nothing we can do. I still think she could have survived. We didn't see her go down."

He gazed up at the rocky slope, and there were several folds in the ground, tiny crevasses in the rock. It was possible, just possible. Except if she'd survived, a little longer wouldn't make a deal of difference. "We need to warn them first."

"But how?" Greg asked, "There's no way."

"There's always a way." It came to him a second later, "We'll mount an attack on the armored column. Set up the Claymores. We'll go part way down the hillside and blast them. It'll make stop and take a second look. That's the best we can do. Then we'll go and see if Sara Carver is alive."

"A Claymore? Are you serious?"

"They're buttoned up. It won't do any damage, but it'll cause them to stop when they know an enemy is in front of them. Take a second look at what they're going into. Let's go."

They scrambled down a rocky slope, heading for the narrow valley along where the vehicles were picking their way past the rocks and obstructions. It made for slow going, making them an easy target for the missiles. They reached a point which Stoner estimated was equidistant from both the column and the ambush, and planted two Claymores, one either side. They were almost too late. The two men were climbing the opposite side to go looking for Sara Carver when the first Bradley came into view. A long burst of heavy caliber shells smashed into the ground where they'd been a second before, and Stoner led the way up a narrow defile, climbing for height. They almost made it, and he turned to detonate the Claymores when a missile smashed into the slope a few meters higher on the slope. Their world erupted in smoke and flame, and the massive blast from the five-kilo warhead.

Even as the rocks tumbled around their heads, he'd worked out what they'd done. Whoever was in command of that lead track had ordered them to fire a missile to bring down the rock over their heads, to either trap or kill them. The surviving Bradley Armored Fighting Vehicle carried a BGW-71 TOW missile launcher as standard. The TOW, or Tube-launched Optically tracked Wire-guided missile was intended to destroy a main battle tank. But against the rocky side of a mountain, it was just as effective.

It didn't kill them, but it worked like a charm. He was fighting his way clear of the cascading rocks to reach Greg, who was half buried in the fall, when something hit him hard on the head, and he blacked out. When he came to, he was staring at the face of an officer who looked more than angry. An infantry colonel, Lieutenant-Colonel Harold H. Brewer, had left his Humvee and climbed the hillside to examine who they'd killed. He wasn't impressed.

"You two! I thought I told you to get out of here. This is a military operation, and you've just endangered the lives of all my men. I ought to shoot you."

The plan had worked as Stoner intended, except they hadn't needed the Claymores. At least they'd stopped. He shook his head to clear the fog enshrouding his brain. "Colonel, we were trying to warn you. There're insurgents ahead of you armed with missiles. Malyutkas, and you were walking right into them."

"I didn't see any missiles," he snapped, "What're you really here for? You didn't make the journey from wherever you came from just to warn us. What're you men up to?"

"Colonel, Sir, look what my men found down on the track." He held up the distinctive green metal casing of the Claymore.

"It looks to me like they were right, we were driving into an ambush."

"Claymores? They'd hardly scratch the paintwork. What kind of ambush is that?"

Stoner cleared his head enough to intervene. "Colonel, I set the Claymore. The idea was to set it off to warn you. I knew they wouldn't penetrate your armor, but it would have brought you to a stop while you investigated."

He gave Stoner a hard look. "You set the Claymores? Whose side are you on, Mister?"

"It was a warning. That was all."

"I don't believe you. What are you doing in these parts? You working for the insurgents?"

They'd managed to dig Greg out. He staggered toward them, in time to hear Stoner shout, "You stupid bastard. We're here to rescue the American officer Sara Carver. The officer you just shot up on that hillside."

"What do you know about Carver?"

"I know she was up there when the lead Bradley opened up on her with a heavy caliber cannon. We were trying to stop you men driving into an ambush, and then go and see if she's still alive."

The two officers swapped looks, and Brewer said, "That's bullshit. What are you really doing here?"

Stoner tried again. "Listen, pal. While you're questioning us, there's a bunch of insurgents less than a klick away, further along this valley, and an American officer up on the hillside, who's either dead or needs our help. What're you gonna do, stand there chewing the fat, or go find her, and kill a few enemy at the same time?"

He knew he'd said the wrong thing the moment the words were out of his mouth. Brewer didn't look at him but glanced at the Captain. "I don't believe a word of their story. It stinks. Put them under arrest until we can work out who they really are."

Stevens looked doubtful. "We did see a person on the hillside, and we gave them a burst from the 25mm. I don't know, Colonel. It could have been anyone. Even Carver."

"Did they carry a weapon?"

"Yessir, AK-47. No mistake."

"Then it was an insurgent. Deal with these men, and join the rear of the column when you're done. If you hurry, you may get a chance to join in the fight. We'll keep going along this track and stay to plan. I don't believe she's up there. She's inside the caves, and that's where we're going. Move your track, Captain. I'm coming past. I'll lead them in myself."

"You're making a mistake," Stoner tried to reason with him. Brewer ignored him, and returned to his Humvee, using the radio to bring up the remainder of his command. The Stryker came in behind him, with the back markers strung out in a long line. Soldiers grabbed Stoner and Blum, hustling them inside Stevens' Bradley, where they forced them to lie on the floor, under the boots of six infantrymen in the cramped compartment.

Brewer gave the order, and the column started moving. Stevens didn't sound convinced, and he stood outside the ramp, trying to make sense of it.

"Are you sure about what you saw? We shot at an insurgent with an AK, but it could have been anyone."

Stoner twisted his head to see the officer and stared up at his face. "I saw her as clear as I'm looking at you. I don't say it was Sara Carver, but I saw a female in a tattered American uniform."

"But carrying an enemy assault rifle?"

"Wouldn't you grab a rifle if you were trying to escape?"

He sighed. "I guess so, but it's too late now. We'll go up and check it out when they've dealt with the enemy in front of us."

"You won't go anyway, Captain. That enemy is just waiting for you with Malyutka missiles."

"I have my orders, Mister. Men, close the ramp. We're moving off. Join the Colonel, and kick some ass."

He didn't sound like he had his heart in it. He looked at the Claymores again, then down at Stoner and Blum. The Captain leapt aboard the Bradley as the ramp closed and climbed into the turret. The engine started, and they followed Colonel Brewer's advance. Stoner glanced at Blum. For some reason, they hadn't searched them. The soldiers took their AK-47S assault rifles, but each man carried a gun under his coat. In Stoner's case, two guns, two big .50 caliber Desert Eagles.

* * *

"Take the armored fighting vehicle first, not the Humvee in the lead. We will leave something for our machine gunners," Rumi Khan chuckled, "Those men will soon join their comrades in hell."

Abdullah passed on the order. "We could capture the men in that Humvee, if the Bradley blocks the track. They would make useful hostages."

Khan considered for a moment and grimaced. "No, kill them all. It will teach them to take us seriously. Then we will talk to the hostage, find out who she is, and why she's so important."

"As you say."

They watched and waited. The Bradley rumbled along the track following the Humvee, and a moment later they reached the narrowest part of the track, where the vehicles had to slow to make a turn. It was perfect. Abdullah waved to the missileer, and a bright streak of flame seared out from the launcher. It struck the Bradley on the side, in the center of the hull. The 30mm spaced laminate armor, combined with an additional layer of explosive reactive armor was enough to protect the vehicle from RPGs and heavy caliber machine gun bullets and smaller shells. The Malyutka was neither an RPG nor a small cannon shell, and it penetrated the hull, to explode inside. No one got out. In less than a second, twenty-seven tons of AFV, costing over three million dollars, ceased to exist, with the crew of four men and six infantrymen.

Rumi Khan smiled at Abdullah. "Give the order."

He turned to the waiting men. "Attack!"

* * *

Inside the cramped compartment of the sole surviving Bradley, Stoner heard the explosion. He knew at once that Brewer had ignored his warning about the missiles and driven into an ambush. Stevens was staring out through the periscope and muttering, "Jesus Christ, Jesus Christ, they hit the Colonel. No, it was the Bradley. He's still alive. Oh, fuck, they're attacking. The insurgents, Jesus, they're everywhere, dozens of them. Driver, advance. We must help Colonel Brewer's retreat. Get the tracks moving now!"

"You sure that's a good idea, Cap? Those missiles can turn this tin can into scrap metal."

Several of the soldiers were murmuring their protests, and Stevens hesitated. Stoner felt the ache of frustration, knowing they were making a mess of it, and more good men were about to die if they didn't do something.

"Captain Stevens, listen to me. I've been here before, and I know the ground. Free us. Give us some men, and we can take them from the rear. They'll run like rabbits. If you want to save your unit, there's no other way."

He stared at him, his face mirroring his indecision, and his fear. "Did you say we should leave the Bradley and go out on foot? That's crazy. We'd have no protection."

"That AFV they hit with the missile didn't protect the men inside. If they hit this one with another missile, you'll go the same way. We must get off this track. It's a death trap. Fight them on foot, flank them, get around back of them, and hit where they're not expecting it."

He was still thinking it through when another missile slammed into the rocks just a few meters ahead of them. An RPG-7 this time, and the fragments of metal and stone rattled against the hull doing no damage, except to the nerves of the crew, who looked at each other in dismay. It made up his mind. If they stayed where they were, they were a sitting target.

"Okay, Mister, whoever you are, I'll take you at your word. Lead the way. Powell, stay with the track. Corporal Wojinski, you're in command. You men in back, open the ramp. We're going in."

A few mumbled complaints, but the ramp opened, and someone handed Stoner and Blum their rifles. He grabbed his AK, cocked the lever, and paused.

"You still have the Claymores? They could be useful."

A man shrugged and handed out the gear stowed in a canvas bag. He leapt outside, searched for threats, but no one shot at them. There was little cover, as the flames from the wrecked Bradley were enough to light up the immediate area. He led them away and they began to climb, away from the ambush site. After twenty meters scrambling up the slope, they reached a narrow plateau he recalled from all those years ago.

So far, the enemy hadn't seen them or shot at them, and his hopes rose that they could pull it off. Get behind them, and turn the tables, unless they had any other nasty surprises, but that was the nature of surprises. You couldn't anticipate or plan for everything.

Greg Blum was right behind him, and a few meters back, Stevens led the six infantrymen. It was dark on the narrow plateau, and they stumbled along, some men cursing as they tripped on loose stones and cracks in the rock. Stevens told them to cut the crap, and they went silent. He came to the end of the narrow plateau, and ahead of them laid the burning Bradley. A shelf of rock less than half a meter wide was the sole option, and he stepped out onto it. Facing the rock, moving sideways, crablike, his rifle slung on his back. They passed the remains of the AFV, and he kept moving. The shelf tilted sharply upward, and the climb became more difficult, but a glance aside confirmed they were still with him. They came to a wider plateau and stepped off the narrow shelf, surveying the target.

The insurgents were below them. By peering over the edge, they could see them, a dark mass of men, moving down to engage the Americans. Further back, more men were carrying two Malyutkas launchers. They'd lost patience, waiting for the Americans to resume their stalled advance. They were going out to meet them, to do battle, and to destroy them.

Stoner indicated a steep, narrow pathway that led down. "Follow me, and we'll be right on their tail. As soon as we're down there, we'll hit them."

"There must be forty men out there," Stevens said, "What do we have, nine? It's not enough."

"It'll be enough, Captain, provided we hit them hard enough. We don't have an alternative. It's that or see your unit massacred."

A pause. "Very well, we'll do it."

"Let's go."

As they descended the steep pathway, he automatically checked the handguns in the webbing holsters. The two Desert Eagles felt reassuring, and he had a strong feeling they were about to see some action. His AK-47S was cocked and ready, and as he reached the track, he walked toward the hostiles. They followed in silence until they were less than thirty meters behind the enemy. He gestured for the men to form up alongside him, and they waited for the order. So far, the robed men were walking eagerly toward the Americans, unaware of what lay behind them. It wouldn't last long. Sooner or later someone would look back. He glanced at Stevens and nodded.

"Fire!"

Stevens and his six men carried M4s. Stoner and Greg, AKs. Nine rifles chattered, and every man had selected full auto over the more conventional burst mode. The roar of gunfire was massive in the night, coming from an unexpected quarter. Men went down in droves, slaughtered by the hammering bullets drilling into their ranks. A few, a very few, dropped their weapons and ran into the darkness, finding narrow pathways to escape the deathtrap, but most succumbed. He led them in a jog toward the fallen enemy, and they checked the wounded. Looking for squirters, men who'd escaped to fire at them from cover. There were none. A few mercy shots finished the wounded, and Stevens started toward his Colonel's Humvee.

He turned to Stoner. "He'll want to confirm the track is clear, so we can advance."

"We should check out the surrounding hillside first," Stoner objected, "We don't know who else they have out there."

"I'll talk to the Colonel."

He nodded. "We're going on to the caves, see if there's any sign of Sara Carver. Assuming she's still alive."

The night sky was lightning, and they saw his face color. "We don't know who it was on that mountainside."

"I do. Good luck, Captain."

He started back to the caves, and when they'd left the scene of the battle behind, they came to the first entrance perched high above the track. Stoner led the way up, and they almost made it to the entrance. Four men stepped out unexpectedly and looked to be just as shocked at seeing the enemy so close. They leveled their AKs, and Stoner and Blum threw themselves to one side as 7.62mm rounds hissed past them. Both men returned fire, and the hostiles dropped to the ground, crawling away toward the cave entrance. They went after them, but as they drew near the entrance, the rifle fire hissed and spat all around them.

"They're well protected in there," Blum observed. "Four of them, and I reckon they can hold us off for a long time. If she's in there, they'll kill her."

"I know she's not in there. She was up on that slope. We need to be sure, and to be sure, we have to get past those gomers ahead of us."

"How do we do that? We don't even have hand grenades."

"We have the Claymores. Cover me."

He snaked across the ground, and the enemy opened fire, trying to kill him before he got close. Greg fired short bursts, enough to put them off their aim. Stoner reached a natural step in the rock less than ten meters from the entrance. Huddled below the step, he felt over the top with his hand to find what he was looking for. A fault in the rock, enough to insert the stake of a Claymore, and the light was still poor enough they didn't see what he was doing. The trick would be getting them out into the open, enough to put them in the lethal arc of the mine.

An Afghan has many flaws, and some are fatal. One such flaw was his stupid, mule-headed Islamic pride. He swore at them.

"Hey, shithead. Do you know what we were doing last night? Us men went to bed with your women. Did you know they were whores? Not very good whores, but you know what we liked best about them? They were cheap."

Silence. He wondered if any of them understood English. Many Afghans spoke enough to get by, so they could screw employment opportunities from the U.S. forces serving in the country. To take advantage of medical aid and various grant packages. Or to deliver the stab in the back, a well-placed ambush when they'd listened to the direction a convoy was traveling. He thought he'd misjudged, just as a reply came.

"What did you say?"

"Your women, the whores. I thought you'd want to know before we kill you, they were a good lay. Said Afghan men had small dicks, so they enjoyed going with Americans, lots of Americans. Say, is that true? Small dicks?"

"Show yourself, infidel. Face me like a man and say those things."

He climbed to his feet. One hand held a Desert Eagle, and the other, concealed in his palm, the detonator. Visibility was poor in the pale morning light, and he counted on them not seeing the thin wire trailing behind him. Their rifles were aimed at him, but so far, not one had the alert posture that speaks of an imminent decision to pull the trigger.

He plastered a sneer on his face. "I was asking about small dicks. That was the biggest complaint from your women."

"How did you know they were our women?" The man who

spoke was older, his face creased with suspicion, but little real intelligence.

"Because they told me. Say, they said to give you a message when we saw you."

"Message?"

"That's right. Goodbye."

He hit the button on the detonator and dove to the ground, away from any ricochets that came his way. The Claymore exploded with a roar, and he hugged the cold rock while hundreds of steel balls ripped through the Afghans. When he put his head up, they were all dead, their bodies ripped to tattered shreds. He raced over and made a check of each body. One was still alive, the man who'd spoken to him. Blood poured from a huge belly wound, and he twisted his head so he could see him.

"Where is she? The American girl, the officer?"

The man groaned at first, a long, low wail of pain-wracked misery, compounded in the knowledge his wound was mortal. "Help me. Please, the pain. Help me."

"I'll help you, but first, tell me where she is?"

The Afghan tried to sit up, and his guts uncoiled out of his belly like a slithering snake. "You will never find her. Never."

"Tell me where she is, and I'll get you to a doctor."

"I'll see you in hell first, infidel." With a huge effort, he hawked a gob of spit that narrowly missed Stoner's face. It was his last act in this world, before he keeled over and sighed his last breath. He looked around hearing a sound, but it was Greg.

"You get anything out of them?"

"Nothing. We'll have to look inside the caves, but that was her on the slope, and if she's alive, it's where we'll find her."

They looked down at the track as the first of the vehicles rolled to a stop. Brewer leapt out of his Humvee, and he surveyed the ground, the litter of bodies, like he'd scored a great victory. He shouted for Captain Stevens.

"Get over here, Captain. Bring your men. I want them to search through the caves, and see if she's inside. The rest of you look around outside, and make sure we got them all. I don't want any mistakes. When we leave here all we leave is bodies." He looked up the hillside and spotted Stoner and Blum. "You men, I was wrong about you, and thanks for the assist. You can get back about your business now. The Army is here, and we'll handle things from here on in."

Stoner stared at the arrogant officer and kept his temper in check. "We'll do that, Colonel. Tell me, how do you plan to go about finding Lieutenant Carver?"

"That's my business, Mister. Leave the Army to do what it does best and move on, while you still can."

"Yeah, right. We'll be seeing you."

They started up the mountain, joining a track that snaked upward, toward the snowline. Brewer called after them. "Hey, that's the wrong way. Where did you leave your vehicle?"

"It broke down. Someone said there's an emergency telephone this way."

His mouth dropped open, and it was almost something to laugh at, were it not for the bodies inside the still-burning Bradley half a klick to the east. He turned away and carried on ascending the steep path, heading toward the spot they'd seen the mystery person. He was certain it was Sara Carver. The question remained as to whether she was alive or dead.

* * *

"What are they doing?" One of Khan's bodyguards, Jamal, watched the two civilians walk away from the American soldiers and climb the slope, "Is there something up there we should know about?"

"Nothing. Be silent," Abdullah murmured from their position less than fifty meters from the soldiers.

He moved close to his boss. "Rumi, we could take them if you wish. Most of our men are dead, but at least they'd have some peace when they see we have revenged their deaths."

"No." He pointed to the two men climbing the mountain, "They know something, and there has to be a reason they're going up there. Could she have escaped that way, the American woman?"

"You gave orders to kill her if it looked like they were getting close to the caves."

He shrugged. "If the man guarding her was as useless as the other men, she will have managed to escape. We climb the mountain, where those men are going. I know of a shortcut, so we can get ahead of them. If the prisoner is up there, we will find her, and we can kill those two as well. A good result."

Abdullah swept his hand toward where so many of their comrades lay. "No so good for them."

"They are with Allah," he said carelessly, "and He will make certain they receive their just rewards. We must move out. If that woman is as valuable as she appears to be, we should get her back."

Abdullah gave him a dutiful nod. He knew his boss was right, for the first time in the last few hours. The Chechen had made some stupid mistakes, but at last he was conserving what few men he had left. If they found the girl, his decision would be vindicated. If not, the men would be unhappy, perhaps unhappy enough to want a change of leadership.

It wasn't all bad. If things continued to go badly, they'd travel to Peshawar where there were many diversions for the weary warrior, booze, for those who ignored the Islamic proscription on alcohol, like most men, good food, and best of all women. Peshawar was home to a huge variety of brothels, whores who catered for the most extreme perversions. Perhaps being forced to abandon the area wouldn't be so bad.

* * *

It was bitterly cold on the hillside, and she shivered inside the tattered remains of her uniform. She'd watched the action unfold and shuddered when she'd watched the men she'd served with incinerated inside first one Bradley, and then a second. It meant for a short time, the Afghans' attention was diverted elsewhere, and she was safe where she was. The cannon fire came close to killing her, but she'd turned to run in panic and stumbled into a crack in the rocks that saved her life. All she needed do now was wait until they killed the enemy, then she could go down, and they'd take her home.

As she huddled in the cover of a ruined shepherd's stone hut, she regarded the action below. It was all over, and the shooting had stopped. The good guys had won, and it would be just a matter of time before she could join them. Idly, she surveyed the slope and froze. There was movement about a half a klick away, and much lower, men moving toward her, six of them, the turbans and AKs visible. She knew she wasn't out of trouble yet. Slowly, carefully, she eased out of her hiding place and bent low. Following the natural contours of the ground, she climbed higher.

* * *

"Jesus Christ, this is hard going."

Greg Blum stumbled yet again, and just stopped himself from tumbling down the thirty meters they'd made. The going was getting more difficult, the temperature plummeting, and the place they'd seen the figure on the mountainside go down looked to be much further and higher than they'd realized. Stoner helped him up without a word, and they pressed on.

"She couldn't be alive, could she?" Blum asked.

He broke his silence to reply. "Anything's possible. An old Russian proverb, Greg, you should know it. 'Don't count your corpses before they are cold.'"

"If they hit that person with the cannon shells, there won't be any corpse to count."

"Maybe. Keep moving."

They were high above the track, maybe a hundred meters above the cave entrance, and the cold rays of the dawn sun had arrived to bathe the landscape. Stoner estimated the position the cannon had hit, and when they arrived, his assessment was correct. The rocks and sparse foliage had been torn to tiny pieces, and nothing remained larger than a ten-cent piece. But no body, nothing to indicate a person had died in that spot. And if she hadn't died...

Stoner pointed to faint marks in the dust and in the fine stone that littered the slope. "She's alive, and she's heading up."

Greg followed his gaze, as if she was standing there in full view. "I don't see anything."

"She's alive, and she's gone that way. We keep climbing, and when we find her, it's our passport to finding the whereabouts of Shahay. Let's go."

* * *

The six men straggled out onto a path, almost a hundred meters above the two men coming below, and well out of sight. Khan went to the edge of an adjacent ledge, and his men held him as he looked over.

They're coming, good. They know she's up here, otherwise why would they come?

He signaled to his men, and they pulled him out of danger.

"It is as I thought. They are coming this way, and the girl is above us. She cannot escape, so now we can kill these men before we go after her. A few meters further up the path there is a place we can wait for them, out of sight. As soon as they appear, we kill them and carry on after her."

He walked off in the lead, and they followed in a straggling line. Soon, they would wreak vengeance for their comrades' deaths. They would happily rest in Paradise, knowing the infidels were dead.

* * *

She could see them clearly now, and she had no doubts about who they were. Six Afghan insurgents, without doubt they were pursuing her. How they knew she did not understand, just that she had to stay out of their clutches. She still held the AK-47 rifle she'd taken from the guard, and a swift check of the magazine showed eleven bullets.

Is that enough to kill them all? In theory, yes, but they'll be seasoned, crafty warriors. It won't be enough, so I'll have to hide, but how?

She cast around for a hiding place, for some way off the mountain. That was when she saw them. Two more men, and although they carried AK-47s, their clothes were different. Paler skin, long, leather coats, one brown and one black. Westerners, and they looked like the men she'd seen fighting alongside the soldiers. They were friendlies. Another glance at the Afghans, just in time to see them go to ground, and a second later, it dawned on her they were about to ambush the two friendlies.

No! I can't allow it to happen. But how can I warn them?

There was one way, and she lay on the rocked ground, curled her finger around the trigger, and waited.

* * *

They'd been climbing for an hour, and for the past thirty minutes seen no sign of any tracks. Stoner considered the possibility the woman they were pursuing had detoured somewhere, and they'd missed it, or even fallen to her death. In places the track was perilously close to sheer drops of up to a hundred meters. Yet he doubted it. She was ahead of them. Or it was all for nothing.

"Where do we go from here?"

He jerked his attention back to the present. They'd reached a fork in the narrow track, and both ways led upward. One was a little easier, snaking its way to the side as it ascended the steep slope. The other went straight up. It would be a hard scramble, but his reply was immediate. "That way. The hard way."

She would have chosen that path. Why make it easy for men who may be coming after you to kill you? They climbed again, and now it was a real climb, not just a scramble. Pulling themselves up, hand over hand, always knowing a misstep could mean the end. The section was less than thirty meters, and once they reached the next plateau, the going would get easier. He looked around, scanning the slope they'd climbed, all the way back down to the entrance to the caves, and found no sign of enemy activity. Far below, the armored vehicles were parked on the track, and the second Bradley was still smoking. American soldiers were prowling around, tiny figures like ants in the distance. But no hostiles, their back trail was clear.

He grinned at Greg. "Almost there, and then it gets easier."

"It gets colder. I reckon the temperature is way below freezing. If that is her up there, she could hit a problem with hypothermia or frostbite."

"So we have to reach her mighty fast. At least no one is shooting at us."

The shot ricocheted off the rocks less than two meters away. For a split second, he was too shocked and surprised to react. The he moved.

"They're ahead of us, the enemy. Either we close with them and kill them, or they'll kill us. We can't fight while we're climbing this path, so move it! Christ, they're below us as well."

They were already moving when the crackle of gunfire echoed over the mountainside. Louder this time, several assault rifles shooting at them. More bullets smacked into the rocks, hitting the spot where they'd been when the first shot fired from above. Stoner led the way, and they almost ran up the final section of track, pursued by more gunfire from below. They made the plateau and flopped on their bellies. Safe from the shooting coming from below, but still wary of the shooter above them.

"It's just one person, so we'll keep climbing and keep watching. When they show themselves, we kill them."

* * *

"The fool," Khan raved as his men, "We had them, and someone warned them by shooting from above." He glared at Abdullah. "Who is up there? Which of our men climbed the mountain?"

"I don't believe it was one of our people, Rumi. I heard a

single shot, and I saw it hit the rock two meters or more from those men. It was a warning shot."

"The American woman, you think she is up there?"

He shrugged. "Who else?"

"Where is she? All of you search the slope. Try to see where she is hiding."

"And when we do?"

"Kill her."

Seconds later, a fighter shouted in satisfaction. "I see her. Look, up on that shelf, about two hundred meters above us. Those men are climbing toward her."

They looked up, and she was standing in clear view on the very edge of the shelf. Still invisible to the men below, but they could see her. She didn't know they were there, but Khan gloated in satisfaction.

She soon will. A moment before she descends into hell, after her body has descended the mountain.

He giggled as he had that thought. He'd suffered a terrible defeat, but somehow, she'd become a symbol for what had happened at Tora Bora. If she got away, it would compound the disaster, but if they killed her, he could snatch a partial victory by preventing the Americans from recovering her. At least, recovering her alive.

"Open fire! Kill her!"

CHAPTER FOUR

She watched the two men climbing nearer to her and stepped out onto the edge of the plateau, so they would see her when they climbed to the next stage. The bullets that punched the air came as a shock, and she'd forgotten the Afghans shooting from below. She stepped back, but too late. A bullet creased her upper arm, tore skin and muscle, and the blood soaked into the rags of her clothing.

She was already cold and conscious of the dangers of frostbite at such altitudes. Now she had the added problem of blood loss, and a bleeding wound to handle. There was another problem. If the Afghans killed those two men, they now knew she was there, and they'd come after her. With a heavy heart, knowing she was mere minutes from linking up with her two rescuers, she turned and climbed again. After the first twenty meters, she encountered the snow line, and the temperature plummeted even further.

She knew of the trail of the blood drops she was leaving behind her. Of her waning strength, and the creeping numbness in her arm. Knowing her chances were fading with every step.

The probability was she would die up on the mountain, and the thought that possessed her was would anyone find her body, or would she lie forever buried in the snow, a cold, unmarked grave never to be uncovered. She took another step, and another. The snow was deeper, but she'd ceased to care. Her mind was fixed on a single action, to climb.

* * *

He'd dropped back and waited to see if the Afghans were still following.

"They're coming up behind us. We need to take them."

Greg came back, and they stared down the slope. Watched the men climbing after them, and any doubts were gone. The first snow had powdered on the rocks, and their footprints had left a trail as clear as a six-lane highway, which the hostiles were following.

"How're we gonna do that? We're on bare rock, hardly any place to hide, and there are six of them. That's not good odds."

"Unless we use the Claymore." Stoner touched the canvas bag he still toted on his shoulder, "We'll find a good place to hide it, and blast them when they get near."

A grin. "Now that's what I call a plan."

They reached a place where they were out of sight, a natural fold in the rocks that obscured the view from below. There was a fine covering of snow, enough to hide the mine, and he unrolled the thin command wire to a position twenty meters further up the slope. They flattened and waited. The wait was short, and after ten minutes, the first hostile came into view. Then the second, and the men walked into the direct path of the Claymore. He held the detonator and smiled at Greg.

"Time to say goodnight to these gomers. See you in hell,

suckers."

He hit the button, and…nothing. He hit it again, and still nothing. "It's not working. The damn thing is faulty; it could be a broken wire or anything. Shit, they're almost on us. Shoot them!"

He leapt to his feet, Greg joined him, and they cut loose with the AKs. A storm of bullets slashed toward the enemy, but they were fast. Two went down, but the other four men ducked back out of sight, and they had a problem. One man toted an RPG-7. It would have been a hard climb, carrying the shoulder-launched missile up the mountainside. Yet he'd done it, and already he'd be preparing the missile to launch. They were trapped. If they climbed higher, they'd be within full view of the enemy. There was nowhere to go. Both sides of the path were impossible to negotiate, still covered by the enemy guns.

He considered his options, and they came down to one. Charge and run at them before the missile launched, because if it detonated on their position, they wouldn't survive it. He explained it to Greg, who looked dubious.

"They'll fill us full of holes before we reach them. There has to be another way."

"There isn't. It's that or we die where we stand."

"So we die here, or we die running down the slope."

"Yes."

He didn't answer, just looked around wildly, as if by magic something was about to turn up. Stoner grabbed his arm.

"Forget it, Greg. We must do this, and do it now. We don't have an alternative."

"What about that guy over there?"

"There is no guy over there, or anywhere else. We don't have time for this."

"But…"

"It's your imagination playing tricks. Make sure you have a full magazine."

"Do me a favor, Stoner. Take a look."

He sighed and swung his eyes in the direction Greg pointed. And did a double take. A man was standing there, but this was no ordinary man. He was like no one he'd ever seen before in his life. A cross between a scarecrow and Bigfoot, clad in rough sheepskins, even his feet were swathed in sheepskins. It wasn't so much he was tall, just that the layers of clothing made him look big; as well as his hair and beard, huge and bushy, as if they hadn't been cut for many, many years.

He was just standing there, staring. Holding an assault rifle, except it wasn't an assault rifle. He moved a fraction and exposed the distinctive butt of a PK, a Kalashnikov light machine gun. A handy tool, when you were facing many enemies.

Who is his enemy? Is it us, is he something to do with those ragheads following us up the mountain? Or are they his enemy? Is he trying to convey a message? I don't know.

Abruptly, the man gestured, a single swipe of the arm, unmistakable, a call for them to follow. Then he disappeared. He couldn't reach him. The path they were on went in the other direction.

Wait!

A few meters further up the slope, he saw a thin slash in the rocks, which could be a narrow, almost hidden path.

Should we trust him, assume he's on our side, or is it a trick? Except we can't be any worse off than we are already.

He pointed. "Greg, we're going there. I think he means to help us."

"You sure?"

"Nope, but if we're gonna die anyway, why not take the chance?"

He was already running, sprinting up the track. He stumbled along the tiny shelf of rock, a few inches wide. If he missed his footing, the enemy wouldn't need to come up to get him. He'd tumble straight down into the waiting muzzles of their guns. He risked a quick look back and down. The missileer was standing in plain view, the nose of the rocket pointed up toward them. They had a scant few seconds, no more. They weren't going to make it, and then a voice said, "In here."

A narrow slot in the rock; so dark and hidden they almost went past it. Conscious of the RPG heading their way at any moment, he shouted, "Greg, get in here." He squeezed through the narrow gap, and Blum tumbled in after him. They were in a dark cave, but inside with no time to examine their surroundings. With a massive roar, the rocket detonated a few meters away, and flames shot past the opening. By their light, they saw the man who'd saved them. The guy they'd seen on the rocks.

The first impression they got was he stank. This was a crazed hermit who lived rough outside even the most basic fringes of society. He was short and wiry, with a massive, long, unkempt beard that had never seen a barber. His skin was dark, etched by suffering and living outdoors, yet somehow not native. The clothing was an odd mixture of military and ethnic. Camo pants, what looked like Soviet jump boots, and the shirt thick wool, over which he wore at least one sheepskin, roughly cut in the shape of a coat.

The eyes marked him out as something beyond the usual. They were blue, a piercing deep blue. Whereas the visage had more than a hint of madness, the eyes were something else. Deep inside, a keen awareness shone through his gaze. He still clutched the PK machine gun they'd seen him carrying, but it wasn't pointed at them, which was a relief. The question was who was he. Some throwback was Stoner's best guess. Genes that went all the way back to Alexander the Great, when he'd conquered Afghanistan, and some of his army were Northern Europeans. Their descendants occasionally threw up blue eyes, even after so many centuries.

"Do you speak any English?" Stoner watched him carefully, to see if he got a reaction. He still wasn't sure.

The man nodded. "Yes." The reply was slow, as if he'd needed to think about the monosyllabic answer.

"Thank you for saving us from that rocket. Those men were trying to kill us."

"Yes."

Does he understand what I said, or is 'yes' the only word he knows?

"They'll be coming after us, you know that? If they find us here, they'll kill you as well."

"Yes."

He looked at Greg, who shrugged. He tried again. "Listen, pal, we're grateful for the help, but can you understand what I'm saying? We're trying to locate an American officer."

"Yes."

He sighed with frustration. "My name is Stoner, Rafe Stoner. This here is Greg Blum. What's your name?"

The answer came so fast he stepped back in astonishment. "I know who you are. You haven't changed much, you know. My name is Wyatt Evers. You knew me as Sergeant Wyatt Evers, 5th Special Forces Group. You were at Tora Bora. As I remember, you were a new Naval recruit, doing escort duty for a U.S. Navy liaison officer."

He stared at him for several seconds, but he didn't recognize him.

"I don't believe it. You're dead. Buried under thousands of tons of rock when they destroyed the original Al Qaeda tunnels."

He opened his hands wide. "Here I am, and I'm not dead yet. They tried, after they captured me during that battle. The bastards held me for a few months, and they were gonna execute me, but I managed to escape. Spent some time getting back here, and went looking around for my buddies, but they'd all gone home."

"But, why didn't you make your way to one of our bases? Why stay on this mountain?"

His eyes stared into the distance, looking at some long, forgotten memory. "It's hard to explain. I had to hole up here while they were looking for me, and by the time they'd given up, I kind of liked it. Been here ever since, both sides of the border. Cross into Pakistan, and then back into Afghanistan. The mountains feel kind of, friendly."

"But what about your family? Your buddies in the 5th Special Forces?"

"They let me down. Didn't look too hard to find me, and I figured what's the point? I got used to being here, and I make out okay. Steal supplies from the insurgents, and I've killed plenty of them since I've been here. Only thing...he looked at Stoner. "What year is it? I kind of lost track."

"Twenty sixteen."

"You're not serious? All those years, damn. Twenty sixteen, I've been fifteen years on my own."

"A long time, Sarge. Maybe you should think about coming in. You've done your duty, more than most would have."

He gave a vague nod, and his eyes darted every which way. "Yeah, maybe."

He was more than a little crazy, both men realized, living on his own in a freezing hell, at least through the winter. Maybe he should come in, but then again, maybe he was beyond rehabilitation. Evers poked his head through the entrance hole, squinted around the outside, and pulled his head back inside. "They're coming. I can't see them, but I know they're there."

"You can hear them?"

"I can smell them. We have to get out, just in case they find this place."

Greg had been examining the inside of the cave and discovered no other exit. "The moment we go outside, they'll see us and start shooting. You know they'll have more RPG rockets."

Evers bared his teeth in a grin. "Then I guess we'd better not go outside. You're on a mountain riddled with caves, you don't think I'd choose somewhere with no rear exit?"

He went to the back of the dark space and pulled a boulder aside, exposing a low tunnel just big enough for a man to crawl through. It was about a meter wide with a roof less than a meter high. "Follow me, and whoever comes last, make sure you roll the stone back over the opening, or they'll find us."

"Where does this take us?" Blum asked him.

"Home."

* * *

She winced, and the noise of the explosion as the rocket smashed into some unknown target stirred some life back into her. The cold was intolerable, and she found it almost impossible to move her limbs other than at a slow, geriatric crawl. Still she kept going, always climbing higher, and higher. Her mind became a kaleidoscopic whirl of jumbled images. She was at home in Washington, and snow had covered the neighborhood, giving it the appearance of a Christmas scene. She wanted to make a snowball and throw it, but she wasn't sure if her father would approve.

Best not to upset him, and besides, she could hear her mother calling her in from the garden. No, it wasn't her mother, but it was someone's voice she could hear. Consciousness returned to her, and she was on a bleak mountain that straddled the Afghan Pakistani border. That much was real, and so was the voice. Even higher up the mountain, and she doubted it was one of her pursuers, although it could still be a hostile. She didn't care, all she wanted was to get warm, to find someone who may help her. Even throw her back inside a dark prison cell. Anything would be better than this.

She put on a spurt and sprinted the next twenty meters where the narrow path bisected a wider track. Wide enough to allow the passage of donkeys, and she knew that because a line of donkey was traversing the track. Bearded men accompanied the donkeys, and she assumed they were smugglers. Men she could offer payment to in return for their help, a big, fat bribe. Her father would pay, even if the military weren't too pleased she hadn't put the request through the right channels.

"Hello!" She waved at the nearest man, and he turned in surprise, unslung his rifle. He saw a woman standing nearby, a sick woman, swaying with cold and exhaustion, and relaxed.

He walked to her and stared hard into her face. Said something, and she shook her head. He wasn't speaking Pashto. She knew that.

"Do you understand American?"

He beamed. "American, yes. I speak good American. You soldier?"

"Yes."

He was instantly wary and looked from side to side. "Where are the rest of your people?"

"I'm on my own. I escaped from the Taliban."

He nodded his understanding. "The Taliban, yes, they bad people. Very bad."

"Can you help me?"

"Help? Yes, I help. You come with us. We take you to where we are going."

She felt a surge of gratitude. "That would be wonderful. You could make a lot of money for helping me."

His face was serious, and something was unreadable in this eyes. "A lot of money, yes, that is true." Then he broke into laughter and shouted something to one of the other men. The reply sent him into paroxysms of laughter. "A lot of money," he repeated, "Come, we must go."

The convoy comprised six beasts, donkeys or mules, she wasn't sure of the difference, led by three men, at least two men, and a boy standing next to the lead animal, staring ahead of them. The animals were loaded with a variety of crates and jute sacks, and she didn't guess at the contents. Something illegal, that was for sure. She didn't care, as long as they took her someplace warm. Somewhere she could get to a phone and call her people.

The man beckoned to her, and she stumbled toward the nearest donkey. He shouted something, and the boy in front turned to look. When he turned, she saw it wasn't a boy, but a young girl. Her clothes were thin rags, almost as bad as Carver's, her face blue with cold and scrunched up in a picture of abject misery. She noticed something else that made her almost forget the cold. The girl wore manacles, steel handcuffs on her wrists. As she came to answer whatever the man wanted, the irons clamped to her legs clanked as she walked with short, shuffling steps.

Carver at first assumed she must be a felon, and she looked at her rescuer. "Is she a prisoner? Isn't it hard for her to walk in those irons? I can hardly walk as it is. The going is so difficult in these mountains."

He laughed, and it wasn't a pleasant sound. "Difficult, yes. But without them she may try to escape."

"So she is a prisoner? Where are you taking her?"

"She is not a prisoner, no. She is a slave."

Her eyes narrowed, and she felt the first real fear since she'd been a prisoner of the Taliban."

"Slavery is illegal." She gave him as hard a stare as her weakened state would allow.

He didn't seem impressed. "So is prostitution, and all sex outside marriage, but it pays well."

"She's a whore? But why is she manacled?"

His smile was oily. "Because it was not her choice to be a whore, so she will need some persuading. She is pretty, yes? Will fetch good money when we reach Peshawar, they are always on the lookout for fresh meat."

She wanted to sob with despair. She'd got so near, and yet she was even further from the help she so desperately needed. "You are taking me to a place of safety? My people will pay a great deal of money for my safe return."

"A place of safety, yes. No need for your people to pay, you will earn us much money. A white Western woman, you will be popular with the men. Some like to inflict pain on white women, and especially one who was an American soldier. Yes, we will be rich. They will queue up for a chance to bed the American whore."

She felt the iron before she realized what they were doing. The other man had come up behind her, and first, he clamped the irons on her legs. While she struggled, the first man held her arms, and they fastened the handcuffs on her.

"Go, join the other whore at the head of the convoy where

we can keep an eye on you."

"But I can't walk in these!"

The weight was terrible, and in her weakened state, she knew she wouldn't get more than a hundred meters.

He wasn't impressed. "It's not a problem. We'll get the donkeys to drag you along until you decide it is better to walk." He kicked her in the small of her back, and she almost fell, "Go, join the other whore. We are already running late, and we have a long distance to travel before nightfall."

* * *

The crawl was long and hard, squeezing through narrow gaps in the rock, always conscious of the thousands of tons of rock above them. After an hour, the crawlspace opened into a larger tunnel, sufficiently high to stand. They emerged a few meters later into a cave. Evers lit an oil lamp, and they could look at their surroundings. He spread his arms.

"Welcome to my home."

Several old mattresses were thrown on the floor. The rest was bare, apart from a blackened fireplace. Gear was strewn everywhere, weapons, crates of food, cans of gasoline, which presumably he used for cooking and lighting. Sheepskins tossed carelessly on the floor, makeshift rugs. And a bible, placed carefully on a side table. He saw the direction of their gaze.

"It's the one thing keeps me sane, all the time I've been here."

"Fifteen years," Stoner murmured, "A long time to be alone."

"Right, a long time. Except I'm not alone, you see. Up here, high in the mountains, I feel closer to the Almighty. Anytime I have doubts about the choices I've made, about the way I live my life, the men I've killed, I read the bible, and then I talk to him."

"Does he ever answer?" Greg asked him.

"Sure, always."

Stoner winced.

He's mad, no question. Mad as a box of frogs, which is no surprise, how could any man live high on a remote mountain for so long, and with no company, without going crazy? Still, it's a puzzle how he passes the time during the long periods of winter when the paths would be all but impassable.

The answer soon came to him, by way of the rank, sweet odor that almost overwhelmed them when they first entered the cave. Opium. As if in confirmation, he picked up a pipe and put a match to it. The sweet scent became stronger, and he seemed to relax, his eyes becoming dreamy.

He allowed him a few minutes, and then tried to question him.

"Sarge, tell me there's another exit from this place? We don't have to crawl back the way we came to get out?"

"Nah, there's another exit, just over there." He pointed to a darker shadow in the rock, "Comes out even higher up the mountain, and there's no need to crawl."

"That's good to know. There's something else. We're looking for an American Army officer. A girl, the Talibs kidnapped her, and they've been holding her prisoner in Tora Bora."

He considered that for a few moments, closed his eyes, and they thought he'd drifted into unconsciousness. The smoke from the opium pipe was a lazy coil that spiraled into the air, and Stoner felt as if they were in some old-time opium den. He worried about the soporific effect. It wouldn't do to fall asleep when so much was at stake. Although falling asleep may not have been much of an option. The temperature was freezing cold. Beyond freezing, and he understood the need for the opium.

Finally, his eyes opened. "I saw a girl. I guess she was the one, going uphill, heading up the mountain."

"You saw her? She's alive?"

"She was alive, yep. May not be now, there's plenty can go wrong up on those peaks."

He nodded. "Like avalanches, and the risks of hypothermia, getting lost, stuff like that."

Another long pause, while he got his answer together. He wasn't used to talking to people, that was obvious. Except to God, and that wouldn't help find Sara Carver.

"Smugglers."

"Smugglers? You mean drugs," he looked at the pipe, "Weapons, things like that..."

Yet another long pause, eyes shut, thinking, puffing on the pipe. Then they opened. "People. There were some guys passing through several hours back, and this is their regular route. People smugglers. They take young women and girls out of Afghanistan and deliver them to the brothels in Pakistan. Most of 'em go to Peshawar, lot of trade there. If they came across her..."

He didn't need to say any more. "Time to go, Wyatt. She could be in serious trouble."

"You want to leave now? You just got here."

"Sarge, can you take us up the mountain, see if there's any sign of her? If we leave it any longer, she could die up there." He thought about the brothels of Peshawar, and shuddered, "Or worse."

He suddenly got to his feet. "Okay, then. Let's go."

He darted across the cave, moved aside a sheepskin curtain, and disappeared through the opening. They followed, and the narrow tunnel felt even colder, with an icy wind cutting along its length. After twenty meters, they emerged onto the mountainside, and the view was spectacular, a vista that stretched across much of Afghanistan. Through a narrow saddle in the peaks, they could look south, and he knew he was staring at Pakistan.

Evers set a hard, fast pace, climbing up a steep, almost invisible path and wading through the snow. After a half hour, they reached the top of the slope and saw more peaks in the distance, even higher. He held up a hand, and they stopped.

"Someone's been here; animals, donkeys, about six of 'em. Three men, no, two men and a girl." He was kneeling in the snow examining the ground and crawling around, putting his eyes almost to ground level. Like a tracker, and Stoner recalled he'd been Special Forces, and so trained to read sign.

"A girl?"

"That's what it looks like. Lighter, smaller feet, smaller steps, although they chain them sometimes, leg shackles. Stops them getting away. Uh, uh, there's something up there. Someone else came and joined them. Another female is my guess, probably your girl."

So she's alive, now all we need to do is find her.

"Where did they go?"

He pointed to the southwest. "Like I said, they're heading for Pakistan. Peshawar, no question."

"Wyatt, can you help us go after her? You know these people, how they operate, and it's vital we get her back."

"She mean something special to you? Girlfriend, or something like that?"

He explained about the deal with Ivan, information about Faria's cousin for the safe return of Sara Carver.

"It's like this. If we do nothing, she won't last long with

those people. And Shahay will die, stoned to death by a medieval bunch of religious nutcases. Two young women, both condemned to a terrible death, and I believe we can save them both. But we'll need your help."

He thought for a few moments, standing in the snow, looking around him like an Old Testament prophet. Wearing his weird mix of clothing and sheepskins, long, straggly hair and beard, like some ancient hermit. But unlike some ancient hermit, he'd once been a kickass Special Forces operator. He was a man who'd spent many years wandering this very region, and who'd seen it all. The people, good and bad, mostly bad. Who they were, where they went, he was a treasure trove of intel.

"Peshawar, you're going there?"

"That's where you said they'd take her. You've been there?"

"I've been there several times, sure. Been most places over the years. Peshawar, you won't find it easy dealing with these people. They won't want to hand her over to you, I promise you that. Place is like Sodom and Gomorrah. A filthy, stinking pit, if you ask me."

"We need you, Sarge."

The title 'Sarge' seemed to make him decide. "Okay, I'll help you, but we'll need transport. Hiking over these mountains isn't any joke, and if you want to get ahead of these people, you'll need a vehicle."

"I have a vehicle," Greg said, "We hid it in a cave when we came in. It broke down, and it was too dark to fix it."

"What kind of a vehicle?"

"A GAZ, the 69 model."

He smiled, a few yellowed teeth showing through the mass of beard on his face. "Piece of shit, the GAZ. Is that the best you could do?"

Stoner grinned as Greg defended his treasured old vintage Soviet SUV. "She's tough as anything, and she'll take us anywhere we want to go."

"Until it breaks down. I've seen a few of them over the years."

"There you go. They go on forever."

"They were either broken down or being towed to a scrapyard."

Greg mumbled something about people who didn't maintain their vehicles, but Evers cut him off. "There's more snow coming in. If this GAZ is down the bottom of the mountain, we'll have to get down there now to retrieve it. Another couple of hours and we won't get off the slope. The snow will be too thick."

"We're ready," Stoner said, "The sooner the better. What about the Talibs who were shooting at us?"

He shrugged. "If they want to get in the way, so much the better. Bring 'em on."

He still held the PK light machine gun, making no secret of the fact he'd enjoy the chance of putting it to work. Before either man could reply, he started down the slope without another word. They struggled to keep up, and the years he'd spent roaming the mountains became obvious. He moved like a mountain goat, seeming to float along invisible tracks, avoiding every obstacle. They slid and tripped most of the way down in an attempt to keep up.

They didn't come across the Talibs, and after an hour, they arrived at the cave where the GAZ waited for them. Silent and cold, and the engine showed no sign of life when Greg pressed the starter button.

"I think it must be a wiring fault, something to do with the ignition."

"It's the carburetor," Evers contradicted him, "In these altitudes and temperatures, the fuel supply gets airlocks."

"It's the wiring," Greg insisted, "I know my vehicle. Give me a minute. Now I can see what I'm doing, I'll soon have it running."

Fifteen minutes later, his head was still under the bonnet, and the engine stubbornly refused to start. He popped his head out.

"I don't get it; I could have sworn it was the wiring."

Evers nodded. "You want me to look? I'll need a hammer."

"What for?"

"I'll show you. It won't take but a minute."

Greg handed over a rusty hammer from the tool kit in the trunk. Evers leaned under the hood, raised the hammer, and brought it down with a hefty 'clang' on the steel. He hit it again.

"Try it now."

He pressed the starter, and nothing happened. Pressed it again, and it stuttered, caught, died, and then roared into life.

Evers' expression was serious. "Russian gear, you need to know how to handle it. Like the people, they don't respond to anything other than brute force."

"I'm part Russian," Greg murmured.

"Figures, buying a heap of shit like this."

Stoner decided it was time to intervene. "We should get going, if we're to reach the border before nightfall. I suggest we take the main highway back toward Jalalabad, and we'll cut the Torkham road before we get there. Stay off the side roads, when the snow comes down hard, they'll become impassable." He looked at Greg. "Even in a GAZ."

Without a word, the half Russian, half Afghan, slammed the lever into gear and roared off. They passed the burned-out hull of the first Bradley to get hit, but the soldiers had gone. He assumed they'd returned to barracks, because of their failed operation to rescue Sara Carver. They reached the intersection where they'd join the Jalalabad road and stopped. They'd blocked it with the surviving Bradley, the Stryker, and a huddle of Humvees. The soldier held up his hand for them to stop, and they had little choice, with their vehicle making an effective barrier.

He walked forward to speak to Greg. "You need to get clearance to proceed. We've just…hey, it's you guys. You were at Tora Bora. I'll go get the Colonel."

Two minutes later Colonel Brewer stomped out from his command Humvee. He nodded in satisfaction. "Well, well, if it isn't the idiots who fucked up my operation to free Lieutenant Carver. What are you doing now, going to join the Taliban? And who's this with you?" He gave a pointed look at Evers in back, "Bigfoot, or his long-lost brother?"

The soldier standing next to him guffawed, and then stopped when Brewer glared at him. "Arrest these men, Private; interference with an authorized military mission, and suspected of aiding and abetting the enemy. Take their weapons, and hold them under guard."

Evers had the PK casually held across his lap, and Stoner squinted behind him, concerned he might be tempted to use it. He'd clarified his contempt for the military he blamed for leaving him at Tora Bora, and there was always a possibility the crazy mountain man might be tempted to open fire. Friendly lives would be lost, and he would not stand by and let it happen. He spoke to Greg in a murmur, without looking at him.

"You see that gap over there, in front of the front fender of the Stryker. I reckon there's enough room to squeeze past and drive over the hillside. If we stay here a minute longer, we're gonna be stuck for the duration. Sara dies, and Shahay dies.

That's if your piece of shit GAZ can make it."

The reply was succinct. "Fuck you, Stoner. I told you, this baby can go anywhere."

On the last syllable, he slammed his foot down on the gas. The engine was already running, and first gear engaged. The ancient Soviet GAZ leapt forward, as if it had gained its second wind, and they left Brewer's shout trailing in their wake. The wing of the GAZ clipped the fender of the Stryker, and then they were past. He swung the wheel over, and they bounced off the road, onto a scrap of hillside that should have been barely passable by four-footed creatures. They climbed a gradual slope, and as they crested the top, the first shots cracked out behind them.

None came near, and he suspected the misses were intentional. Brewer's men were no fools, and they'd be more than aware of their Colonel's failings. A stickler for spit and polish he may have been, but he was no judge of men, and no genius at military planning. They cleared the top, and the GAZ went airborne for a few brief moments, crashing down with a force so powerful he felt the tremendous jar in the base of his spine. Greg floored the gas pedal when they touched down and steered the SUV along a rocky hillside, weaving in and out of huge boulders, before he sighted the road and turned the steering wheel to bounce back onto the smoother surface.

He kept the vehicle flat out on the road to Jalalabad and didn't slow until they were approaching the turn off for Torkham, the crossing into Pakistan. Evers hadn't said a word, had been silent ever since they'd got the GAZ started and moving. Sitting in the rear with his back upright, like the Sphinx, gazing into infinity, as if for all time.

As he eased off the gas, Blum turned to Stoner. "Doesn't it strike you as strange?"

"What?"

"Your involvement in what we're doing. I mean, considering the trade you're in."

"Surplus machinery?"

A chuckle. "Ma Kelly's. You recruit girls to work in the brothel you part own, and here you are risking your life to save a girl from a brothel."

"I know Ma Kelly's."

The voice came from the back; Evers. "I went there when we first arrived in country. Good place, decent girls." Stoner turned, and he stared at him. "That place is yours?"

"I own a part of it, yeah. So what?"

"So nothing, I had some good times there, before Tora Bora. Plenty of girls wanted to work there, as far as I could see, and they made a good living. Thing is, the Peshawar brothels are different. You ever been in one?"

"Never felt the need."

"No, I guess not. Thing is, those places cater for the worst desires of the Islamic male mentality. Men who like to hurt their women. To inflict wounds, beat them, cut them, or anything else that takes their fancy. Women die in those places, which is why no one wants to work in them. So they must keep grabbing unwilling girls to work in them. Replacements, I guess. They have a reputation, those places, and it's not one to be proud of."

"How long would she last?"

A shrug. "Who knows? They'll give her drugs to make her develop a habit, and then she'll find it more and more difficult to leave, even if they allowed her to, which they won't. A year if she's lucky. A lot less if she isn't. And the longer she stays, the harder it will be to shake the habit."

"She won't be there that long. We're getting her out."

"They won't like it, you going in there to remove one of their girls. They'll try to kill you."

He gave Evers a grim look. "They can try all they like. I'm still taking her out of there. You still up for helping us?"

He shrugged. "I'm up for anything that comes along. Life has been a bit boring on the mountain, so I guess a bit of variety will be good for me. I just hope you understand what you're getting into, is all. You done much killing lately, since you left the Navy, I mean?"

"Some."

"What about the other guy, Greg?"

"Some."

He stared back at Stoner for long seconds, as if measuring something, his abilities, perhaps, or his determination. He seemed happy with what he saw.

"Then I reckon that little lady will be going home, as long as you realize it'll be on top of a pile of corpses."

"No sweat."

* * *

The airfield looked deserted, and the light had very nearly gone. Ivan looked at Captain Narwaz Aziz and almost felt sorry for him. He was just a regular guy who had got caught up in the Islamic craving for revenge and punishment of anyone who failed to follow their preconceived notions of religious laws. In his case, he was gay. In the West, he could have lived out life with protection from the law. Inside Pakistan, the law would hammer him into the ground.

"What can you do for us, Captain? You know we're looking for a gunship."

"We are mainly a training squadron here, and most of our

aircraft are unarmed. There is one, an IAR 330. She's Romanian built," Ivan winced, but Aziz went on, "She's really a Puma, a copy of the Aérospatiale troop-carrying gunship. They were using her on the range, practicing gunnery, and when they landed, fueled and armed her up ready for a dawn training mission."

"What kind of weapons does she carry?"

"Two 23mm single barrel cannons, pod-mounted on either side of the fuselage. In addition, they have equipped her with two 7.62mm caliber door-mounted machine guns. There are boxes of spare ammunition inside the cabin, so should you need more to finish your target, you could reload."

"Sounds good, so how can we do this? What about guards?"

"The corporal who completes the guard roster made a mistake and sent the sentries off duty without replacing them. There will be no guards."

"How much did you pay that corporal? He's taking one hell of a chance."

"I paid him nothing. He and me are…"

"I get it. Okay, we'll stroll over there and get the engines started. Good luck, Captain, and you haven't mentioned how much you want for this."

He shrugged. "You will pay me what you consider it is worth. And of course, forget you ever saw me, or even heard of me."

"A quarter of a million."

His face fell. "Rupees?"

It was about two and a half thousand dollars. "Not rupees, no, U.S. dollars."

"That is enough to pay for silence from those who would expose me." He held out his hand, and they shook, "Thank you, whoever you are."

"Call me Santa Claus."

He smiled. "Very well. Good luck with whatever you are doing."

He left them, and Ivan tried to gauge the best time to cross the airfield and board the gunship. The darkness was almost complete, although the perimeter security lights would be enough for anyone to see them make the approach, if they were looking. He looked at his men, Gorgy, Akram, and the two Afghan Taliban deserters, Daud and Habiba. Good men, handy with a gun, and no qualms about killing. They used to be Taliban.

Gorgy, you and Daud come with me. Akram, take Habiba and approach the aircraft from the flank. Make a wide circle, and if you see anyone try to ambush us, you know what to do. But do it quietly."

"We'll use knives," he confirmed, "Habiba is good. Knows what he's doing."

"He'd better be. I pay him enough. Look at that watch he wears, a Rolex Submariner, top of the line. He could buy a couple of young wives with what that cost him."

The Afghan grinned and flashed his wristwatch. They called it a Submariner with good reason. The dial had enough gadgets to outfit the control room of a nuclear sub. Ivan decided the best way would be to stroll out across the field, as if they had every right to be there. The lights almost turned the night into day, and he felt at any moment someone would challenge them, or start shooting. They didn't, and he reached the gunship and climbed into the cockpit. Behind him, the cabin had enough space for sixteen troops, and the door-mounted machine guns looked as if they would do the business. He left Gorgy and Daud to slip behind the guns and familiarize themselves with their use. Moments later, the other two men entered the cabin, and he set to checking out the controls.

He was no stranger to rotorcraft and anticipated no special problems with the Puma. The cannons were another matter. He'd noticed them when they approached, long, black barrels poking out from the nose. He'd need gunners to operate them, and he called Akram and Habiba, showed them the guns, the sighting mechanisms, and the triggers. Then he turned his attention to starting the engines.

The two massive Turbomeca Turmo IVC turboshaft engines roared into life as he depressed the starter buttons. Above the fuselage the rotor blades turned, slowly at first, and then they gathered speed. He watched the engine temperatures rise, and before they'd even entered the green, he shouted a warning to his men and throttled up to maximum. The revolutions rose, and the rotors whirled into a fast blur. He applied collective, corrected with the tail rotor, and the Puma soared into the air. And dropped like a stone. He'd moved the collective the wrong way, and he hurled it over to reverse the fall. Someone shouted in alarm, but he ignored him and fought to gain height.

At one time, the helicopter actually touched the ground. He felt the impact as the undercarriage struck, and the telescopic leg compacted as it took the weight. Then he managed to get it moving upward, and in a few seconds, he'd gained a hundred meters of height and was arrowing away toward the north. Due north, not the direction for Chitral, but he'd get a few klicks before he altered course. As he left the airfield behind, he looked in the mirror, and nothing had changed. The security lights were still on, and no one was moving. No vehicles rushing across the field, flashing lights of military police, no lines of troops doubling to their alert stations. Nothing. Satisfied, he stayed low, following the contours of the ground, below the radar horizon. Leaping over pylons and tall buildings, until he estimated he was five klicks from Peshawar.

Then he turned due north, hugging the border on the Pakistan side. The journey would be short, a little over two hundred klicks, destination Chitral, and time to settle the score with Batu. If all went well, his business problems would soon be over. If they ran into an inquisitive Air Force jet, his problems would still be over. Just in a different way.

He looked over his shoulder, and they were all crouched at their stations. They knew the risks of running into trouble, should the Paks discover someone had stolen their aircraft. So they were watchful and ready.

"Test your guns, and make sure you know how to use them. We could run into trouble."

"And if we do?" Bukharin asked, sitting behind the port side cannon.

"Deal with it."

"Deal with it?"

"Shoot the bastard down, preferably before they get a chance to use their radio."

"Whatever you say, Boss. Say, do we get a bonus for this one?"

"Sure you do. You keep living."

CHAPTER FIVE

Torkham, the border crossing into Pakistan, was virtually abandoned. Inside the heated guardhouse, they could see the soldiers supposed to be doing guard duty playing cards. The snow was falling in thick, white clumps. The single guard at the barrier raised the pole and waved them through. There were no passport or document checks, no inspections for illegal weapons or drugs, just one bored soldier wishing he were anywhere other than standing guard in the frozen mountains.

The distance from the border to Peshawar was sixty klicks, and even in the slow-moving GAZ, they arrived in just over an hour. The snow was falling heavier when they got into the city, and the miserable, broken slums were hidden beneath a vast expanse of white. He'd been there before and found it to be one of the most depressing places on Earth. The city attracted the worst elements across Asia. The priority was parking the GAZ. Not that it was worth much, but in the pits of the Islamic world, even a worn-out Russian relic had value. They paid a garage owner to store it inside his lock-up, half up front, the other half when they collected it. Just in case he got any ideas about making a quick profit. A long look at Wyatt Evers and his machine gun was enough to dissuade the most hardened and ardent thief.

The three men walked through the streets of the city, and it wasn't a pleasant place for a stroll. Those fleeing the violence in Afghanistan, who were to be pitied, the smugglers, the economic powerhouse that kept the city a financial ruin, and the inhabitants, poverty stricken, many hopelessly addicted to drugs. Disease was rife, as was malnutrition. Any efforts to alleviate the problems by injecting money were a waste of time. The men with the guns simply took it off those in need.

One main economic engine that drove the city was the brothels, bordellos of every type, catering to every need, every perversion. There were no limits, save one, the ability to pay. Once the client parted with his hard cash, he could indulge himself in whatever he pleased. Many did so. Young girls suffered the most terrible pain to satisfy the demands of their john. Some eventually died from continual abuse, and all became hooked on hard drugs, supplied by the management to keep them pliable.

Evers was looking around keenly, scenting the air like a hunting dog. He ordered Greg to stop outside the Qissa Khwani Bazaar, scene of a massacre during the time of the British Raj. Several protestors against British rule were arrested, and a crowd gathered at the bazaar to demonstrate. British Indian troops moved into the bazaar, and the crowd pelted them with stones. A British Army dispatch rider was killed, and the crowd cheered and burned his body. Two British armored cars drove into the square at high speed, knocking over and killing several people. The crowd tried to gather up their dead and wounded, provided the British troops ceded the square. They refused, so the protestors remained.

Frustrated with the native disobedience, British officers ordered their troops to open fire with machine guns. The violence continued for six hours, and afterward, the exact number of deaths was disputed. Some officials claimed as few as twenty dead, others suggested the figure was nearer four hundred. Following the massacre, two platoons of a British Indian Army regiment threatened to mutiny. The NCOs served sentences of up to eight years in prison.

There were no mutineers now. People in Peshawar were too cold, despairing, and hungry to consider anything other than the next meal. Buildings were in disrepair, and those who braved the cold weather huddled into an assortment of old blankets and sheepskins. In the case of the women, thin cotton burqas. They were women. Allah would keep them warm.

Evers prowled around the square, looking inside the coffee bars, watching the people who came and went. He even spoke to two men, who seemed to nod their heads in agreement with something he'd said.

He came back. "They're here, got here ahead of us."

Stoner stared at him. "How the hell could they do that, a donkey train?"

"They'd have had transport waiting on the far side of the mountain, so they'd drive the final part of the journey. I checked around. They've just received a new consignment of opium, and the price has dropped, always does. I'd buy some myself if I didn't have more than I can use back home."

Home, in a cave up in the mountains!

He shivered. "Any ideas where we could start looking?"

He nodded, although his gaze was far away, staring at the distant mountains, the place he called his own. "Right here, that's why I wanted to come here first. Worst brothel in Peshawar, so I figured this would be the best place to start."

He pointed across the square to a building on its own, four stories high. Two men stood outside the front door, both armed with AK assault rifles. While he watched, a man went past them and through the front door, which opened as if someone was waiting and watching the other side.

"You're sure she'll be inside?"

"Not one hundred percent, but close. It'll be a tough one to crack, plenty of guards around."

"What about the rear?"

He grimaced. "They're not stupid, these people. Guards front and back, and more inside the front lobby, a couple more patrolling inside, I'd say eight or ten all told. The minute we try to get inside, they'll start shooting."

"If we give them the chance."

Stoner pulled aside his long, black leather coat and exposed the Desert Eagles. "I don't plan to go in there and ask nicely. Either they play it our way, or they die."

"No more than they deserve. Okay, how do you want to play this? Go in through the front or the rear?"

He'd been thinking about nothing else, and he still wasn't sure. Until his eyes lit on a truck that had just stopped outside what looked like the one decent building, a bank. The truck was armored, and this late in the day they'd be collecting cash. Armored meant heavy, which suited him just fine.

"We drive in. Front entrance."

"There ain't no way you can drive in through the front."

He grinned. "Trust me. I'll find us a way."

The guards watched him warily as he strolled toward the armored truck. They passed sacks of cash from a hand truck and gave them to a third guard positioned in the vehicle. They continued to work, but their attention switched when they saw another man stroll up to the truck they were working on and grab a sack of money; a wild-looking man, long hair, huge beard, and wearing the clothing of a vagrant, a mix of military surplus and sheepskins.

The man in the truck dropped a hand to his holster as his two colleagues raced after the thief. He didn't draw the gun. Another man, a Westerner in a long, brown leather coat, was pointing a gun in his face. An AK-47S, and he froze, praying to all his gods he would not go down in a hail of automatic fire.

The other two guards rounded the truck, handguns already drawn, and stopped. The wild man hadn't continued running. Instead, he was facing them, but no longer clutching the bag of money. He held a machine gun. A Russian built PK machine gun, and if he twitched the finger they could see on the trigger, they'd be dead. Even if they survived by some miracle, the other man was enough to stop any ideas they had about shooting it out.

He wore a long, black leather coat, and slung across his chest, an AK-47S. He wouldn't need the carbine-length assault rifle because he had two huge automatic pistols, one held in each hand. Pointed at their bellies, and from a mere two meters away, the muzzles looked huge. Neither guard needed anyone to tell them a single bullet fired from those monster guns would do mortal damage, and they dropped their pistols, and put up their hands.

The older man attempted a smile. "Sirs, whatever it is you want, you are welcome to take it. I have a family and seven children."

"I, too, have a family," the younger guard stuttered, "Eleven children."

Stoner stared back at them and didn't answer for several seconds. The men shook, waiting for the bullet. When he spoke, they flinched, until they heard the words.

"Drop the guns, and I won't kill you."

"Yes, Sir, of course. Take the guns, the truck, the money, everything."

"We will. Lie flat."

They obeyed, and he scooped up the guns. Evers picked up the bag of money, went to the rear of the truck, and tossed it inside. He jumped into the back after it, while Stoner climbed behind the wheel. Blum joined him in the shotgun seat. He started the engine and drove toward the brothel, taking it slow, so they didn't attract the attention of the men inside. Behind the truck, there was a great deal of attention. The square was already crowded with people, scores of people. By the time the truck had traveled fifty meters scores became hundreds. They raced in, crowds of shouting, gesticulating, excited people.

The reason was simple. Wyatt Evers playing Santa Claus in back of the armored truck, tossing out bundles of money, removing the rubber bands that held the notes together, and flinging them out into the breeze. The notes flew out like confetti, and eager Pakistanis pursued the truck, grabbing at the precious paper. By the time Stoner jammed his foot to the floor on the gas pedal, the square behind them was blocked with the freeloading throng. Greg shouted at Evers, "Hold on, three seconds and we hit."

He grabbed for Stoner's seat belt and fastened it, and did the same for his own. He grabbed a handhold with one hand, his AK with the other, and held on. They were hitting almost top speed, and the two guards outside the door stared in astonishment at the armored truck bearing down on them. Disbelieving, they stood their ground, and left it too late. The truck brought them down beneath the front wheels, and the tons of steel rolled over them as it mounted the two steps and slammed into the building. The door didn't stop them. The walls surrounding the door didn't stop them. Tons of steel tore down all before it, and when he jammed on the brakes, they were inside the bar.

Men turned in astonishment, dropping their glasses of booze in alarm. Girls squealed and started to run. Two armed guards appeared from a doorway behind the bar. They raised their rifles, and Stoner unsnapped the belt, leaned out of the open door, and hit them with a .50 round apiece from the Desert Eagles. Both men flopped back through the doorway they'd come through, and he didn't need to worry about a follow up shot.

Evers clambered from the truck, and the men in the bar watched him warily. He was scary enough to look at, with his wild, mountain-man appearance, but the PK he held rock steady in his arms was the clincher. He didn't speak, didn't need to. Stoner leapt out and surveyed the room. It comprised the entire first floor of the building. The sole exits the rear door, which was closed, and the remains of the front they'd demolished. Apart from the door behind the bar, and he gestured for Greg to check it out while he kept the remainder of the room covered.

That left the wide staircase leading to the upper floors, the bedrooms, and the whores' places of work. Greg came back a second later and shook his head.

"Just the two bodies, the guys you shot. Nothing else, and no other doors."

"They're dead?"

He glanced at the Desert Eagles. "What do you think?"

"Right. Sarge, we're going upstairs. Keep them where they are. Anyone moves a muscle, shoot them dead."

"Copy that. I could shoot all of them, just to be on the safe side." An odd expression came over his face, "Or maybe I should ask Him first."

Stoner winced. He was mad, a loony armed with a gun. Then again, he was their loony, which made him useful. "Just watch them. Only kill anyone who moves."

"You got it."

He led the way up the stairs, his boots pounding on the wood, and they came to the second-floor landing. Blum covered him while he went from room to room, kicking them open, and where a girl was inside with a client, a gesture with the pistols sent them racing to the staircase to join the crowd in the bar. They found no sign of Sara Carver. He raced to the third-floor landing, and Blum did the same. Just two girls this time, both with clients, and he sent them down the staircase. Raced up to the fourth and top floor, for their last throw of the dice. If she wasn't there, they'd missed her.

His mind reeled with the implications if they'd raided the wrong brothel. Whoever held Lieutenant Carver would have plenty of warning there were armed men in town, looking for her. They'd spirit her away, or even kill her.

She must be here, has to be!

He opened the first of the closed bedroom doors, and not surprisingly, the people inside hadn't heard the rumpus on the first floor. She was tied to the bed, on her back, staring up. The man who stood over her, naked, held an erect penis in one hand, and in the other, a thin cane he was using to slash across the girl's breasts. With each stroke, she squealed in agony, while he shouted at her in Urdu. When he learned of another man in the room, he turned and snarled at Stoner.

Who slammed the barrel of the Desert Eagle on his skull, reversed his grip and took it by the barrel, slamming the heavy butt down on his head. The blow wasn't intended to stun. He intended to hurt, and it worked. He felt the give in the bone as it cracked under the weight of heavy steel, and the man slumped to the floor, unconscious, blood pouring from his shattered head.

"I'll get someone to untie you later, Ma'am. Right now I'm in a hurry."

He didn't wait for a reply, but rushed out and into the next room. He put his hand on the handle and turned as a shot whistled past him. Greg had identified an armed man racing out of a room further along, probably a guard. He'd snapped off a quick shot. The guy wasn't hit, but he froze, and Blum fired again, a three-shot burst. This time he went down. Stoner entered the next bedroom. He found was a girl lying on the bed, face down, her buttocks raw and bleeding after a hard beating, and her sobs were pitiful.

"I'll be back, Ma'am, and get you out of there."

Then he was outside the room, back into the hallway, and the next bedroom had two stout locks on the door. He put his boot against it and tried to kick it open. All he managed was to come close to breaking the bones in his foot. Mumbling, "Okay, we'll use the key," he squeezed off two .50 caliber rounds, one into each lock. The kinetic force of the impact broke the locks and pushed the door slightly ajar. He went in and found the space empty of people, but not entirely empty.

He was inside a storeroom for drugs; the chemical restraints that would stop the girls from escaping, at least, from developing any desire to escape. Plastic bags of white powder, and he didn't need to work out they contained heroin. Syringes and other equipment for administering the drugs, the chains that would bind the girls to the brothel keeper, as much as hardened steel and toughened padlocks.

He left the room and tried the handle on the next door along the passage. It was locked, although with a simple door lock rather than the high security devices next door. He stepped back, hurtled at the door, and slammed his shoulder to the woodwork. The door crashed open, and a girl was chained with one hand to a steel radiator. Crouched on the floor, naked, bleeding where she'd taken a hard beating. She looked up at him with glazed, drug-fueled eyes.

"Please, don't hit me again. Don't touch me. You can do what you like with the injection if you wish. I won't put up a fight, but don't hit me again."

The room was cold and bare. Bare wooden boards on the floor, bare, roughly plastered walls. No furniture, none. The radiator was cold, and besides the bleeding, she was blue with cold, shivering uncontrollably. Her wrists and ankles displayed dark bruises, like those sustained by prisoners who'd worn shackles locked on too tight. The language was English. The accent was American. Her face was unmarked. They'd only beaten her on the body. Her face was her prized asset, a beautiful, European face. Just like a girl he'd intended to marry, so many years ago.

Her name was Madeleine Charpentier, and an IED detonated beneath the ambulance she was traveling in. Killed her, and destroyed the Red Cross emblazoned vehicle on the way to carry out a mercy mission inside Afghanistan. He'd found Second Lieutenant Sara Carver.

"I'm not here to hurt you. I'm here to get you out."

She looked up warily, and her eyes struggled to focus on his face. Regarded his body, took in the coat, the guns, the face, and recognition dawned. "You."

"Me, yeah. Listen, the keys to the cuffs, do you know where they are?"

"No."

The voice was faint. He knelt beside her, and she flinched

at the proximity. He took her hand, and she didn't pull away. Her small hand was frozen, and he tried to rub some warmth into it.

"We're going to get you out, but first, I have to remove the chains."

"Yes." A whisper, "But you don't have a key."

It was a risk, and he didn't want to take it. But Greg shouted from the landing, "Stoner, we got trouble. Evers just called up from downstairs. There's a bunch of guys coming in, and they don't look like they're customers."

"Copy that. Hold them off for a few minutes."

"Any sign of her?"

"Yes, I found her, and she's alive. I just need a few minutes to free her."

"Make it quick. Wait, they're coming through the door. They're…"

The chatter of a light machine gun was loud inside the building, and he knew Evers had opened up. He would have had good reason to shoot. There had to be more men rushing to join the fight.

"I hear them, Greg. Start looking for another way out. A window, anything, I'll be right there."

He gripped the big pistol and put the muzzle close to the shackle, less than an inch from her hand. If it went wrong, a ricochet could chew a big chunk of flesh from her hand. Even kill her. Then again, when a person is facing death, the risk of death doesn't seem such an issue.

"Turn away and close your eyes."

"What…"

"Do it!" He raised his voice to a shout. There wasn't enough time for debate. She turned away, and he pulled the trigger.

The girl screamed, and the 'boom' of the shot was enough

to shake piles of dust and flaking paint from the ceiling, but the handcuff had split into two, and she was free. She wasn't dead, and her hand was still intact.

"Where are your clothes?"

"I…I don't know. They took them."

"Okay, we'll find some later. Come with me, and make it fast. We don't have much time."

"But, I'm naked."

"I promise not to look. Lieutenant, move your ass, if you want to live."

He dragged her to her feet and ran to the door. A man was rushing past, his face flushed with fear after the gunfire from below. He wasn't armed, and Stoner grabbed him as he tried to avoid him.

"Coat and pants, get them off!"

"What do you…"

He slammed the barrel of the pistol against his head. "Next time you get a bullet."

A minute later, Carver was pulling on the clothes, and she staggered as he dragged her away. "You can do the buttons later. We're going downstairs. Can you shoot an AK?"

Some memory of her past life came back to her. "I'm a Second Lieutenant in the U.S. Army, Mister. Of course I can shoot."

He gave her the AK 47S. "Use this. The magazine is almost empty, so use single shots. If you get a chance, grab another mag if you see one."

"Another magazine? Where would I see one of those?"

"Next to the corpse of the guy it belonged to. Now move it."

Greg was guarding the top of the staircase, and he stood aside to let them pass. He followed them down the three flights of stairs, and they reached the first floor. Abruptly, the gunfire started again. Evers was at the front of the building, firing short bursts at whoever was outside. The customers were lying prone on the floor. Bullets smashed through the ruined windows, and many splattered against the concrete wall outside. Several rounds impacted the body of the armored security truck, and Stoner reckoned they were facing at least twenty men outside, all doing their best to kill them.

He pushed Carver toward the truck. "Get in the cab, and keep your head down. We're leaving."

"In this?"

"Correct. Sarge, Greg, go one each side of the truck and start blasting. When we go, I don't want them so close we make it easy for them to kill us."

They nodded and squeezed past the truck. Both men opened fire, and the incoming fusillade died away as the enemy ran for cover from the unexpected counterattack. He took the opportunity to start the engine, ram the gearstick into reverse, and move backward. He glanced out the side window, in time to hear a scream, and an assault rifle flung into the air as its owner went under the wheels. The square was rapidly emptying of people, and the threat of gunfire overcame the lure of free cash. He hit the gas pedal and roared past the armed men who'd come to the aid of the stricken brothel.

A gun barrel poked through the passenger window, but Greg pushed his head through the hatch connecting the driver's cab with the rear and put two bullets into the snarling man holding the weapon. The barrel disappeared, but more were pushing toward them, and several shots whistled past Carver and Stoner before they exited the other side. Evers' machine gun roared, and most dropped back, but on the driver's side, a bunch of men flung themselves into a loose charge, firing from the hip.

A bullet grazed his forehead, and he immediately wiped the blood as it trickled down toward his eyes. He held the wheel with one hand and emptied the Desert Eagle with the other.

He had four rounds left, and each bullet punched a big hole in one of the shooters crowding in to the truck. The firing pin clicked on empty, and one of their pursuers understood what had happened, increased speed, and ran alongside the cab. The muzzle of his rifle pushed through the open window, and he shouted something in Urdu. He was the hero of the moment. Nothing could stop him claiming credit for the death of the infidel who'd invaded their city, and attacked the vital brothel.

Nothing could stop him except a second Desert Eagle. Stoner dropped the empty gun beside the seat and snatched out the other. Seven .50 caliber rounds in a full clip, and he aimed and fired in a split second. Fired again, and the man went down in the dust, dead or dying, he couldn't give a shit either way. Then he ripped up the parking brake lever and brought the vehicle skidding around in a tight turn. Straightened the steering wheel and headed for a wide gap between buildings, his hand on the horn, blasting a warning to those stupid enough to stand in his way. Two seconds later, they were charging away from the square, and he followed a twisting path toward the outskirts of the city. With so many enemies eating their dust, irate brothel owners, savage insurgents, cheated of their moment of lust, and cops chasing the men who'd hijacked the armored truck, there was a single place he wanted to be. Out of Peshawar.

* * *

Mohammed Abdullah turned the corner into the square and immediately stepped back as the armored truck roared past him. He'd heard the shooting, and the shouts and screams of wounded and panicked people, but in Peshawar, such sounds were nothing new. People needed to let off steam. He understood that. If a few civilians got caught up in the crossfire, it was just too bad. People lived, people died. It was part of the grand design of Allah. Who was to question what happened?

Except what he saw as the truck roared past was emphatically not part of Allah's grand design. The man in the driving seat looked remarkably like one of the two men he'd last seen on the slope above Tora Bora. The girl in the passenger seat was even more familiar. Second Lieutenant Sara Carver, their prisoner. The girl who'd escaped, the one they'd come after with their troops and armored vehicles, which meant she must have great value to someone in Washington.

He was so startled he didn't have time to unsling his rifle. When he managed to ready it for firing, the truck was past him, and there were two men in the back. They stared at him for a moment, and one man, fierce and wild-looking, raised his weapon. Abdullah recognized the PK machine gun and jumped back, dropping flat an instant before a stream of bullets chewed up the ground where he'd been a second before. The truck took the corner on two wheels and careered away through the city.

I must get back and tell Rumi Khan. This could be important, and he'll want revenge for what they did to our home at the Black Caves. I want revenge. We all want revenge for what they did, and the surest way to take revenge is to get that girl back, the American officer. Find out who wants her so badly, and then bleed them try in return for getting her back.

* * *

The most direct route to Afghanistan lay to the northeast, the highway they'd driven into the benighted city. In the armored truck, they'd have been lucky to make two klicks before the cops stopped them. He headed back to the lock up where they'd stored the GAZ. Sara stayed in the truck while he put a different proposition to the owner. Storing a beat-up wreck was legal. Storing a stolen armored truck was not.

"No, I cannot. It is impossible. If the police find it on my premises, they will put me in prison for many years. Sorry, but you'll have to remove it. Take it away," he raised his voice in an angry shout, "I do not want it in my shop. Not for anything, not for a king's ransom. Not for all the gold in Pakistan."

"Stoner."

He looked up as she called to him from the cab. "Not now."

"Yes, now. We have a problem."

"Not now, Lieutenant. If we don't get this truck off the street, any second someone will see it and report it to the cops." He turned his attention back to the sweating Pakistani, who looked more nervous by the second, waving his arms, as if to bat the offensive vehicle away from his shop. "Tell me how much you want."

Carver wasn't giving up. "Stoner, listen to me. They've gone."

"Who've gone?"

"Those men who were with you, the ones in the back of the vehicle. I think they must have tumbled out when you took that last corner."

He raced around and looked in the back. Nothing, she was right. "Jesus Christ, they could be anywhere."

"Could those men who were chasing us have captured them?"

"It's possible. We have to go back." He looked again at the Pakistani and back into the truck. Something caught his eye. A canvas sack, of the kind they use for carrying large amounts of cash. It was full, bulging with something. He leapt inside the vehicle and opened it, bundles of cash.

A huge amount of money for the locals, is it enough for a bribe?

He looked at the garage owner.

"How about this? Take the money, and dismantle the truck. Sell it for scrap. That has to be worth a bit more cash."

"Let me see." The man examined the contents of the sack with an expert eye, "Done. I will make this truck disappear. Drive it inside my workshop quickly before anyone sees it. I will drive your GAZ outside to make room. Hurry!"

Stoner restarted the truck, and as the GAZ came outside the shop, drove it inside. They closed the outer door, and he climbed into the old Soviet jeep. Carver leapt into the passenger seat, and he didn't object. They were going back, and she carried an AK-47S, which could come in useful.

"I don't have any shoes."

He glanced across and noticed her bare feet, already covered in blood where she'd run over broken glass or something similar. "We'll find you some boots as we're going along. All we need is for someone to get in our way with small feet like yours. No time to stop right now. They're on their own and could be in trouble."

She nodded, and he drove furiously back toward the square. They almost reached it when in the distance they saw a bunch of insurgents, and they had to face the truth. They'd taken them. He'd got Lieutenant Carver out, but now his best friend and the man from the mountains above Tora Bora were prisoners of the insurgents. Somewhere in Peshawar, they were holding them, and there wasn't a chance in hell he'd return to Afghanistan without them. Not his way, not the way they trained him in the SEALs.

"I'm going back." He stopped the GAZ and turned around. He'd talk to the guy in the garage. Someone would know the location of Insurgent Central, the local Taliban HQ. It was that kind of a city. Everyone knew, and no one talked about it, except for money.

"Right, we don't have a choice." She slipped out the magazine and counted the rounds, "Almost full, I'm set to go."

He stared at her. "Lieutenant, we just freed you from those people. I'm sending you back to Afghanistan. Your people need to know you're safe. If you think I'm about to take you back into enemy territory, you're wrong. It isn't going to happen."

She stared back at him, her expression filled with anger, and it reminded him of long ago. Many years back, when he'd been with Madeleine, before the IED that took her life. It wasn't just that Carver looked like her in every way, she even shared the same facial expressions. Uncanny. But there was a big difference. Madeleine was dead. Sara Carver was alive, and he intended to keep it that way. She wasn't giving in easily.

"I'm not leaving this place, not without those men!" It was weird, as if he'd gone back in time. "I'm a United States Army Officer, Mister. I don't consider the mission over until I've brought all my soldiers home, dead or alive. You can forget any quixotic notions about sending me back to Afghanistan. I'm in this to the finish."

He started to speak. "You don't get it, Sara. I can't..."

"You don't get it! Listen to me. Watch my lips. I do not go home without those men."

He spoke without thinking. "That's just what she..."

Her eyes lit with understanding. "You lost someone close to you, I guess."

"That was a long time ago, and it ain't happening again."

"You're right. Thing is, Mister, I'm not close to you, so it's not happening again." She saw the direction of his stare, "Oh, right, I get it. I remind you of her."

"Some, yeah."

"Uh, huh. Well, you'll have to go past it, get over it. I'm not her, and we're going after those men of yours. Do you know where they are?"

"I soon will."

The garage owner wasn't happy to see them. "If it's about the money, I don't have it anymore. I put it in a safe place."

"It's not about the money. I want to know the location of the Taliban Headquarters in Peshawar."

His face dropped in alarm. "I know of no such place."

"Sure you don't. Where is it?"

"I don't know, I told you. Even if I did, it would be madness to tell anyone. I'm sorry, I can't help you."

"You'll tell me inside the next thirty seconds. If you don't, I'll find a phone and call the cops."

He sneered. "And what, report me for not telling you about the Taliban?"

"I was thinking for stealing an armored truck and hiding it in your shop."

His eyes changed, and the expression was almost comical. He went through the gamut of emotions, from anger, astonishment, calculation, and then fear. His mouth opened to protest until he saw Stoner's determination. At that moment, he knew he wouldn't get another dime out of him. Besides, the woman with the bare, bloody feet was holding the AK-47S in a casual grip, inches from his belly.

"Soekarno Road, the junction with Bajon Road. Not far from the square. It's the big yellow painted house, three stories. They'll have a guard outside. They always do."

"Thanks."

He turned away, and the Pakistani shouted, "Don't come back. Our business is finished."

"It's finished when I say it's finished. You've taken the money, so live with it. We'll be seeing you."

He drove away and looked at Sara. "Assuming you do come along, we need to think about things. This won't be an easy one. They'll be expecting something, and they're wide-awake after the ruckus we caused in Qissa Khwani Square. We'll need something different, something original to get in there and get them out."

"I concur. What did you have in mind?"

"One thing's for sure, we can't drive right in the front door."

"Then try the back door. Mister, it's so simple they may not be expecting it."

"It's Stoner."

"No first name?"

"Stoner is fine."

"Is that what she called you?"

He was about to ask whom she meant, but Carver was too perceptive to fool. "Yes, she did."

"Right. I suggest we make sure it doesn't happen again." She shot him a wry grin, "I'm not in any hurry to die. Hey, stop!"

He jammed on the brakes, and she pointed to an open storefront. "In there, and tell them I'm a size seven. Lace up trainers, something that won't fall of when we're running, dark color."

He was back several minutes later, and she laced them onto her injured feet, wincing as she fastened the ties. Then she glanced up at him and grinned. "Done. We should check out this building. There has to be a way in. Back door would be fine, or..." She looked up at the rooftops. They were flat, as was common in this part of Asia, "or we could use the roof."

"Let's go take a look."

He drove through the teeming streets, and people were emerging as the excitement of the events in the square faded. They reached the building inside of ten minutes and drove past without slowing. There wasn't a guard outside the front door. There were three men, all armed, all viewing the surrounding area with suspicion. Up on the rooftop, two more men were on watch. They were ready for trouble.

He guided the GAZ to the rear, and it was no different. Three more men, and he stayed at the end of the street, in case they were suspicious. Then they drove away. It was a no go. He stopped two blocks away, and they talked over the problem.

"We can't go in front, back, sides, or roof. I doubt there's a basement entrance, so it looks like we're screwed."

She nodded her agreement. "The best way would be to do the unexpected. Come at them from where they least expect it."

"Like how?"

She was thinking it through as she spoke. He could see her eyes coming alive with excitement, as if the weight and pain of her captivity was sloughing away in a matter of minutes. "I'm coming to that, but first, we must find out where they're holding those men, what were their names?"

"Greg and Wyatt."

"Right. We'll grab someone and ask them where they're holding them."

He nodded. "Sounds like a plan. And when we do know, what then?"

She grinned. "That's the best bit. I'll save it until last. We find a likely candidate first, and we'll take it from there."

They parked the GAZ outside a coffee bar and strolled toward the target building. On the way, Stoner found a store selling used clothing, and he bought a huge, sheepskin coat. It stank like it had spent most of its life in a dumpster, but it was cheap, and he donned it over his leather coat. Looking like two smugglers from the Pakistani badlands, they continued along Soekarno Road until they were a hundred meters away. A man walked away from the front door, but they left him. He looked like a gofer, and they wanted someone with real information.

They sat outside an empty, semi-derelict building, two vagrants enjoying the sunshine, until the right man came along. They didn't have to wait long. His clothes were of better quality, his beard neatly trimmed, and he sported an expensive watch on his wrist. A man of substance, a squad leader, and he would know what was going on inside the building. Sara did the initial approach. Stoner waited inside the doorway. She walked away, stumbled, and fell against him, just as he was level with the open doorway.

He scowled and turned toward her, not recognizing her as a woman, and cursed. He threw out a hand to push her away, and Stoner moved. Grabbed his coat with one hand, dragging him backward, and in the other hand he screwed the muzzle of a Desert Eagle into his neck.

"Nice and easy, feller. We're not going to hurt you if you keep it quiet."

He shouted, "What…"

He didn't get another word out. The gun barrel moved a fraction and came down on the side of his head. He collapsed to the floor unconscious, and Stoner dragged him inside. Sara closed the door, or what was left of it, and helped him to tie his arms and legs. As he regained consciousness, Stoner added a strip of cloth to gag his mouth and stop him calling out. He recovered after a few minutes, struggled, and gave up when he realized there was no point. The squirming stopped, but his eyes made it obvious he wouldn't be an easy proposition.

"We want to ask you about the two Westerners you took prisoner about an hour ago. Where are they?"

He unfastened the gag, and the man spat at him, narrowly missing. He put the gag back in place and tried again. "Listen, I don't want to hurt you, but I will, and you'll never be the same again. A lame eunuch would have a hard time in this neck of the woods. How about we try again? Where are they? Are you going to behave?"

The prisoner nodded, and he unfastened the gag. "Okay, what's your name?"

He gave him his name, Abdul Sattar, and smiled an evil leer. "But it will do you no good. They are where you will never find them. Not in the building you saw me emerge from. Our commander sent them to the deepest, darkness hole in Peshawar, and they will stay there until the day they are brought outside to die. That is the penalty Rumi Khan has decreed for captured Westerners. You are infidels, all of you. You will die and go to hell."

Stoner nodded. "Sure we will, but you haven't answered. Where are they?"

The leer stayed fixed to his face. "We took them to the one place you cannot hope to free them from."

"Where is that?"

"Go to hell, infidel. I will never tell you."

He took a half hour to get what he wanted. Sara Carver had to excuse herself to vomit in a dark corner. Stoner felt no remorse, stripped the prisoner naked, and tied a thin piece of line around his testicles. Several blows from the heavy Desert Eagle threatened to smash his genitals forever, and the final crunch was when he pressed the knife blade against his manhood. In Stoner, he'd come up against a man for whom there were no rules. No morality, except to win. He surrendered.

"The Peshawar garrison of the Army of Pakistan. They have close links to the Taliban, and they give us help when we need it."

"Which part of the barracks?"

He sneered. "The room at the rear of the armory, they put them in a deep well. They may not even be alive, who knows?"

The sneer deepened, "It depends on how well they can swim."

He ignored the taunt. "How many troops inside the garrison?"

"Too many, infidel, about five hundred, at the last count. Your men will never get out of there, until they are carried out for burial. They're dead, and that whore who's with you will die as well, after they've used her body to satisfy their basest lusts."

He wasn't talking about Carver. In that moment, Stoner still had Madeleine in the forefront of his mind. The girl who men like this one had brutally murdered. Not content with that, he wanted to brutalize the girl who resembled her.

He delivered a hard strike to the back of the neck and felt the 'crunch' as the vertebrae in the top of his spinal column collapsed. He choked and writhed, trying to reach up and repair the damage. Stoner hit him again, and he stopped moving. He heard a sharp intake of breath from the girl.

"You didn't need to do that."

He felt tired and didn't want to explain. It was like the Talibs had wanted to kill her over again. With an effort, he faced Madeleine's ghost. "You wouldn't understand."

"Try me."

He told her, or tried to tell her, but he never knew if she understood the whole story.

CHAPTER SIX

"You cannot leave them here indefinitely," the Pakistani Major explained to Khan, "We are subject to occasional inspections from Islamabad, and how can I explain the presence of these two men?"

Rumi Khan shrugged, looking around him and enjoying what he saw. The solid confidence it gave a man of having thick stone walls, artillery gunships, and hundreds of troops. When his own organization had won their battle inside Afghanistan, he would have such a place as this, legions of uniformed troops, pledging allegiance to him, and to Allah.

Outside the window, parked in the cobbled courtyard, an old gunship, a United States built and supplied Huey, the venerable UH1 of Vietnam fame. Two machine guns, one at either side, in the open door, and as the nose pointed toward them, he could see the forward-facing chain gun. A formidable weapon, and he smiled to himself as he thought of the terrible fusillade of heavy caliber bullets it could hurl at an enemy. One day, he would also have one of those machines.

He realized the Major was still speaking to him. "What was

that?"

"I was asking you about your plans to remove these men."

"They stay here. I have reason to think an attempt may be made to free them, so I want them to be kept in this secure location."

"But I just told you, if the inspectors come and see unauthorized prisoners, they could ask questions."

"In which case you will refer them to the ISI. Or would you like to speak to them?"

He blanched. The Directorate General for Inter-Services Intelligence, or **Inter-Services Intelligence ISI, was the premier intelligence service of Pakistan. Their role was to provide intelligence critical to** national security, and pass it on to the Government of Pakistan. That was the theory. In practice, they were brutes, thugs, and bullies. Something like the Gestapo of Nazi Germany, they had absolute power over every person in Pakistan, civilian or military. They were also avowed supporters of the Taliban regime in Afghanistan. The Major had no doubt this man would have strong links with ISI, enough to make his life very hard indeed.

"There's no need," he answered hastily, "They can remain here. We will make arrangements if anyone turns up for a snap inspection."

Khan suppressed a smile. "That's very kind of you, Major Qureshi. I will be certain to speak to my friend in ISI, and praise the help you have given us." Qureshi smiled in relief, "Tell me, where are you holding them?"

This time the officer smiled. "Where? The man who brought them here, Abdul Sattar, approved my arrangements. They are in the armory, the strongest and most protected part of the barracks." He pointed out the window, "Look, across the parade ground. That building is used to store ammunition and explosives, so we like to have it separate from the main operational areas."

Khan glanced across the expanse of beaten earth. Men were marching and wheeling in precision rows, and at a shouted command from their NCO, they stamped to a halt. A hundred meters past them was the armory that adjoined the perimeter wall on the opposite side, guarded by two men with fixed bayonets on their AK-47 rifles.

Only two men! I don't feel comfortable, and an armory is the worst possible place to hold prisoners. If they should get free, the destruction they could do is incalculable.

Qureshi watched the frown appear on his face. "You're thinking if they escape they could cause damage to this place, yes?"

"It did cross my mind."

"You can forget it. At the rear of the armory, separated by a security locked, thick steel door, there is what used to be the old well, which supplied the barracks with water. After they installed the main water supply, we stopped using it, but kept it in case we should need it should there be a failure of supply. The well is twenty meters deep, and getting out would be impossible. The one place they could be more secure is if they were dead and buried in a cemetery. They cannot climb the well, and even if they did, they cannot escape the room. In addition, there are the guards. Two inside and two outside the armory, always, as well as a man inside the well room, should they sprout wings and fly out. Day and night. You need have no concerns about their security."

He wasn't convinced, but he gave the man a nod of acknowledgment. "If you say so, Major. What happened to the water in the well?"

He got an answering chuckle. "Nothing happened. It is still

there."

"So they are floating in the water?"

A shrug. "Either that or they drown. Yes, Rumi, they are treading water to stay alive. The last man I sent to check said they'd found rough handholds in the side of the shaft to support them. But I can assure you, every minute of their confinement will seem like an hour."

He felt more reassured. The men were suffering, which was as it should be. From this moment on, their lives would be one, long, continuous scream of agony. Their death would be almost too terrible to contemplate. Almost.

"Very well, Major, I accept your arrangements. I will notify you when we have captured the men who were with them. If they are still alive, we will reclaim them, and take them to our headquarters."

"They will not be alive, I promise you. No one could survive for long in that well. The water is icy cold, and there is nowhere secure to hold onto the sides. When they are exhausted, they will drown. Their remaining hours will be an agony of terror, and when Allah wills it, they will die."

He frowned. "I think it a question of how well they can swim, more than the Almighty."

"Yes, of course."

They said their farewells, and he left, out into the stinking, teeming hell of Peshawar. The entire city seemed to be on the move at once, a huge river of swirling humanity.

* * *

It looked to be impossible. They were on the roof of a high office building, overlooking the barracks lit by floodlights. The armory was obvious, separate from the offices and accommodation, adjacent to the perimeter wall. Outside the door, two men were on guard with rifles at the ready. The open square in the center, the parade ground, was busy with men. Marching, coming and going, some just sitting around doing nothing. Early evening, and the bulk of the day's activities were drawing to a close. Many would soon go off duty, but they would be close. Ready to react in a second if the alarm sounded.

"We need more men," she murmured, lying alongside him, "There's no way two people can pull this off, and you don't need to be a soldier to understand the problems. Look at it! We wouldn't even get across the parade ground before they start shooting at us. I could contact my unit. See what they say."

"Pakistan is an ally," he said, "The Paks would deny they're holding them, and that would be the end of it. They'd be warned we know where they are, and they'll either reinforce the guards or move them."

She grunted. "That's probably true, but we can't get them out. We need to think of another way, maybe bribes."

"They won't take bribes, not just like that. This is a tie up between the Talibs and the Pakistani Army. Any soldier who took a payoff to let Taliban prisoners go free could count his remaining days on the fingers of one hand."

"Do you have a better idea?"

He was thinking, and thinking hard. It was so confusing; lying next to this girl was like being reunited with Madeleine. As if he was with his fiancée again. Being with Sara was like opening a wound. He forced himself to put her out of his mind and concentrate on the job. He had the germ of an idea, and he said the words before he could work it all out.

"We need a truck."

"A truck. Right, that's interesting. You don't think it would stand out a bit when we try to leave the city. Wouldn't it be better to use the GAZ? It's not fast, but it's nondescript and anonymous."

"We're not using it to escape the city."

"So what, you're planning to go into the haulage business? Make some spare cash to pay for more men to help us get them out."

"No. It has to be a big truck, one of those things they used to carry goods across Asia. Monster things, weighs about forty tons or so."

"Stoner, you're going crazy."

Maybe he was, and maybe he wasn't. But it was all he could come up with, so he explained it to her, and she nodded her agreement. "You're right. We need a truck."

* * *

Greg had never been so cold in his life. Even up on the heights above Tora Bora, he hadn't been so cold. They'd dropped them down into the well from the top, and the fall seemed endless. They didn't know what was at the bottom, and both men braced for the bone-shattering impact with hard concrete. The cold water came as a surprise, and then they were floundering to keep afloat. Evers swam around, looking for something, and then he shouted to Greg, "Over here, we can hold onto this."

They'd covered the head of the well, and darkness closed in. But he followed the sound of the voice, and Wyatt guided his hand to a thin crack in the shaft.

"Grab hold of this. It'll help you stay afloat. We can't both tread water indefinitely."

The crack was barely wide enough for one man to insert the fingers of his hand.

"What about you?"

"We take it in turns. Five minutes each. You can manage that?"

"Sure, but how we gonna get out?"

"We wait until they come back, and see how it looks."

"They may not be back for some time. It could be days. Can we stand this for all that time?"

"I can stand it, my friend. I've been up on that mountain for a long time, and it teaches you many things."

"You mean survival against the odds."

"That, too, but it isn't what I meant. It teaches you to be patient. Like when your biggest ambition is to grab hold of the men who did this to you and rip out their guts. I'm working out who to kill first, and so far, I haven't decided."

He did his best to think about revenge. About the pleasure of killing the first man he came to who was responsible for putting them down here. He failed. All he could muster was to think about Faria back home, the kids, Ahmed, Kaawa, and Rahima, his dog, Archer. All of them waiting, trusting him to get back to them safe and sound. And here he was, almost drowning in a deep well inside a Pakistani barracks. Despite everything, he knew the chances of Wyatt Evers getting the revenge he craved were remote. If they left them here long enough, they'd grow weak and exhausted, and they'd slip into the water and drown.

He heard Wyatt's voice calling to him. "Hey, Greg, you're not giving up on me, are you?"

"Er, no."

"You thinking about revenge."

"Yeah."

A chuckle. "You're a liar. But it doesn't matter, because there's something else you haven't thought of. That pal of yours, Stoner, he was a Navy SEAL once, wasn't he?"

"Once, yes."

"He'll find a way to get to us, count on it. That's what they do, SEALs. The impossible."

"Sure."

Not this time, Wyatt. We'll stay here until we drown. They won't come for us. No one will come for us, except to fish out our bloated corpses. I'm sorry, man, but you should have stayed on that mountain. Freezing your balls off, but at least you were alive.

* * *

The Romanian-built Puma zoomed across the harsh terrain of Northern Pakistan. They were flying at low level, relying on the terrain following radar, and Ivan's skill as a pilot. The radar was Romanian, like the aircraft, and he had little faith in the hitherto communist nation's ability to get anything right. His skill as a pilot was something he had even less faith in. Although when Bukharin tactfully suggested they climb for a little more height, he laughed in derision.

"Scared, Gorgy? This is nothing. I can go even lower if I... whoops, that looked like a mosque. Could have caused us a problem if I hit it."

"Like we'd have crashed into the ground?" the Russian grated.

"I was thinking more about a bolt of lightning from the heavens. I don't think old Allah would be too happy if we destroyed his real estate."

"The least of our problems," he grunted, "How long before we reach the target?"

Ivan leaned closer to the complicated control panel. Alive with scores of digital readouts, lights of all colors and enough switches, knobs and levers to control the traffic signals in New

York City.

* * *

The truck was perfect, a Chinese-built FAW heavy tipper, bright orange, and loaded with around twenty-five tons of scrap iron. Added to the weight of the truck itself, he estimated a total of over forty tons. Even better, the driver was asleep in an opium-fueled haze, lying under a blanket in the cab. Stoner lifted him out and laid him on the sidewalk. He didn't even stir.

The engine started on the button, and Sara climbed into the passenger seat. She gave him a nod, and he engaged first gear and started the big vehicle rolling.

"You think this'll do it?"

"If it doesn't, nothing will."

She lapsed into silence as they drove through the almost deserted streets. He couldn't help but think how the darkness covered so many things. The ramshackle, sordid poverty, the rundown nature of the buildings, all desperate for a lick of paint and some attention with sand and cement. Maybe some new timbers and roof shingles. Nothing expensive, but the will was lacking. The will of the people, that is. They relied more on the will of Allah, as in most Islamic countries. If he wanted the buildings repaired and maintained, he'd bring it about. Or so the thinking went. Meantime, they lived like paupers.

"I don't have much ammunition, just the one magazine."

He grinned. "Me neither, but we're about to go into an armory. We'll pick up all we want when we get inside."

"And if we don't get inside?"

"Then we won't need the ammo."

"Right."

He drove past the barracks first and confirmed the street

was clear. No parked vehicles to block what he planned to do. No groups of homeless people sleeping where he intended to strike. He reached the end of the street and performed a complicated maneuver to spin the ungainly truck around. Engaged first gear and hit the gas pedal. The three hundred and eighty horsepower roared, and he watched the rev counter. When it reached maximum revolutions, he dropped the clutch. Sara squealed as they took off with a massive jerk, as if they'd been catapulted off the deck of a carrier.

He aimed at the spot he'd identified earlier, about twenty meters from the corner of the perimeter wall, watching the needle as the speed rose. He made a few last-minute checks, and Sara gripped both rifles. When they hit, they could be tossed around inside the cab. His Desert Eagles were snug in the canvas shoulder rig. Seat belts fastened, and then they were out of time. He swung the wheel over to hit the wall head on, and the crash as they hit was loud enough to awaken a cemetery. For several seconds, everything was chaos. Stone blocks cascading down on top of them, the windshield reduced to shards of reinforced glass, and dust swirled into the cab like a sandstorm.

They were in. Lights inside caged surrounds burned in the vast room, and racks and racks of weaponry lined the walls. Two men stared at them, their expressions stupefied, as if a genie from hell had burst into the duty station, and they had no response. The soldiers stared at the orange apparition; unable to make any sense of what lay in front of their eyes. One had a mug of some liquid in his hand, half raised to his lips, and he held it there, frozen into immobility.

Stoner pushed the door open, threw chunks of broken stone blocks aside, and climbed out. This time they reacted. A man standing in front of them was something they understood.

He was flesh, living and breathing, and their response was automatic. They came to life, and made a grab for their rifles that lay propped against the wall next to where they'd been sitting. He drew a big automatic and put a bullet into each as he ran.

"Sara, watch the door. They'll be trying to get inside at any moment."

"Copy that. Hey, they have plenty of ordnance in here, enough to hold out against an army."

"That's just as well, because any second now, we'll have an army coming at us. Help yourself, and watch that door."

"I've got it."

He rushed toward the side of building where their prisoner had told them the well room was located. He threw the door open, and it wasn't locked, which surprised him. He rushed inside, and the reason for their lack of security became evident. A guard fired a shot as he walked inside, the Sara screamed in shock and pain as the bullet by chance smacked into her as she was pulling weapons and ammo off the racks. At the same moment, the entrance door burst open, and the guards who'd been guarding the outside door burst in.

He snapped off a shot, taking down the soldier who'd fired, and raced back through the armory, firing alternately with the .50 calibers. He hit them both several times, and the heavy rounds knocked them back. They were dead. They'd have to have been wearing armor plate to withstand those bullets, and he ran to Sara. She was kneeling on the floor, groping for a dressing to staunch the flow of blood from the top of her leg.

"How bad is it?"

"Nothing to worry about, once I stop the blood. Go get those men."

"You're sure you can manage?"

She pointed to the weapon lying on the floor beside her. The one she'd been helping herself to from the racks when the bullet hit. A relic from the past, the Soviet so-called 'record player.' A light machine gun, with a characteristic pancake magazine mounted on top. A Degtyaryev, the 7.62mm squad automatic weapon that helped the Red Army repel Hitler's invading hordes during World War II. Sixty rounds in the magazine, and she'd pulled down a wooden box of spare mags to go with it.

"I can manage, once I get that into action. How long do we have, Stoner, before they come?"

"They'll be on the way already."

"That's what I thought. Go get those guys out. I can hold here."

Don't die on me, Sara. I lost Madeleine before. I couldn't stand seeing her ghost die on me.

He hesitated, torn between wanting to help her shore up the defenses against the troops that even now must be rushing to the armory, and to get Greg and Wyatt out of that well before they drowned. Their prisoner, Abdul Sattar, had expressed doubts about whether they could survive, and that was one reason he'd hit him so hard. The Islamic predilection for torture and agonizing death made a man want to hit back.

She was staring at him as he looked at her. "Stoner, go! I can manage. Get them out of there before they drown."

He nodded and ran back to the well room. He peered over the low wall down the shaft and saw nothing. His guts turned icy. It looked like they'd succumbed.

"Greg, Wyatt, are you down there? It's me, Stoner."

A pause, and he feared the worst. Until a voice shouted back, "It's about fucking time. We're freezing down here."

"I'll throw a rope. Hang on."

"We're not going anywhere."

He smiled at Wyatt's ironic reply and went hunting for a long rope. It was hung on the wall in a neat coil. As he removed it, the shooting started. A short burst from an assault rifle, and then a long, shattering volley echoed inside the armory as Sara opened up with the Degtyaryev. Several cries of pain meant she'd hit something, and then he laid his concerns to rest to concentrate on getting the two men out.

He fastened the rope to a metal hoop cemented into the wall and tossed it down. Two minutes later, Greg climbed out, and in a few seconds Wyatt joined him. Both men were blue with cold, and Greg was shaking almost uncontrollably. But they were alive. Blum grinned.

"Am I glad to see you, Stoner. Never more than now, believe me."

They were still soaking wet, and he could do nothing to help. No towels, no blankets, they'd have to bear it, except they were breathing.

"No sweat, but we're not clear yet, Greg. We busted in here with a big truck, but getting out may not be so easy."

"How many troops are we facing on the outside?" Wyatt asked.

"A couple of hundred. Maybe more."

"Shit."

"Shit is right, but we have one thing going for us. We're inside an armory, the walls are thick, and we have plenty of weapons. Sara Carver is keeping them back for now, but we should join her, try to push them back, and then get out the way we came in with the truck. I'll see how we're doing out there."

They were jumping up and down, trying to restore their circulation, but they stopped and followed him into the main room. Bullets were flying through the entrance door, and Carver was crouched behind a stack of wooden crates, the Degtyaryev machine gun poking through a gap between them. Two empty magazines lay on the floor beside her, and she was firing again as more bullets ricocheted all around them. Wyatt took stock, whooping with delight when he found a PK and dragged it off the rack. The magazines were nearby, and less than twenty seconds later, he'd joined Sara and was firing repeated bursts out through the door.

Greg took down an AK-47 and went to join them, but he stopped him. "We have to leave them to it. I want you to climb out past the truck and guard our exit. If they come at us from the rear, we're screwed."

"Leave it to me."

Stoner doubted he'd be able to hit anything much. He was still shaking with the cold and wet. Then again, a few long bursts would at least deter an enemy from getting too close. He crawled out through the broken masonry, and a moment later he was back.

"We have a problem."

"You don't say."

"Soldiers, running toward the opening you made. I can hold them off, but there's about twenty of them. Too many to kill, and one of them's carrying a machine gun. The moment we reverse out, they'll..."

He didn't get any more, the voice was drowned out by the noise of turboshaft engines, and it increased to a roar as the Huey UH-1 outside took off, removing itself from the shooting.

"They'll riddle the cab with bullets," he completed the sentence.

He nodded. "Okay, I'll work something out. Hold them off, and don't let them get any closer."

"Okay."

He snaked back through the gap, and his AK-47 fired. The enemy answered, and more bullets smashed into the rear of the truck. Some came through the gaps in the broken masonry, but at least he was buying them some time. Stoner rushed back to the racks of weapons. He'd seen something that would hold them off for longer, RPG-7s, several, and crates of rockets. He broke out two, loaded a rocked in each, and took one to Greg, who took it and grinned, and joined Wyatt and Sara.

In time for a massive burst of heavy machine gun fire to smash inside and tear huge holes in the barricade they were sheltering behind. When the burst ended, he peered out. In the floodlit courtyard, he saw the AFV they'd brought up with a mounted DShK 12.7mm, the .50 caliber equivalent. The weapon could almost tear apart the masonry by sheer weight of lead it could throw at them. The gunners were reloading, and in a few seconds, they'd be inundated with lead.

He dragged Sara further back into cover. "Keep down. In a moment, they're going to unleash hell."

"What…"

The roar of the machine gun interrupted her. This time they emptied a full fifty-round magazine that tore more huge chunks from the flimsy barricade. When the burst stopped, Wyatt was ready, and he jumped up with the RPG-7, aimed, and fired. The rocket trailed smoke as it hurtled toward the target, and it struck the base of the gun. It exploded into flame and scrap metal, and then the awesome destructive power of the heavy machine gun ceased. They were safe, for the time being. They all knew the respite wouldn't last long.

"They'll bring up a tank next," Wyatt said, his voice grim, "Anything modern and these things won't touch it, won't even dent the armor. You got any other ideas, Stoner? As rescues go, this one looks pretty bad."

"I'm thinking."

As he said that, more machine gun bullets hacked at the truck from outside, and Greg was under pressure. The 'whoosh' of the RPG rocket launch signaled he'd fired at whatever was shooting at them, and the weight of fire eased. But it didn't stop, and he knew they had two choices. Come up with something different, or die.

Madeline's still firing, but no, it isn't Madeleine. It's Sara. Madeleine is dead, and she'll go the same way unless I do something radical, but what?

He dropped his hand to his side and felt the device in his pocket. The satphone Ivan had given him.

Is it possible he could help us?

He was one of the most resourceful men he'd ever encountered. It seemed impossible he could bail them out of this one, but he had nothing to lose.

If Ivan can't help, what then, reverse out in the truck, take the bullets, and hope for the best? A million to one shot, and million to one shots rarely come off. Never come off. I need something else, a miracle, and if Ivan isn't a miracle worker, he's always full of surprises. Probably can't call down a Coalition airstrike against a friendly power, but who knows? Maybe, just maybe, he can do something.

He hit the speed dial number.

* * *

"Yeeah ha! Like taking candy from a baby. Damn, I haven't had so much fun since…"

"Since you flew for Russian Frontal Aviation?" Bukharin shouted to Ivan, his lips split into a grin. He was enjoying himself and couldn't resist the dig about Ivan's supposed Russian origins. No one knew where he hailed from originally, but one thing was for sure. It was somewhere between the East and West coasts of the Continental U.S. of A.

He wasn't fazed. "Something like that. Button it, and keep shooting."

"There's nothing left alive down there. We've hammered them into the ground."

"Hammer them again. This is better than Coney Beach."

A rare slip, and Bukharin said, "Would that be next to the Moscow River?"

He didn't hear him over the roar of the powerful turboshafts, then they'd come around again, and the guns were firing. He'd kept the target, Batu's Chitral camp, on the port side, to give Gorgy a good target, except for when he wheeled to come back, and Daud was ready and waiting with the starboard cannon. Akram and Habiba kept the 7.62s chattering, and if anyone dared to show their face, the sheets of lead hurtled down to blot out their lives.

He came around again, rejoicing they'd found it so easy. Batu had made it easy for them, not expecting an attack from the air. Why should they, Pakistan wasn't a country at war, was it? When the Air Force gunship flew over, the assumption it was a routine flight, nothing unusual. SOP for the military that liked to keep an eye on the insurgents who operated from their territory. The Mongolian had made his headquarters in a crumbling fort that dated to the nineteenth century, to the days of the British Raj. Despite the decay, the place was still a formidable defensive position, with stout walls enough to deter any but a determined attacker. The roofs of the buildings were not stout, made of timber and bamboo, insulated with woven rushes. Back in the day, there was little need for anything more. Back in the day, there were no gunships.

He brought her round again as the guns ceased chattering,

and his men hastened to reload, but there was little moving below. As far as he could tell, they were all dead or dying. Inside the square perimeter walls of the fort, the ground was littered with bodies, and flames licked out from anything that was flammable. And some things that were not flammable. The job was done, and Batu Amar's dreams of dominating the illegal arms and drugs trade of Asia were over.

"That's it, men. We've done enough here. Time to go home before the Pakistanis decide to investigate who's shooting up their buddies."

Bukharin climbed up to sit in the left-hand seat. "It didn't seem fair, Ivan, not giving them a chance to shoot back."

He grinned. "Seemed pretty fair to me." He glanced back, and his expression changed, "I'll be damned."

"What is it?"

"Batu. The bastard, he isn't dead. Look!"

As he spoke, the threat alarm sounded for the first time since they'd begun the raid. A man was standing on top of the gatehouse, and he'd fired an RPG at the departing gunship. Neither man had any doubt it was Batu. A huge beard, and the characteristic Mongolian pants and pointed hat; his personal trademark. The missile reached its apogee and fell away. Ivan spun the gunship in the air and headed back.

"What are you doing?"

"Going back to finish him."

"You were worried about a Pakistani fighter buzzing us to take a look?"

"I'm more worried about him. All of you, man the guns. Fill the bastard full of lead."

They bored in at the maximum speed of one hundred and eighty miles an hour, and seconds later Batu was staring up at them. Knowing his fate was sealed; he shook his fist in a final gesture of defiance. Then they pulled the triggers. First Bukharin and Habiba, and then he wheeled the aircraft around, giving the other two men a clear shot. Below, the sheets of lead smashed into the Mongolian warlord's body, and Ivan watched in satisfaction as the corpse jerked and kept jerking, and yet the storm of bullets kept coming. Until caution reminded him they could face their own problems.

"Cease fire, he's gone. We're going home, but keep an eye out for fighters."

He almost set course for Afghanistan, southwest, where he'd be partway home. At the last minute, some notion made him head due south, back toward Peshawar. He'd clear the region of Chitral, and halfway back to Peshawar, make a dogleg of the mountains. There cross into Afghanistan away from the bigger population centers. It seemed like a good idea until he had to jerk the controls over to put them back onto an even keel after the fighter jet roared past them, twenty meters off the port side.

The JF-17 Thunder, made in China, looked impressive. Capable of Mach 1.6, and Ivan recalled seeing the ordnance list; more than enough to deal with one rogue helicopter. A GSh-23-2 twin-barrel cannon and several Piranha short-range air-to-air missiles, together with any other goodies they'd bolted on. If they tried to fight, they'd be like David with his slingshot facing Goliath. Except this time, there'd be no Biblical miracles.

"Jesus Christ, what's he up to? Is he blind, can't he see we're Air Force just like him?"

"Apparently not," Bukharin said with a trace of irony.

A second later, the radio squawked on Guard channel. "Pakistani Air Force IAR 330 gunship, identify yourself. Which airfield did you take off from?"

Ivan clicked the transmit button. "This is PAF IAR 330.

We're out of Islamabad."

The voice growled back a moment later. "No, you are not from Islamabad. You took off from Peshawar, and you're flying a stolen helicopter. You will continue flying south to Peshawar and land at the indicated helipad."

He glanced at Bukharin, who was impassive. "We don't have much choice but to do as he says. He's faster and he outguns us."

"That's true. But is he sneakier than us?"

The Russian looked suspicious. "What did you have in mind?"

"Get back on the guns. Make sure they're all locked and loaded. This sucker is going down."

He looked appalled. "You're taking on a supersonic fighter interceptor in this?"

"Unless you want to spend what's left of your life in a Pakistani jail."

He climbed from the seat and moved to the gunner's position. "Tell me what you want us to do."

"I'll get him close, and when I say, blast him. If I get this right, standard tactical doctrine would make him lose height to get away from our guns. When he does that, I'll bank to starboard, and we'll give him a burst from the other side. If that doesn't bring him down, nothing will. It all depends on getting him in close. Real close."

He concentrated on flying straight and level to lull the pilot of the jet into a false sense of security. Make him think he'd won the fight, so the next bit wouldn't alarm him. He gave it ten minutes, enough for him to relax. To think of how he'd tell his fellow pilots back at base how he'd scored a bloodless victory over the gunship. The time had come, and he twitched the collective, touched the rudder bar. The helicopter tilted over to the side and dropped fifty meters. The response from the fighter was instant.

"IAR 330, you will resume straight and level flying. Any attempt to change course will result in my opening fire. I will shoot you down."

"Negative, negative, we have a technical problem. Something came loose. We heard a loud mechanical noise, like something broke off. I don't know if I can keep her in the air."

"You will maintain course. I don't care what your problems are. You will fly straight and level."

"Pal, believe me, if I could I would, but this bucket of bolts is about to fall out of the sky. What do you want me to do?"

"Resume straight and level."

Trouble with this guy, he hasn't got a sense of humor. Not yet.

He twitched the controls again. "Listen, I can't hold her. I have to land. It's an emergency."

"You will..."

"Yeah, I know, I know. Thing is, pal, if I fell out of the sky, that'd be the end of everything. You won't get us back to your base, and we'd be dead."

No bragging over drinks in the mess.

"How about you look, see if you can see what the problem is."

A pause. When he answered, he was suspicious. "Me?"

"Yes, the problem seems to be coming from the area of the main rotor shaft. It could be damaged. See if you can see what's causing the problem. If it's nothing serious, maybe we can make it back."

And you'll be able to boast about the captured helicopter.

"Very well. Hold the aircraft as steady as you can. I'll see if any damage is visible. Hold your craft steady."

"I'll do my best."

The JF-17 drifted closer, hit an air current, and drifted away. They were near the mountains, and close formation flying would be difficult. A challenge to the ego of this fighter jock, and how could he resist it, something else to brag about, playing chicken with a stolen gunship. He shouted across to Gorgy. "Any moment now, but don't move the guns. Don't give him any suspicions we're not on the level."

"Yob tvoy mat, we're not amateurs."

He smiled. 'Fuck your mother,' the Russian insult that rolled off the tongue of native Russians several times a day.

He watched the Thunder move even closer. When he estimated the gap to be less than thirty meters, he gave the order, "Open fire! Shoot the bastard before he gets us!"

The door gun joined the slow, deep beat of the cannon as they blazed away, and the heavy barrage of lead tore chunks as it ripped through the airframe of the Thunder. But the fighter wasn't finished, and the pilot tilted the wings over and started to bank and speed away. Ivan worked the controls and spun the rotorcraft over, exposing the guns on the other side. They didn't need the order to open fire, and more lead smashed into the Pakistani jet. This time he saw the pilot slump as the bullets found their mark, and at least ten cannon shells smashed their way into the cockpit. The guns ceased fire as they ran out of ammunition, and he maneuvered to bring her back for the port side guns to bear. It was unnecessary. The nose of the elegant fighter jet tilted over and dove for the ground.

They were still low, at less than a thousand meters. Seconds later, the stricken craft impacted the ground and exploded burning jet fuel over a wide area. He put the nose back down to get below the Pakistani radar cover and flew on, making an immediate turn to the north and fly out of Pak airspace. Home to Afghanistan where there was never any doubt about friend or foe. They all carried guns, and you assumed they were all about to shoot you. It was the kind of assumption that made life easy. Simple and uncomplicated, the way he liked it.

Goodbye Pakistan, and I'm not coming back for anything. Nothing would persuade me, and besides, if they got their hands on me, they'd tear me apart. Literally.

He was still smiling when the call came in on his satphone, just as he'd nudged the nose around to fly north.

"This is Stoner."

"Uh, yeah, you get her out?"

"That's a yes and a no. We got her, but we're trapped inside the armory of Peshawar Barracks. We're in deep shit, Ivan."

"Can't help you, buddy. I've got problems of my own. We just kind of tangled with the Pakistani Air Force."

"You're in Pakistan? Ivan, you have to help us. For Christ's sake, man, we need you. We've got half the Pakistani Army outside, and they're getting closer. If we don't get help very soon, we're all dead."

He felt a qualm, just for a second, but qualms didn't keep you alive. Not in his business.

A pity about Sara Carver, they want her back real bad, but I can't help out this time. Just can't.

"Sorry, pal, you're on your own."

He ended the call and flew on.

CHAPTER SEVEN

The stolen Puma droned on through the night sky, and Ivan began to enjoy himself.

Pity about Stoner and his pal, they're good guys, but shit happens, the way of the world. As for the girl, they'll have to swallow her loss back in Washington. I've no idea who she is, or why she's so important, but if she dies, that's the end of it. No hostage for them to use as a bargaining chip, a reasonable outcome.

He gave the engines more power. He was in a hurry to get home and climbed to cross the mountains into Afghanistan.

Who knows, I could do a repaint job, register, and even keep this handy little aircraft. It'll be useful for my business.

That's when the satphone rang again. He checked the display, assuming it would be Stoner calling again, but it wasn't. This time it was important. He hit the receive button.

"Ivan."

"Langley. We're calling for an update on that hostage."

No surprise they'd called, but he needed to word it carefully. He knew of Bukharin watching him, and his gaze carried a measure of accusation.

Fuck him, it's for the best.

He turned his attention to the call. "The guy I sent after her, he messed up. I'm sorry. Nothing to be done, he's dropped them all in the shit. A firefight with the Pakistani Army that they can't win, I'm afraid they won't be coming back."

The silence on the other end lasted forever, or at least it seemed that way. Then the voice spoke again; a voice he couldn't ignore, a man who occupied a position close to the Head of the National Clandestine Service, the Directorate of Operations, a man many pay grades above him. "That won't do, Ivan. We want her back."

He sighed and hoped he'd used the right emphasis. "We all want her back, Sir. The problem is, we can't. The Paks have them all surrounded, and they don't stand a chance."

"Her father is Bruce Carver."

He grinned. "Say, that's the same name as the President's Chief of Staff."

"That's because they're one and the same. The President is Lieutenant Carver's godfather, and he takes a personal interest in her welfare. You with me so far, Mister?"

Shit! Of all the bad breaks, this is the worst. The President and his Chief of Staff involved personally. Shit.

"Yessir."

"Good. So don't go telling me there's nothing you can do to get her back. Say, the work you do for us in Afghanistan, we're looking for someone to set up a similar intelligence gathering operation."

He'd been in this Asian shithole for enough time, and a change was tempting. "Where would that be, Sir?"

"Northern Alaska, on the shores of the Bering Strait. You could wave to your Russian pals across the ice."

"It's a generous offer, Sir, but I think I'm more valuable

here."

"That remains to be seen. Don't let the President and his Chief of Staff down, Ivan."

"I'll get onto it right now, Sir."

"See that you do. Call me when you have some news, and it better be good news."

The phone went dead, and he hit the disconnect button. Bukharin was still staring at him, and he grimaced. "We're going back to Peshawar, Gorgy. Like I said, it would be wrong to make a run for it when those people are in trouble."

The Russian's face was impassive. "I knew you'd do the right thing, Boss, never doubted you. She's a real VIP, this Carver?"

He explained what they'd told him about her father, and her godfather. "I guess you could say she's a real VIP, yeah."

"Not that it makes any difference," The Russian said, "You'd have gone back for them anyway."

"That's right."

"You never know, they could give you a medal for this one, Boss. Showing courage and bravery under fire, setting an example to others."

Ivan glared at him. Bukharin was enjoying himself, and didn't seem to give a damn about the certainty in Ivan's guts that they were heading into disaster.

"Shut up, Gorgy. Make sure the guns all have full loads. Where we're going, we're gonna need them."

"Sure. What is it they could give you, the Congressional Medal of Honor?"

"Shut the fuck up and do some work."

* * *

A bunch of Pak soldiers with more bravery than sense mounted a suicidal charge. It was so unexpected it almost succeeded, eight men, firing from the hip, rushing the main door in the teeth of Carver and Evers' machine guns. They were in process of reloading. Evers shouted to Stoner and rushed to assist. They'd got within a meter of the door. Five men lay dead outside, and the other three, one of them bleeding from a bloody wound in the abdomen, pushed through into the armory.

He'd just fitted a new mag in the AK and then raced to help them. Emptied the full load of bullets into the men, and they went down. One was merely wounded, a slight nick to the ankle, and he got up and kept coming. The firing pin clicked on empty, and he dragged out a Desert Eagle. The guy was too fast, and he closed with him, his gun empty and his arms outstretched to grapple. The next moment, he was fighting for his life.

The Pak soldier tossed his empty rifle to the ground and snatched out a knife, a slim, stiletto like blade that some soldiers keep for the messy business of silent killing. The blade went past his chest, missing him by less than an inch, and with no room to shoot, he slammed the barrel against the man's arm. Except he'd switched knife hands, a feat of trickery he shouldn't have fallen for, but all the same he missed it.

The blade slice into his neck, and he felt the blood trickle out, but he dodged aside and prevented a deeper cut. He lashed out with the pistol again and connected with a blow to the head. The guy dropped to the floor, stunned, but now he was reaching for the gun holstered on his belt. The .50 caliber bullet from the Desert Eagle stopped him dead, a heart shot. He watched the blood spurting from the wound, and then the flow eased as he breathed his last and was still. Sara rushed to him.

"You're hurt. He cut you in the neck."

"It's nothing. Stay here, and make sure no more of them get

close. Wyatt, don't let that happen again."

He pulled a face. "That was an amateur mistake, sorry. I'll grab some spare guns. It's not like we don't have enough to choose from. Did you come up with anything we can do?"

"We can't stay here."

"You don't say."

"I'm working on it."

He went looking for Greg, to find out if he'd succeeded. His friend emerged from the back room, wearing a downcast expression. "Not a chance. I've searched everywhere. I even found a flashlight and played it around the shaft inside the well. Just in case there were any tunnels or shafts in the side, but there's nothing. Other than the stream that keeps it supplied with water, but without scuba gear I guess that's not much of an option."

"No it isn't. We'll take another look at getting out the way we came in. If we could drive the truck through the wall, there's no reason we shouldn't go out the same way."

Greg's glance was filled with skepticism. "Apart from fifty soldiers waiting outside to fill us full of holes,"

He shrugged. "Better odds than the two hundred men out in the courtyard. They're lined up ready to put even more bullet holes in us. You remember that old movie, where they were trapped inside a building, and they decided to come out shooting? Butch Cassidy and the Sundance Kid, as I recall. That's the way we'll do it. Drive out the back entrance in the truck, pouring gunfire on their heads."

"Except last time I saw the movie, they had enough troops outside to make it a quick way to commit suicide."

"Butch and Sundance didn't have a forty-ton truck. We do, and there's a chance we could make it."

He met Greg's eyes and knew he hadn't fooled him. The

reality was they weren't going to make it out of this trap, short of an artillery piece to rip apart the enemy, and they had no artillery piece. He looked back at the entrance as the shooting became heavier, and after a quick glance to make sure they were holding, he ran to the truck. Didn't start the engine, because that would warn them something was up. But he wanted to make certain it hadn't taken too much damage when they drove it through the wall. It hadn't. It would drive out of this place, as far as the waiting soldiers. Then, they'd have swapped one deathtrap for another.

Something crossed his mind, something he could put a name to, and he sent Greg to join Wyatt at the front.

"Soon as you reach them, send Sara back here. I have some things to sort out."

Greg didn't look happy, but he ran to join Wyatt. Seconds later, Sara joined him.

"You wanted something?"

"We're going to make a last-ditch attempt to crash out with the truck, but I wanted you to know the odds are not good. I'm sorry."

"Forget it, you tried. What choices do we have?"

He gazed back at her, once again reminded of the astonishing similarity to Madeleine Charpentier. "We could surrender to the Paks, and I think you know what they'll do to us. It'll be brutal, painful, and in the end, they'll still kill us."

"I get it. In that case, it doesn't look like we have a choice. It has to be the truck." She continued looking at him, and her expression puzzled him, "You know, Stoner, we make a pretty good team."

The comment hit him in the guts. It was almost a pickup line. There was something else. When he first met Madeleine, she'd said much the same thing. He remembered her face, and her cute French accent. 'We could make a pretty good team, Stoner. You and me.' He was already half in love with her, and when she said that, he was hooked.

Before he could answer, they had to duck as bursts of gunfire smashed through the gaps in the wall. They were coming, and they had to race to the bigger gaps in the ruined wall to return fire and keep the enemy troops back before they got inside. The shooting became heavier, and they edged back inside, still firing. The enemy was closer, encroaching, and they both knew they had little time left.

He felt the pull, the magnetism that sucked them together, and he felt a searing regret it should have happened when their lives were about to end; even worse to another girl as brave and pretty as Madeleine. He'd met her, and soon, he'd lose her. Life was tragic, but then again, he'd known that for a long, long time. In Afghanistan, life and tragedy were the same.

With an effort, he gathered his thoughts, forcing himself to work through the problem.

This is no way to go. No way for her to go. Think! I'm a soldier, so fight like a soldier, Stoner.

She was peering out through the gap, and with a startled cry, she said, "It's him, the man from Tora Bora! The one who captured me, and kept me prisoner. Rumi Khan."

He felt his fury surge, the man who was behind all of this. "I'll kill the bastard."

He slammed a new magazine into his AK and watched the man in the distance, about two hundred meters away. He was standing next to another man, and from beside him, she said, "That's Mohammed Abdullah, his second-in-command."

"I don't give a shit who he is. He's going down."

He pulled the trigger and sent a long stream of bullets toward the two Talibs. He also noticed the army uniforms that surrounded them. He'd have liked a video camera to record the scene, so the world would know just how truthful the Paks were when they talked about the measures they were taking to fight the Taliban.

Two hundred meters was too far for accurate shooting, and the Taliban leader stepped away quickly when he saw the gun pointing at him. The soldier standing behind him crumpled as he took the full force of Stoner's bullets. The Talib briefly looked out, ducked back inside, and shouted an order. Another machine gun opened fire, and bullets whistled and spat all around them. He dragged her back behind cover.

She was still struggling to get out and return fire, and he had to grip her ankle to stop her crawling into the open. She twisted around, face-to-face, her mouth open to reveal perfect teeth, and her eyes narrowed to furious slits. Even in anger she looked beautiful, just like Madeleine, and he wondered about her features.

Could it be she also has some French ancestry? A pity I'll never find out.

He knew the plan to leave in the truck was doomed to fail. The moment they reversed out, they'd riddle the cab with bullets, and anyone inside would die. Even if he made a space for her in the back, amongst the piles of scrap metal to keep her safe from the bullets, it was a no go. Whoever was driving would be dead, the truck stopped, and they'd search and find her. He shuddered as he thought about the eager, brutal hands ripping at her clothing, and he'd never felt more wretched in his life. He should have kept her away from it, tied her up, and knocked her out, anything to stop her coming to get Greg and Wyatt out of this place.

His frustration peaked, swept over him like a wave, but with an effort he calmed himself.

There will be a way out of this trap. There must be.
Even as he had that thought, a crazy idea came to him.
If we could spoof the Paks into thinking we've left, it might just work. Find somewhere we can hide. Wait until they leave the armory, and then slip away. No, that's a million to one shot. How often did they come off? Never. Still...

"Sara, stay here, and make sure no one gets close. I need a word with the others."

"I'll be here, Stoner. I'm not going anywhere."

A girl with a sense of humor, like Madeleine.

He went to the front door. Wyatt had found a case of bottled water and broke it open. He stuffed one in his pocket for the girl, and greedily drank down a liter. He didn't bother mentioning spoofing the Paks. It was too stupid to even consider.

"Guys, we need to come up with something. We can't sit here and wait for them to kill us."

"A miracle," Evers snorted.

Greg was more practical. "Has to be the truck, you never know, we may just make it. If we're lucky."

"With fifty assault rifles and machine guns firing at us? I'd like to say yes, we'll try it, but if they take the girl alive, you know what happens next."

Both men nodded. They knew. He was about to toss the idea over more when her voice cut through the room.

"Stoner! Get here, now!"

He raced over to the truck and climbed up to where she balanced on the top of the cab, peering out through the broken masonry. He heard something, but he couldn't say for sure what is was. She said one word, and he knew they wouldn't be going anywhere ever again.

"Gunship."

He looked out, but still couldn't see it, although he could hear it. No question, a gunship, which meant cannons, machine guns, missiles, and rockets. They'd standoff and turn the small armory building into tiny pieces of rubble, with them inside. He turned to the girl.

"Get back. They're coming in to make an attack run. It has to be the Huey they had parked outside in the square. I heard it take off shortly before the shooting started."

They both slid back inside the armory building, not a second too soon. The rotorcraft opened fire with the nose-mounted cannon. 30mm rounds slammed into the masonry around them, smashing holes into the truck. In seconds, the armory was a nightmare of flying fragments of lead. He flung himself over her and stayed on top until the burst ended. The moment it went quiet, he pulled her down beneath the truck, where the bulk of the vehicle and its load of scrap metal offered some protection.

"What can we do about it?" she asked him, "Can't we bring it down with an RPG?"

He shook his head. "There's just one place we can get out into the open, and that's the gap in the wall. The moment anyone shows their head outside, there's a platoon of soldiers itching to blast it off. As for using an RPG, forget it. It's not going to happen, not unless someone wants to commit suicide."

She was silent, and she seemed to huddle closer to him. For reassurance, warmth, human contact, or for something else, he wasn't sure. But her suggestion had given him an idea.

"There is one chance. I could wait behind the broken masonry. And sooner or later he's going to come down to try and fire through the gap. Stay here. I need a launcher and a rocket."

He bounded to the weapons racks, took down what he

needed, raced back, and climbed onto the top of the cab roof. She was already there, waiting for him. He felt a surge of anxiety.

"Get down from here. All hell is going to break loose any second."

She ignored him. "You need a spotter, Stoner. That would be me."

"You can't..."

"I can, and I am. Get on with it. He could appear in your sights any moment."

He sighed and didn't waste his time arguing. He propped the launcher on the rubble, lay down behind it, and waited. The wait was more than uncomfortable, with frequent machine gun and rifle fire chewing up the ground close to him, but he stayed clear of the line of fire. And waited. Waited more, and the roaring of aircraft engines became louder. The aircraft was descending, and he was certain he was about to get a shot. Maybe it wouldn't get them out of the trap, but it would sure feel good. The noise was louder and louder, and then the nose of the helo appeared in front of him. Less than a hundred meters away, and the big aircraft was a sitting duck. Yet he was also quick.

The cannon was mounted below the nose, and its multiple barrels moved slightly, before fixing their aim on him. They had him, target acquired, and all they needed was to pull the trigger, except he fired first and waited for the roar of the rocket motor igniting. He anticipated the jet of flame as the missile hurtled out of the tube and crossed the short distance to the Huey. Nothing happened. He fired again, and still nothing. Of all the bad luck, he'd picked up a dud, or maybe a system that had taken damage during the fight. He lay there and waited for death to come. There was nothing left. It was all over, or it would be in the next couple of seconds. A storm of heavy caliber shells would turn the inside of the armory into a charnel house. He'd be dead. They'd all be dead. He pulled her close to him.

"I'm sorry."

"What?"

The noise was incredible, and he could hardly believe anything could make that much of a racket. The 30mm cannons fired, and the noise was like a hundred blacksmiths beating on monstrous iron anvils. The cannon fire was a shattering machine like rhythm, yet none of the rounds came inside the armory. Then he saw the reason. The Huey was going down in flames, torn apart by incoming fire from yet another gunship.

Was it a mistake, has someone fouled up? Have U.S. forces come to our aid? No, that is impossible; Pakistan is a 'friendly' ally. About as friendly as a wounded rattler, but that's another story.

There had to be a reason, even if he couldn't work out what it was. The UH-1 hit the ground, and a ball of burning kerosene trailed along the street, engulfing many of the soldiers who'd been besieging them from close by. The rest ran, some with their uniforms on fire, and the screams of the fleeing men were an unearthly chill. The roaring of engines became louder, and to his astonishment, he watched a Pakistani Air Force helicopter perform a landing, a very shaky landing, but a landing nonetheless.

What the hell's happening here, is this some kind of a trick?

"Stoner, get your people out here, and get aboard!"

He recognized the voice, but it couldn't be, it was impossible. The starboard gun barrels were moving around, looking for targets, and he still didn't believe it.

"I said get out here, and make it mighty fast. You do have Lieutenant Carver with you? Because if you don't, I'm going without you."

Ivan, but how? Does it matter how? The hell it does. He's here. That's all that counts. A miracle, Wyatt Evers said was what we needed. Okay, maybe he was right.

He shouted across the darkened room. "Wyatt, Greg, get over here. We're getting out. The cavalry's here."

He moved, knowing the Puma would come under attack once they realized what was happening. Something made him hold back. Ivan was visible through the window of the cockpit, grinning at him and waving. He didn't relax. This was Ivan, and anything could happen when he was involved, and usually did.

He shouted at Greg, "We need weapons and ammo. Just in case. I don't trust Ivan not to have an alternative agenda."

Blum looked astounded. "Like what? Look at the armament on that gunship. Cannons, machine guns, and we've seen what they did to the barracks. We don't need more weapons."

Greg was right, but he was also wrong. The guns fitted to the Puma were awesome, less useful once they landed. Or were brought down by enemy fire. All they had were two AK-47s and a PK machine gun, all of them almost out of ammo. He raced to the armory racks and tore down a half-dozen AKs, two PK machine guns, and shouted at Greg to bring boxes of ammunition.

Sara stared at them as if they'd taken leave of their senses. Ivan was waving like a madman for them to get aboard. They bounded through the door of the Puma, where Ivan was already gunning the engines. A moment later, the craft was leaving the ground. Abruptly, they shot up into the air, and he looked down in astonishment at the damage and destruction the battle had wrought upon the barracks. Close by, the wreck of the Huey was still burning. Inside and outside the walls, there were bodies. Many bodies. He didn't make a count, but at a rough guess there were sixty or seventy men who would never get up again.

"Where's Wyatt?"

Sara was staring around the cabin, looking for the man who'd been with them since Tora Bora. The man without whom they couldn't have made it, and he wasn't there. Left behind, and when Stoner looked down at the ground, he couldn't see him. He looked at Greg.

"What happened to Evers?"

"I don't..."

A burst of gunfire punched holes in the helicopter as they clawed for height and distance, and he saw him then; a tiny figure far below, running across open ground carrying something on his shoulder. Then he disappeared into the shadows of a nearby building. The weapon stopped firing as a rocket ignited, sending its fiery trail across the short distance to the machine gun position. The explosion threw up a mixture of masonry, shattered machine gun, and broken bodies. The figure of Evers appeared again for a brief few seconds, and he waved. Stoner could swear he was smiling, white teeth bright against the dark beard, and then he was gone.

"We have to go back."

Ivan jerked his head around. "You what?"

He explained about the man they'd left behind.

"Him? You're kidding me. The crazy bastard, he didn't need to do that. You want my opinion? He wanted to throw it all away on one, last, insane show of heroics. He'll take a few more of them with him, and then all that's left is a footnote in history. That's it for Sergeant Evers. He got what he wanted, and now he's gone. Forget going back, Stoner. We're out of here."

He kept looking, but he didn't see him again. But he couldn't take his mind of the half-crazed hermit they'd encountered in the mountains above Tora Bora. Ivan was right. He harbored a death wish. What else could have sustained him over the years? He'd said he didn't need to fire that missile to take out the machine gun, and maybe he was right. The Puma was a tough ship, but all rotorcraft could be vulnerable to ground fire. And human flesh certainly was.

He closed his eyes for a second, sad at losing such a brave and colorful man, who for all his mad eccentricity had become a friend in a short time. Out of that friendship, he'd sacrificed himself for his friends, given them the ultimate gift, their lives. And paid the ultimate price, his own life.

"He had the courage of a lion," Sara said, her voice sad.

"Yeah, he did that, a mountain lion. They're the fiercest."

He glanced back at the place they'd just left and wondered how they'd done it. How they'd fought off the Pakistani troops for so long was hard to explain from up in the air. He put it down to a combination of luck, the stout walls that had been more than adequate to shield them from the bullets, and the bravery of Wyatt Evers. Then there were the contents of the armory, without which they'd have been unable to fight back. They'd been more than lucky, and now the miracle had arrived to save them. They flew higher, and he waited for ground fire to creep up toward them. The four men manning the guns, Gorgy, Akram, Habiba, and Daud were wary. But no shots came at them, no missiles launched. They were in a helicopter that bore the markings of the Pakistani Air Force. Despite the destruction they'd carried out, the soldiers would be confused. Not knowing whether shooting down or attempting to shoot down the Puma would bring them a medal or a court-martial and summary execution.

Ivan flew low, and when he was far outside the city limits swung the nose to the northwest, heading for home, for

Afghanistan. Friendly territory. At least, a little friendlier than the place they were leaving behind. When they were flying over the countryside, and he considered the immediate threat lowered, he entered the cockpit, taking the seat next to Ivan.

"I guess we all owe you a deal of thanks."

A grin. "I guess you do. That's one you owe me."

"We also owe Evers. A lucky hit from that machine gun and we'd have lost it all."

A shrug. "Maybe."

He was hard and cynical, was Ivan. Still, he'd been there for them, arrived in the nick of time.

"Why did you come back for us? Or was it just the girl? Who gave you the order?"

"Dammit. Stoner, we go back a long way. I came back for all of you. How could I have left you in the shit?"

"That's exactly what you did before when I called, and you left us in the lurch. It didn't bother you then. What changed?"

He grunted. "It was a mistake, is all. I told you, I'd never have left you down there."

Yeah, right. What's going on, Ivan?

He watched Ivan flying the cumbersome machine, and he showed a fair degree of skill, although flying low, his inexperience showed when he needed to make sudden alterations in course and trim. Still, he relaxed. They were heading in the right direction, and Peshawar was falling back into the distance. It came to him, then.

The reason for the chance of heart must be down to a high-level connection. How high?

"Who is she, Ivan?"

He glanced back in the cabin to make sure she was okay. She was battered and bruised, but she smiled to reassure him. He waited for Ivan's answer, knowing Sara Carver was no ordinary officer.

"The Chief of Staff, she's his daughter."

"Chief of Staff? Which Chief of Staff?"

"As in the President of the United States, Chief of Staff."

He nodded in understanding. It had to be something like that. "So that's why you decided to turn back."

"It was part of the reason," he admitted, "But you should be more positive. It ended well, and now we're taking her back to Kabul. The job's done, and she'll be home, safe and sound."

A new voice intruded on their conversation. "What was the price?"

They both looked around, and the Puma wobbled in the air before he regained control.

"The price?" His puzzled expression was almost believable, "You were in trouble, and your people wanted you out. That was enough for me. You think I'm that mercenary, that I'd want payment for rescuing one of our own!"

She looked at Stoner. "Is this true?"

"No." He explained the deal he'd made with Ivan, information in return for getting her out of Tora Bora.

"Information about what?" She looked from one to the other, her expression making it clear she was determined to get answers.

He pointed to Greg. "It's his wife's cousin. She's under sentence of death from a bunch of Islamists for some crime they say she committed. Ivan said he'd use his resources to find out where she is so we can free her."

She was silent as she digested what she'd just heard. Then she glared at Ivan. "Do you know where she is?"

"Well, yeah, I do now. I went to plenty of trouble. You know, I splashed some money around and called in some favors…"

Her glare was like a laser gunsight. "Crap. Where is she?"

He cleared his throat. "They are holding her in a Madrassah in a town called Panjab, in the middle of Afghanistan. That's where they plan to stage the trial, and there'll be no doubt about the outcome. The people in that place are real believers. Long beards, turbans, and they don't even go for a shit without a copy of the Koran in their back pocket."

She closed her eyes momentarily. "And now you expect Stoner to go in there and get her out? What about you, why aren't you helping him?"

He gave her a look of surprise. "Me? My job is done. They wanted me to get you out, and here you are." He fixed her with a stare, and the aircraft wobbled again, "It's not the way I work. You know, a favor for a favor, then me and Stoner are square."

"They gave you the task of getting me out of Tora Bora, didn't they? Instead you passed it across to Stoner and Blum. I reckon you owe them a lot. Like helping them get this poor woman away from the Islamists, and take her home. Like me."

Stoner noticed Gorgy Bukharin had moved closer, and he'd overheard some of the conversation. He was grinning, and he knew when Ivan was hooked. Knew when the guy was pinned like a housefly to a board. She'd called him out, and now he had no choice but to show his hand or fold. There was silence in the cockpit for long minutes as he chewed it over, and then he gave her his most charming grin.

"Look, lady, of course I'm going to help them get her out. It never occurred to me to do anything else. Listen, we'll go back to my base, get some rest, a shower and a shit, and we'll be ready to give these bastards a big surprise. Yeah, we'll get right onto it. You can tell…"

He stopped as the turboshafts stuttered, and one cut out completely. The other ran ragged for several seconds, and then it too fell silent.

"What's up?" Stoner said, automatically making a grab for Sara to keep her safe.

Ivan was scanning the gauges, and he cursed. "Damn, I forgot to check the fuel levels. We're out of gas."

"Does that mean we're going to crash?"

"That's what it means, lady."

"What do you want us to do?"

"Hold on tight. There's nothing else you can do. Make sure you're strapped in, and with any luck, we'll autorotate down and make a landing."

"Will this be a soft landing, the kind we can walk away from?"

He didn't look at her, as he concentrated on preparing for the crash. "I said a landing. I didn't say what kind of a landing." He continued to play with the controls and looked up at the rotor blades, "All I can tell you is we'll hit the ground, somehow. Hold tight. We're going down."

CHAPTER EIGHT

They tightened the straps and found something solid to hold. Above the fuselage, the rotor blades spun slower, but by the magic of aerodynamics, the turning blades spun enough to slow their descent. Lower, lower, and Ivan fought to keep the craft level. A few kilometers away lay a small village, and on either side of them loomed the harsh, sheer sides of a deep valley. Stoner knew it, knew it well, as did Blum.

"The Torgan Valley," he shouted to Ivan, "You know what we're dropping into."

"I've heard there's insurgent activity around here."

"You could say that. This is Taliban country, so we'll need to get out fast and find a good defensive position. Wait until the light goes, and then make our way out. Assuming you get this craft down in one piece. If not, it won't matter."

The speed of descent was picking up, and there was little they could do about it. Lower, lower, the stricken Puma fell faster as they neared the ground. They hit with a rending crash that almost shook them out of their seats. In the cabin, one seat, where Akram and Habiba had been sitting, ripped from its mountings and tossed them across the cabin. The Puma slid along the ground for several meters, hit a rock, and tilted over on its side. But they were down, and without gas in the tanks, the threat of fire was non-existent.

He unstrapped and rushed to help the two men in the upturned seat, although by some miracle they'd suffered no more than bruises. The windshield had shattered, and one by one they crawled outside. Habiba and Daud took longer, unfastening the 7.62mm door guns and passing them out. Akram and Gorgy slung belts of ammunition around their bodies and crawled out last. They'd made it. They'd landed, and they were alive, for now. In the distance, he'd seen movement, and he squinted to get a better look. Armed men. The iconic banana-shaped magazines on their assault rifles, the usual mixture of black turbans, shabby robes. Taliban.

Ivan nodded his agreement, and he took another look. "We're about twenty klicks from Ghazni. I'll call my people on the satphone and get them to send transport, but it'll be a while getting here. In the meantime, I suggest we start walking."

"I concur. Now would be a good time to beat it."

A single track existed that led toward Ghazni, and as they walked, Ivan made the call on his satphone. When he'd finished, he explained his people would arrive in three or four hours. "In the meantime, we have to keep ahead of those folks."

He pointed back down the valley. They were getting nearer, and starting to encroach on them. Three men were climbing the steep, valley sides. Their intention was obvious, to get level with them, and snipe from the heights. Slow them down, and give their buddies time to catch up with them and kill them. They were strangers in the valley, and these men did not take kindly to strangers on their territory. The fact they'd come down in a military helicopter was enough reason to kill them. Insurgents didn't use helicopters. Government and Coalition forces did.

They tried to hurry, but the going was hard, strewn with rocks and debris, and the risk of twisting an ankle or breaking a leg was severe. Severe enough that each knew to sustain an injury enough to prevent them walking would be a sentence of death. The men on the valley sides had no such constraints, and they got closer. After the first half hour, they were close enough to open fire, and bullets began to whistle around them. He looked at Ivan.

"It's just a matter of time before they get near enough to start hitting us. Keep them moving as fast as you can. I'm going up there."

Sara heard him and protested, but he had peeled off to dive behind a larger fall of boulders that had tumbled down over the centuries. They would give him cover to climb. The move was fast, so fast the hostiles didn't appear to notice, and they kept up the inaccurate fire on the party moving along the track. He looked back as someone cried out. Habiba was clutching his side, with blood pouring from a wound that had grazed him. He didn't falter, and they kept moving.

The cover petered out when he was halfway up the side, but he slipped behind some scraggly bushes, enough to screen him from the hostiles. The last twenty meters would be a problem. Down below, they could see all the way up, and were ahead of him. They'd seen his predicament, and how close he was to the enemy. As he was about to make a sprint for it, and pray they didn't hit him, the machine gun spoke. Akram was behind the 7.62mm, pouring bullets at the hostiles up on the slope. They had little choice but to scuttle for cover, and he took advantage of the confusion, raced the last few meters, and dove to the ground. There was little cover, just a slight dip like a shallow foxhole, and he went to ground.

The gun ceased fire, and the hostiles leapt to their feet and ran toward him. Within two minutes they'd be on top of him. The machine gun fired again, but this time they could stay clear of the gunfire by using a narrow ledge that ran along the top of the slope. He waited for them to come. When they were close enough, he'd start shooting, but they stopped again. They were directly above where Ivan's party was crouched next to the track. They'd taken cover behind a natural cleft at the bottom of the rocks, which kept them out of sight of the main group of insurgents advancing along the track. Although the moment the insurgents came nearer, they'd see them, making them an easy target.

He waited for the moment, knowing he'd have one chance. The firing from the machine gun stopped, and in a lightning movement, the three insurgents ran to the edge. A second later they opened fire on Ivan's almost defenseless party. He catapulted to his feet and ran at them. Firing from the hip, his first burst took one man in a slating line of bullets that impacted across his body, from the hip to the shoulder. He was already dead when he hit the ground, but the other two had jumped back into cover. Now he was out in the open, and he had no choice but to keep running.

His AK would be running low on bullets, and he switched to single-shot mode, lacking the time to slam in a new magazine. Kept running, and when a head appeared above the rocks, fired twice and ran on. The head disappeared, and another popped up. He got off two shots before he repeatedly pulled the trigger. One of his bullets tore into the man's face, throwing him back in a welter of blood and brains. He ran on, and when he was a meter from the last man, the Talib popped up and opened fire on full auto. Stoner hit the deck and returned fire. Two bullets came out of the barrel, and then he was empty. He desperately grabbed for another magazine. The enemy fighter had guessed he was out, and he charged. Spewing out bullets, and they missed. The shooter's eagerness for the kill made him shoot high, the barrel jerking around as he sprayed bullets everywhere except at the target.

Stoner survived, but the man was on him, and as he prepared to pull the trigger, the Talib leapt on him. Screaming his fury and determination to kill him, and now he too was out of ammunition. It was too close to take aim, and as the man swung his rifle like a club, he had no choice but to block the massive blow with his own rifle. It promptly broke in two, as the breech separated from the barrel. He tossed away the useless pieces and closed on his enemy.

The man struck again, and this time he had to take the blow on his shoulder, as his hands reached out to grapple. The butt of the rifle came in again, and he grabbed for it, stopped the blow, and kicked out. His boot caught the man on the thigh, and the blow was hard, but the target was not hurt enough to incapacitate him. For a third time, the butt flew toward him, and he had to drop low to avoid it knocking him unconscious. This time the Talib saw his opening and used his own boot to slam into Stoner's belly. The pain was incredible. He tried to swerve aside and succeeded in offering his left kidney as a target.

The Talib knew he'd done serious damage, and he snarled a vicious shout of triumph as he came in again. Stoner was fighting for his life, and his opponent was a man more skilled than any he'd encountered in the past. A veteran of countless fights, he instinctively knew how to wound, to weaken, to disarm. This time he dropped the rifle and used his fists, hitting him with a hard blow to the same kidney, and Stoner grunted in agony. Using the single move he had left, his hands reached out to grab, and he caught a fold of cloth from the guy's robe. Pulled him toward him, and used his momentum to hit him with a raised knee. His target was the area of the groin, and his hard kneecap was precisely on target.

The man screamed, and the wail was like it came from the very depths of his tortured soul. For two seconds, he was out of it, and Stoner took advantage. Ignoring the pain of his tortured kidneys, he straightened and whirled, bringing his boot into the man's neck with every ounce of force he could muster. The guy had to abandon trying to favor his tortured genitals to protect his neck, and so exposing his belly. They were close to the edge, and the former SEAL took advantage of the exposed belly. Hit him twice, three times, and the third time the punch was into his already bruised crotch. Another piercing scream, and his eye glazed with agony. He slammed another punch into the now defenseless Afghan and drove him to the edge. A final hard blow sent him toppling over, and he tumbled head over heels down the steep slope, landing in a crumpled, broken heap next to the track at the bottom.

Stoner straightened and massaged his aching body where his kidneys were hurting like they were on fire, almost missing the fourth man who'd climbed the slope to rush to his companion's aid. The bullet whined over his head, and the man chuckled to himself as he moved the selector to full auto to give the American infidel a bellyful of lead. The long burst hissed past him, and to his astonishment, he was still alive. The bullets came from behind him, and he whirled, ready to jump clear to avoid the shooter. There was no shooter, save Sara Carver, standing five meters away.

"I thought you might need a hand. That last guy was sneaky; he'd climbed higher and slid down to take you from behind."

He nodded. "Yeah, thanks. How'd you get up here?"

"Same way as you. Akram put down a long barrage from the machine gun of his, and kept the others occupied."

He smiled and nodded. "It's appreciated, Lieutenant. Thanks."

"No sweat, you've put your neck on the line enough for me. Call it a present from the Big Red One."

He scooped up a dropped AK, took four spare magazines from the fallen man's pouches, and tucked them into his pockets. They began the climb back down. Akram saw them coming, and put down heavy covering fire with the machine gun. They reunited with Ivan and the others.

He frowned. "It's about time. I've had a call from my people. They've made good time, and they'll be here in about thirty minutes. It's time to get out of Dodge, and we're...oh, shit!"

Another enemy fighter had appeared at the top of the slope, and his intentions were obvious. He wore the characteristic suicide vest, a crudely constructed garment of cheap canvas, with sticks of explosive tucked into the pockets. He held up one hand to show them the detonator, ducking back as they fired several shots toward him.

Ivan grimaced. "Stupid bastard, he won't climb halfway down the slope before we rip him apart."

"He's not about to climb down the slope," Stoner said, his voice grim, "He's going to jump."

"Jump?" He stared at him for a moment and swung to Akram, who was still covering the enemy further along the track. "Up there on the ridge, there's a guy about to jump at us. Nail him, now, for fuck's sake."

He swung the machine gun around and took aim. They all took aim, just as the guy stood on the very edge, arms outstretched, like a diver in an Olympic event. They could do nothing to stop the fall, and their weapons opened fire and spoke as one. Automatic fire from assault rifles and machine guns tore into the man's body, a fraction of a second after they'd heard him scream, "Allah Akbar!"

The body jerked as the rounds smashed into him, but he was already tumbling down the slope toward them. In two seconds, his bomb would explode in their midst. It exploded, but not where the would-be suicide had intended. There was one man amongst them whose shooting skills were very different, Greg Blum, his specialty sniping. His Spetsnaz father had taught him the intricacies of military marksmanship, and now he used those skills to deadly effect. His target was the explosive, and he fired single, well-aimed shots to slam into the C4 and the detonators inserted into each deadly stick.

The AK-47S he used was no sniper rifle, but as the range closed, it was good enough. Seven shots left the barrel, and the eighth hit the vital part of the target. A second after he'd jumped, it was incredible shooting, and required a speed of computation within Greg's brain beyond belief. The body tumbled down the slope, already dead from the barrage of gunfire, hit a rock, and bounced in the air. Greg Blum's bullets hit, and a moment later the would-be bomber literally split into hundreds of tiny fragments.

The shockwave from the explosion slammed into them, punching them back, dust and stone chips showering them with the remnants of human being. For a few seconds, the shooting died. The hostiles on the track expected their sacrificial lamb to do the work for them, and they weren't ready for failure. They started to assemble, to form a new group to make yet another desperate attack. But Akram's bullets sang their song of death, and slowly, they disappeared into the distance.

Less than an hour later, the Land Cruisers driven by Ivan's men arrived, and they clambered aboard. They left the Torgan

Valley behind them, and the vehicles stopped briefly at Ghazni. There, they found a café on the outskirts of the town for some much-needed food. They took two hours, luxuriating in the knowledge they'd escaped the trap in the valley. Ivan promised them all a hot shower and a night's rest when they reached his base, and Stoner began to think things were on the up and up at last, until the satphone buzzed.

"Ivan."

They watched as his face tightened, and his eyes narrowed.

"When is this?"

More words they couldn't hear, and then he ended the call with a snapped, "Keep me posted."

He glanced at them and lowered his voice. "We got trouble."

* * *

Shahay Pazira crouched on the floor of the cell. She wasn't alone. Twenty women, all shared the cell with her. The stench was terrible inside the cramped, stone room. Designed to hold two prisoners, or a maximum of four if conditions demanded, the twenty females packed inside the tiny room had insufficient room to lie down. They'd been there for days, what seemed to some to be a lifetime, and they shared the cell with something more than the other women.

Fear. Fear was a living entity, something they felt, they smelled, an evil force that reached out and touched each one. The execution was scheduled for the following day, and the prospect of any last-minute reprieve was zero. The Mullah had addressed them from outside the bars an hour before, his face wearing an expression part grim, and part joyous. The purpose of his visit was to pronounce sentence.

"You are guilty, all of you, crimes against Allah, apostasy, worshipping a false god, and failure to wear correct Islamic dress! In two cases, your crime of adultery is enough to condemn you a hundred times over. There can be no doubt about your guilt, and the punishment is unalterable. You will be taken out together and stoned to death. May Allah have mercy on your souls."

He turned to walk away, but Shahay had had enough.

I have nothing to lose, and besides, if this worthless piece of shit wanted his say, I'll have mine. What can he do, stone me again?

She shouted out loud, "What about the men?"

He paused and looked around. "What men?"

"Adultery requires two people to make it happen, so what about the men?"

He spread his hands in confusion. "Men are different."

"It wouldn't be adultery if they were the same as women," she responded, to hoots of laughter from her prisoners, "What punishment do they get?"

"It is none of your business," he snapped, "Be silent, and make your peace with God."

"Tell us first what punishment they get."

A sigh. "Very well, they were forced to sign a document admitting to their guilt, and promising not to commit a similar crime in the future."

"That's it?" someone shrieked in despair, "That's all they get for doing the same as us?"

"Yes. It is the law."

A hubbub of voices broke out, all shouting and chattering at once, but he fled through the outside door. The guard slammed it shut behind him, leaving them in their dark, fetid misery.

"We should try to escape."

The voice was a whisper, and she looked at her fellow prisoner, Fatema Akbari, sentenced for adultery. She was a big woman, tall and stout for an Afghan, with a twinkling smile that even in these circumstances never entirely left her face.

"There is no way to escape," Shahay murmured, "The door is locked, and these walls are impossible to break down."

The jail was a former store, divided into several rooms. The walls were of stone, and the door to their cell built of timbers two inches thick.

"In that case, we must persuade the guard to open the door. Or are you so anxious to die you want to sit here like these women and wait for the end?"

She looked around at them and realized they almost seemed ready to meet their fate. The brief excitement of shouting at the Mullah had gone, and now they'd lapsed back into silence. Like cattle, going to the slaughterhouse, almost as if they were unaware of how terrible the execution would be.

She shook her head. "I am not anxious to die, no. But what you describe is impossible. The guard would never take a bribe to open the door and release us. They'd kill him. Besides, even if we did get out, you know we're a long distance from Panjab. How could we escape? They'd come after us in vehicles and recapture us long before we got halfway."

"We can worry about that when we get out. Perhaps we can take a vehicle, and disable the others to stop them coming after us."

Shahay was about to object when she thought better of it.

Any chance, no matter how remote, is a chance. And what do we have to lose?

"How do we get to the guard?"

A smile, and the other woman whispered, "You are younger and prettier than me. You must offer him what every one of these filthy animals wants. Sex."

"You think he would..."

"For you, yes, for me, older and fatter, perhaps not. Use what you have, Shahay. Call him. No, I have a better idea."

She regarded the other women, her sisters in suffering. "I need you to make a noise. Shout, scream, make it sound as if we're dying in here."

"We are dying," someone snorted, "There's no need to make it sound like we are."

"Whatever. Shout and scream. Get the guard to come inside here."

"What for?"

"For me, please, sister. My friend Shahay wants to talk to him."

"He is a pig. Why talk to him?"

"The reason does not matter. I ask you to do this for me. We do not have much time left."

The woman shrugged. "Why not? Perhaps it will make this endless waiting go quicker. Shout, all of you. Scream."

They shouted, and they screamed, and Shahay had to clamp her hands to her ears to screen out the worst of the cacophony. Inside the packed cell it was more like Dante's inferno, the entrance to hell, with the ringing screams of tortured souls condemned to suffer for all eternity. Moments later, the door crashed open, and the guard rushed inside the darkened corridor. He came to their cell door and leveled the muzzle of his rifle to point at them.

"What's going on here? You must stop this noise, or I will call the Mullah!"

A woman laughed in derision at his empty threat, but the others became quiet, all except for Fatema. "My friend wants to speak to you."

His eyes narrow in suspicion. "Which friend?"

She pointed to Shahay, and his eyes fell on her slender body.

She'd pulled in her robe to tighten over her breasts, and they pushed out the material, rising and falling as she breathed in and out in terror and excitement. He watched her at first, and then came nearer.

"Is this true, you want to speak to me?"

His eyes were wide, and his voice slightly hoarse with arousal. She read the signs, as would any woman. "It is true I am to die tomorrow, and yet I have been admiring you each time you come into the cell. My body longs for yours, to feel the passionate embrace of your strong arms. What is your name, soldier?"

"Mohammed."

"Mohammed." She rolled the three syllables around her mouth, and each came out as an alluring murmur, soft, sensual, and difficult for any red-blooded man to resist.

"You want me?" His surprise was justified. He was paunchy, short, bandy-legged, and stank of body odor. His face was repulsive, pitted with acne scars and pimples that looked ready to burst their contents of septic pus.

"I want you, Mohammed. Do this for me. Let me join you for a single time before I go to my death. Allah would look on you favorably for doing this favor for a woman who is about to die."

The hesitation was momentary. He shouted an order, "Get back from the door. All of you, or I'll shoot."

As they pressed backward into a tight throng, he produced a large iron key and unlocked the door. He beckoned to Shahay, who swayed out toward him, her robe coming loose at the neck to expose her upper body. Her coffee-colored breasts were in full view, inches from his face, and he goggled at them, bemused, and captured by their spell. She came closer, hypnotizing him with a glimpse of the forbidden fruits of her body. So much so he didn't see Fatema move.

She slithered behind him, and still his eyes were fixed on Shahay's breasts. They were still fixated when she struck with the pistol she'd deftly eased from the holster on his belt. The blow smashed into his head, and he dropped to one knee, stunned. She hit him again, and again. As he fell to the floor, she followed him down, and now she was raining blows on him. She didn't stop until Shahay held her wrist.

"That's enough. Can't you see he's dead?"

Fatema spat on the bloody body. "Good, he deserved to die. Pick up his rifle. I have his pistol. Sisters, we're going home."

They took a second to understand they had a chance to live. Then they were surging out the cell, along the passage. Some opened the outer door, raced outside, screaming in relief at getting out of their cell and into the fresh air. Their relief didn't last long. Four men, Talibs, were staring at them, their faces as implacable as the steel barrels of the rifles they clutched ready to open fire. Behind them, the Mullah surveyed them with a grim expression. He spoke one word, enough to stop them in their tracks.

"Aim!"

Rifles went up to shoulders, and selectors slid into the full auto position. He regarded Shahay clutching the rifle. "Drop the weapon!"

She didn't drop it, but a guard she hadn't noticed came up behind her and smashed a wooden club on her head. She went down, seeing stars, and blacked out for a few moments. When she came to, it was all over. Fatema's pistol lay in the mud, and the women were filing back into the cell. Two guards plucked her up to drag her inside, but the Mullah shouted at them to stop.

"Not her! I have a special place for this one, far out in the wilderness, a narrow hole in the rock where we will leave her to reflect on her fate. There will be no escape, and you will remain there for two days without food or water after the other women are executed. Then it will be your turn, and I promise you, your death will be worse than even Satan himself could imagine. Take her away!"

They dragged her to a truck and tossed her into the bed. Climbed up beside her, and the Mullah seated himself in the passenger seat. Another fighter took the wheel, and they set off into the barren wasteland that lay outside the village. She despised herself for failing, for not pulling the trigger of that rifle before they took her. Now she had to contemplate only a death as agonizing as this sick-minded bastard could make it. A death that had already begun, which would force her to endure hell for many, many days before that blessed, final release.

* * *

They waited for Ivan to explain the call he'd just received.

"They moved them out of the city. Someone told them a military unit was heading in to investigate reports of the mass execution, so they've changed the location."

"Do we know where?" he asked.

Ivan shook his head. "So far, we don't have a clue. Our best bet is to head on into the city. I do have a contact who may have heard something, or alternatively we could grab one of the clerics and beat it out of him."

"That's my favored option," Stoner said grimly, "What are we waiting for? Time's awaiting, and we have some distance to cover."

Ivan nodded his agreement, and the Land Cruisers sped away from Ghazni toward their destination of Panjab. Because of the dire nature of the Afghan roads, they had to detour away from the city and head northeast toward Kabul. Before the capital, they turned west, and began the final stage of the journey, the last one hundred and fifty kms to Panjab. They made twenty kilometers when a roadblock brought them to a stop. It wasn't the Taliban staging one of their frequent raids on passing traffic. It wasn't the Afghan Army or police, checking documents in an attempt to stem the passage of insurgents across the country.

"It's the Big Red One," Second Lieutenant Carver exclaimed, "That's my own outfit."

Blum was staring ahead, and he identified the red-faced man standing with hands on hips, watching them approach. "I'll be damned. It's our old friend, Lieutenant-Colonel Harold H. Brewer. Let's see what his grouse is today."

Akram was driving, and he braked to a halt a meter from the officer's polished boots. Brewer stood glaring at them, as one of his men rushed to the driver's window.

"State your business, Mister."

Ivan leaned over and smiled. "Nothing for you guys. We are heading into Panjab to pick up supplies. I'd be more than grateful if you'd move your vehicle so we can pass."

The soldier looked around at his Colonel and repeated what he'd just heard. Brewer walked over to the passenger side, and Ivan lowered the window.

"I understand you men think you're on the way to Panjab, is that correct?"

This time, Ivan's smile was even wider. "You got that right, Colonel. Just routine trip, nothing of any interest to the military."

Brewer looked inside the vehicle and did a double take when he recognized Stoner and Blum. "You two men! Going to visit more relations, is that it?"

"We're doing nothing illegal," Stoner said, working to keep his temper in check, "Why don't you search the vehicles if you have any doubts?"

Even as he said it, he recalled that each of the Toyotas had a 7.62mm machine gun stashed in the trunk. They'd brought them along, just in case. But Brewer wasn't interested in a search. He was that kind of an officer, a man who wanted to assert his authority, no matter the reason.

"I don't need to search your vehicles, Mister. You're not passing this point. I want you to turn around and head back to Kabul."

"Ghazni," Stoner corrected him, "We didn't come from Kabul."

He stared back at him, his eyes glacial. "I couldn't give a shit if you came from Tibet. Turn around now before you piss me off any more." He turned his gaze to the other occupants, and his jaw dropped as he recognized the missing junior officer.

"Second Lieutenant Carver, you managed to get out."

"I did, Colonel, thanks to these men."

He grunted. "The how or why doesn't matter, but now you're safe. Were you injured or harmed?"

"Nothing too serious, Sir, but all patched up. I'm fine."

"Then you can step out of the vehicle and rejoin your unit."

Her return gaze was cool. "I'm sorry, Sir. I can't do that. There's a woman facing execution, and we're going to save her. I made a promise to these men in return for getting out, and I couldn't live with myself if she suffered the kind of fate I was facing. The moment she's free, I'll be right back."

His jaw tightened. "Lieutenant, you don't give the orders here. I do. You will rejoin your unit now."

"I'm sorry, Sir, no can do. Akram, turn around and drive."

"Yes, Ma'am."

The engine was still running, and he backed up, swung the wheel over, pushed the lever into drive, and stomped on the gas. The Land Cruiser picked up speed, and behind them they heard Brewer bellowing with anger. Sara chuckled.

"You know, I never did like that man. I have a feeling it's mutual."

"He'll cause you problems when you rejoin your unit," Stoner observed.

She waved away the comment. "I really couldn't give a damn. Besides, if I need someone to tell him to back off, Daddy will have a quiet word with his Commander-in-Chief."

Ivan chuckled. "It must be nice to have friends in high places."

She looked at Stoner, a long, slow, inspection. As if she was measuring up. For what, he had no idea. "I'd sooner have friends like you. People I can trust." She paused, "People I'm going to like a lot."

She locked her gaze with his, and there was a message there he didn't need to work too hard to interpret. Except it wasn't right time, or the right place.

"We still need to find a way to reach Panjab. That road is the only one passable, as far as I'm aware. Short of taking on the United States Army, we're screwed."

"Cross-country," Akram said. He looked sideways at Ivan, "You know the route. We used it to…"

"Never mind what we used for, you think you can find it again?"

"I can find it."

"In that case, what are we waiting for?"

Akram stamped on the gas, and the swift Toyota SUV ate up the distance until the roadblock was out of sight. He drove on for a further five klicks, reaching a narrow track that branched off the main highway to the left. It was narrow, little more than a footpath or route for goat herders to use when moving the animals from place to place. He didn't slow down, and within minutes, they were hugging the edge of a steep slope, with a fifty-meter drop to one side and the rock wall to the other.

He didn't let up, and the wild ride was like a white-knuckle rollercoaster, with one vital difference. Rollercoasters didn't threaten to kill you if you took your attention off the route for a split second. Somehow, he kept the careering SUV from plunging over the edge and killing them all. The vehicle behind dropped back, as the driver took a more careful approach to the prospect of imminent death.

Far below, and to the south, they had a fine view of Brewer's roadblock. Stoner wondered how useful it would be when bypassing it was a cinch for anyone who knew the region. Provided they didn't mind taking a gamble with their lives, although dicing with death was par for the course in Afghanistan. Three hours later they sighted the city of Panjab, and after another fifteen minutes of furious driving, Akram slammed his foot on the brake pedal. The powerful vehicle half spun on the road, before he corrected and brought it to a halt.

The outskirts were no surprise, the usual squalid slums of cities across most of the Islamic world. Besides, they'd been there before, and that time it had been another young woman facing a barbaric execution. Stoner got her out, and enjoyed a short but pleasurable relationship before she disappeared with a large quantity of gold, the property of the Afghan government. This time, it was different. The streets were thronged with armed men, and there was a definite buzz in the air. As if these people were there for a festival, Islamic style.

Not music and games, booths laden with food and drink for everyone, but the grim business of ritual execution. Not one girl, but twenty. And one, Shahay Pazira, was the cousin of Faria Blum, Greg's wife, to whom he'd given his word to get her out. They'd gone through hell to get this far, and a few hundred armed fanatics, who'd turned up for a front seat to see the show, would not deter him.

He tapped Ivan on the shoulder. "Now would be a good time to look at your contact and see what he knows. The execution ground can't be that far away. Otherwise, these people wouldn't be gathering here. But if we can't find out in advance, we won't know what we're up against."

Ivan nodded. "He runs a coffee shop about two blocks away. Gorgy, you come with me, and stay sharp. These people look as if it wouldn't take much of a spark to set them off. I'm sure they'd love to add a Westerner to the list for execution."

Both men exited the vehicle and walked through the crowd. As they passed along the hard-packed earth of the street, men jostled them, darting venomous glares. It was proof enough, should anyone be in any doubt, this was Islamic territory. Kabul may think they ruled here, but they were wrong. The men who dictated the law in the city were hard-line Islamists. If asked, most would give allegiance to a single organization, known as the Taliban.

They waited for almost an hour, and the wait was more than uncomfortable. Frequently, young men peered through the windows of the vehicles. Few were too young to carry a weapon. At one time, scores of armed Afghans crowded them, and Akram even suggested dragging the 7.62s from the trunk. Just in case. Stoner dissuaded him. They had problems enough, without making any kind of aggressive move. The men moved on, and all they had to contain with were small groups of three or four who gave them hard stares. Leaving them in no doubt how delighted they would be to turn the Land Cruiser into a bullet-riddled coffin.

Eventually, Ivan returned and stepped back inside the vehicle.

"I think I got it. It's a small village a few klicks outside the city. When the Soviets were here, they found it was home to a bunch of mujahideen, and they staged a raid, almost destroyed the place."

"What about the people who lived there?" Sara asked him.

"All dead. You'll understand when you see the place. They surrounded it with tanks and APCs. Sat and watched while the bombers came in and unloaded enough ordnance to destroy a major city. Then the armor opened fire, and when they were bored, the infantry went in and finished off any survivors. There weren't many. Afterward, no one bothered to live there. They just left it. I guess it became a symbol of bad luck. The poor bastards were in the wrong place at the wrong time."

"There weren't any mujahideen in the place?" Greg Blum asked.

"Not one. It was either faulty intelligence or downright murder. Most of them didn't even own a gun."

"What's this place called?"

"Sangdar. A word of warning, my informant told me that since the bombing, there's no cover, and no way to approach without being seen. After they destroyed the buildings, there's nothing standing more than a meter high. They'll be holding the women in an underground cell, little more than a deep hole in the ground covered by bars at the top. Getting in will be anything but easy. Getting out is likely to be much harder. The moment they know a rescue is underway, there'll be nowhere to hide, and they'll shoot the shit out of anyone they don't like the look of. Which I guess goes for all of us."

They talked over the best way to approach the place, and they'd go in between 02.00 or 03.00; a time when sentries were at their lowest ebb, and if they were careful, they wouldn't see them coming. That at least was the theory. They had a few hours to wait, and Ivan directed Akram to drive to his informant's coffee shop. His man was the owner, a big man with a huge beard and an even bigger belly. He presided over the cash register, with a smile for everyone that walked past, and a cautious squint when men made to leave without making any overt move to settle the bill.

Ivan greeted him, and the proprietor directed them to a table in the corner. They ordered coffee, but what they needed was a few hours' shuteye before they went in, and once again the owner was more than helpful. No doubt for a price, and Ivan would settle later, using his normal currency. Information.

He showed him, Sara, and Greg to a pair of tiny bedrooms over the coffee shop.

"You may rest here until you are ready to leave, my friends, as long as you want. Any friend of Ivan is a friend of mine."

Greg went into the room on the left, and Stoner went to follow him. He didn't make it. Carver took hold of his arm, dragged him into her room, and closed and locked the door.

He raised his eyebrows. "What gives?"

She didn't release his arm. "I think you and me have some business to attend to."

"Business?"

She put her finger to his lips to silence him, then took hold of his coat, and pulled him toward her. Her lips locked onto his, and her kiss almost made his knees tremble.

She murmured in his ear, "Take your clothes off. You'll be more comfortable in bed, and you need rest if we're going into

Sangdar."

"Rest, yeah. Okay."

He removed his coat, feeling just a tad disappointed.

"Stoner."

He looked at her, and she was undressing, too. "What is it?"

She was smiling. "I always found I rested better when I'd done something to help me relax."

His interest sparked. "Like what?"

"How about a fuck? I find it never fails."

He undressed quicker. "Me neither."

CHAPTER NINE

Colonel Brewer was unhappy. He was bored and fed up with standing around in the middle of nowhere, waiting for something to happen. Nothing had happened, except for those two civilians who'd showed up and tried to get past him. He snorted with amusement.

That was a laugh. When I put a roadblock in place, no one gets past, not without proper documentation. Not anyone, Nosirree. It was a pleasure to send them packing, and hot damn, it was fun, seeing off those cowboys.

But now he was bored. The operation had been intended to look for Second Lieutenant Sara Carver, and monitor evidence of any other unusual activity. Intel had reports of a big gathering planned, somewhere over Panjab way. No one knew the reason, so they wanted to know more. So far, all he'd seen were these groups of civilians, and none appeared overly belligerent. Quite the opposite, they were excited, as if they were going to a party. Good for them, but of no more than passing interest.

Okay, he'd seen Carver with his own eyes in the company

of those civilians, and she'd ignored a direct order to rejoin his unit. Not that he could do anything about it, she was armor plated. A female with connections to the top, his sole option was to keep his mouth firmly shut, even if it rankled. He wasn't a believer in women serving in front line units.

The little ladies are good for the rear echelon stuff; manning a desk, transport drivers, that kind of menial work. And a girl like Carver, I wonder what she'd be like in bed. Hot, by the look of her. A pity I'll never find out. But as fighting soldiers, no way!

He beckoned to his adjutant, Captain Leonard Stevens, and he doubled over. "Colonel, what is it?"

"I've had a gutful of this place, Captain. I want you to contact HQ and ask for any updated intel on that Islamist activity we're supposed to be monitoring. I'd like to hunt some of those bastards down and get payback for what happened at Tora Bora."

Stevens' look was quizzical. "Sir, they said to block the road here, and stop anyone getting past. There was nothing about hunting anyone down."

Brewer reddened. "Did I ask you a question, Captain, or did I give you an order?"

"Yessir, right away."

He doubled away, and Brewer looked at the road, which was empty of vehicles. Groups of Afghans came past, men in robes, turbans, and all manner of peasant clothing. Women, too, and most wore burqas, which was unusual. In these post-Taliban days, no more than a minority of women wore the tent-like dress. Although almost all these people passing by the roadblock wore traditional dress.

Weird, it's as if they're going to some religious ceremony. Maybe it's something like that, something I haven't heard about. Whatever, it isn't my business.

Stevens returned, and his face betrayed his excitement. "They asked me about Carver, and I told them we'd found her, and she was alive."

He nodded. "Good, good. Anything else?"

"Yessir, they've had a drone up over the Panjab region, and they've seen signs that suggest insurgents may be gathering a few klicks outside the city. A village called Sangdar, destroyed by the Soviets, and never rebuilt, but they're gathering there. The overheads picked up a fair size crowd, and it's building. Their best guess is they're performing some rite or ceremony, although quite what it is they don't know."

He felt a rising tide of excitement.

We could get moving again, and maybe, just maybe, there'll be some real action. Not that sneaky ambush stuff like happened at the caves, but a chance to charge down the enemy, guidons streaming in the breeze, and the autocannons spitting bullets.

He nodded to Stevens. "Get 'em formed up and ready to move, Captain. We're heading for this Sangdar place. You have the coordinates?"

"I do, Sir. It's difficult country, but we can make most of the way before nightfall, and make the final leg at dawn."

"Good man. Jump to it. We're going into action, Captain. We'll travel to Panjab, and stop before the city for the night. As you say, at dawn, we'll drive in there and see what out Talib friends are up to. If it's something bad, the motherfuckers will regret it for the rest of their miserable lives."

Minutes later, he mounted his command Humvee and followed the lead and his sole surviving Bradley along the highway. The Big Red One was going into action, and by tomorrow, there wouldn't be a man in Afghanistan who hadn't heard of Colonel Harold H. Brewer.

* * *

The alarm on his watch beeped, and he came awake still unsure if it had all been a dream. Sara Carver's sleeping form next to him made it clear it was no dream. He touched her smooth skin and traced a finger around the outline of her face. Her eyes flicked open, and she gave him a long, slow grin.

"Good morning, Stoner. Sleep okay?"

"For about an hour, yeah. You?"

"I'm good." Her expression changed in a second, and she was all business, "We have a lot to do, so we should get started."

She got out of bed, and he checked his watch. "It's 01.30, and the village isn't far away."

"Good, then we have time to reach Sangdar. Catch them napping, and get Shahay out of there, along with the other women. You should wake the others. Tell them to hurry."

She didn't wait for an answer, just threw on pants and a shirt, and went to find the bathroom. He dressed and gave Greg a knock.

"What is it?" His voice was full of sleep.

"We're moving. Five minutes. I'm going to rouse Ivan and his men."

"Okay, I'll be there."

Stoner went down the stairs and found Ivan and his men slumped in chairs around the coffee shop, dozing. His eyes opened when he heard the footsteps. He reached for a weapon and relaxed. "Is it time already?"

"01.30, we're moving."

"I'll kick them awake."

Fifteen minutes later, they were boarding the Land Cruisers. Sara appeared, carrying a cloth bundle he didn't question, and she climbed into the first Toyota. Akram drove the lead vehicle, and Daud the second one with Gorgy Bukharin. A man was missing.

"Where's Habiba?"

Ivan shrugged. "No idea. When you came down just now I saw no sign of him. Bastard's gone off somewhere."

"Any idea where?"

"None. I'm guessing he found a woman and spent the night in her bed. We can't wait."

"You don't think it's a problem?"

"No, no problem. He's reliable, one hundred percent."

"Okay, time to go."

He took the front seat, with Carver in the center. Ivan rode in back with Greg, and they brought out the 7.62mm machine gun and made sure it was loaded and ready. At 02.00, they stopped two klicks outside Sangdar to work out how they'd go in. Carver had it all planned. She unwrapped her bundle and produced a mass of black cloth.

"It's a traditional burqa I found in the room where we stayed." She ignored Ivan's look of interest at the word 'we' and went on, "I'm going in on foot to find out how many guards they have, if any. That'll determine how we do this. Give me a satphone, and I'll call in when I have some information."

She didn't wait for a reply, but shrugged into the voluminous garment. Stoner stared at her transformation from a pretty American officer to a shapeless, formless Islamic female.

I don't like it, don't like it at all, but what she said makes sense. We have to know what we're facing, without blundering into hidden defenses or even an ambush. Still…

He took out a Desert Eagle and handed it to her. "Take this. Stash it under that robe."

She stared at the .50 caliber automatic and winced at the

weight. "You don't think this is excessive?"

"If you get into trouble, you'll need something with stopping power, and a .50 caliber bullet has plenty of stopping power."

After a brief hesitation, she smiled and nodded, tied a piece of cloth around the trigger guard, and hung it inside her robe. "Thanks."

Her eyes flashed, and he assumed she was giving him a grateful glance.

Burqas are a bastard. How's a guy supposed to know what signals a girl's giving him?

"No sweat. Just don't lose it. That's my lucky gun."

"Why this one? Why not the other?"

"They're both lucky."

The black face veil crinkled, and he assumed her mouth had formed a smile. Ivan rummaged in the glove box and came out with a spare satphone. He switched it on and checked the display. "You can use this. Call the moment you hit any problems. Even if you think it's just an outside possibility, call."

The black-cowled head moved up and down. "I will. How near can you take me without them hearing the engines?"

"Another klick," Stoner said, "After that, you'll have to walk. It may be better if someone went with you. Just in case."

The eyes stared at him. "And tell any guards I come across an American is on the way in? I don't think so. I'll be fine, and I'll call as soon as I know anything."

They drove as far as they dared. Without a word, she climbed out, gave them a wave, and started walking along the track. Minutes later, she'd disappeared into the darkness. The night was moonless, with even the stars obscured by thick cloud. He felt as if the night had swallowed her up, and for a brief second, he thought she'd never return. It was crazy thinking, and he made himself relax. Estimated how long she'd take to travel one klick, take a swift look around, and call in. *About thirty minutes, no more. Any longer, and I'm going after her.*

* * *

She walked for less than ten minutes before she saw the village in front of her, or what was left. Not so much a village, more a heap of broken stone; like an archaeological excavation. She saw a single light in the center, coming from a tent someone had erected. For what reason, she had no idea.

Just as she was entering what had once been the main street, a man stepped out in front of her and shone a flashlight on her face. He said something in Pashto. She had no idea what he'd said. He spoke again, and this time his voice was louder, peremptory, demanding. She still hadn't a clue, but she'd anticipated being stopped, and had picked up several large stones. She clutched them in her hands. He played the flashlight over the stones, and his thick lips parted in a wide smile. He said something else, and without waiting for her reply, waved her onward into the village. She'd made it.

The stones were the sole currency she could think of to get her past any guard. The following day, they were executing the women by stoning, and she'd reasoned many would bring their own ammunition. He would have taken her for a devout Muslim, and no doubt assumed the reason she'd declined to speak was because he was a stranger. And a man. As she walked through the dark piles of rubble left decades ago by the Russian attack, the clouds suddenly cleared, and the moonlight lit up the ghostly scene.

She was approaching what had once been the village square. Two more guards watched her approach, but she'd passed the outer guard, and they made no move to stop her. The wide area of beaten earth was littered with lumps of stone from the bombardment. Bushes had poked through, giving it the appearance of an abandoned Old West ghost town, except it was not in the Old West. Ranged around the square, women were stretched out, sleeping, and she concluded the guards were to protect them, to protect their honor should a man decide to take advantage.

What greeted her in the center was macabre. Twenty shallow holes dug in the ground, like foxholes, about a meter deep. They'd bury the women up to their armpits, ready for the stone throwers to lob their missiles at the unmoving targets. She thought of the bloody scene that would take place here if they didn't get them out. Screaming women, suffering endless agonies until finally they succumbed to their wounds and died. She felt sick and fought down the urge to puke.

It's always the women who suffer in places like this. Never the men!

She prowled around the ghostly remains, careful not to trip on sleeping men who lay in the dark spaces. The tent was her first target, but when she got near, she found a single guard sitting cross-legged outside the doorway. Without doubt he was guarding someone of importance, hence they'd erected the tent for his comfort. She continued scouting the village, walking a mere thirty meters before finding where they were holding the women. The smell alerted her first, the stink of ordure, of people held in a place for a certain time without sanitation.

The second clue was the bars set over an opening enclosed by a stone wall, no more than half a meter high. She saw no guard, and she walked to the edge. A hinged iron grating was fastened at one side, locked with a heavy iron padlock, and on the ground next to the wall, a wooden ladder. Down inside the dark depths, she could hear them, a couple of snores, and the odd fragment of murmured conversation. Low moaning, the sound of women who had no alternative but to face up to the reality of what awaited them, whose fear has overwhelmed them, and sometimes driven them into early madness.

She had what she needed and was about to put the stones down in order to use the satphone, when a man loomed from the shadows. He barked questions, and once again she held up the stones. He gave her a curt nod and sat by the grating, staring at her. She decided it was time to move on. She couldn't use the satphone. The village was almost silent, and they'd overhear an alien voice. She retraced her steps to the Land Cruisers. Stoner was waiting.

* * *

He watched her return and let out a long sigh of relief. He'd been about to go in after her, although he knew it was the wrong thing to do. She was an Army officer and deserved credit for being able to make good decisions, and carry through her mission. They listened as she explained what they faced, and Ivan said what they all knew to be true.

"We go in on foot. Leave the vehicles here."

"The women," she objected, "They'll be in a bad way, maybe not able to walk after what's been done to them."

"They'll walk," he said, his voice careless, "They'll know the alternative, so they'll walk if that's what it means to stay alive. First, we deal with the guards."

"That's my job," Stoner murmured, "Leave them to me."

"Not on your own, Stoner. You'll need at least one man to watch your back."

"That'll be me," Greg said.

"Okay, I'll give you thirty minutes, and if you haven't called in, I'm driving into the village, and we'll use the machine gun to cut through the opposition."

"We'll call." Sara handed him back his second Desert Eagle without a word. He tucked it into the holster, took out his combat knife, and started walking.

"I don't have a knife," Greg murmured.

Ivan nodded to Akram, who handed him his own blade. A six-inch-long thin, straight dagger, with the blade darkened so as not to reflect the light. Greg nodded his thanks, shouldered his AK, and sped after Stoner. He caught him up halfway to the village.

"Listen, we…"

The American held up a hand for silence. Used a hand signal to tell him to stay in place, and he went on alone. Blum waited in the silence. A second later, he understood what had alerted him, a faint spicy odor, the familiar scent of opium. Someone close by was smoking, probably a pipe, for a cigarette would have showed a glowing tip.

Stoner dropped to the ground, crawled forward, and saw the man five meters away. Probably the guard Sara had encountered, but he'd moved further away from the village. No doubt so he could smoke without his companions becoming aware he was neglecting his duties to get stoned. He snaked along the ground, edging toward him, and then cursed. Something alerted him, some noise in the distance, and he looked up toward where Stoner lay in full view, bathed in the moonlight.

His mouth opened, and his rifle came up. With no other choices, the American catapulted to his feet, took aim, and threw. The blade flew unerringly to the target, the center of the man's chest. Except at the last instant, he moved to get a better grip on his rifle, and the blade embedded itself into his shoulder. He put up a hand to wrench it out, and Stoner moved, crossing the distance between them at a run. As the Afghan pulled the blade free, he leapt the final gap, using his weight to take him down. Punched him in the face, but the guy brought up his knee, and he just managed to twist aside to avoid a crippling blow into the groin. But he took it on the inside of his leg and felt the shock of the impact.

His opponent was quick, a fit, young, veteran fighter, and he gave no quarter. He smashed his fist into Stoner's belly, and as the pain redoubled, swept his wounded leg from under him. With an effort, he threw out a hand, gripped the man's robe, and dragged him down with him. Thumped another hard fist into his face, but in the dark he'd missed the man's other hand, hadn't seen him bring out a gun, a big automatic that appeared from nowhere. He didn't need to put a bullet into him, to end everything. A single shot would alert the entire village, they'd lose the advantage of surprise, and they'd all die; the women, Ivan and his men, Greg, and him.

They were so close he could smell the spices from his last meal on his breath, the stink of his body, his unwashed clothes, and then his mouth opened. To shout a warning, probably, and he couldn't allow it to happen. His good leg was jammed under the man's body, but with a huge effort, he kicked out with his injured leg, wincing at the pain. His boot connected with the man's neck, and he grunted in pain. Stoner used the surprise to press home the attack and punched out with one hand, grabbing for the automatic with the other. He missed, and frantic to stop him firing, he reached out again.

This time, he got a finger through the trigger guard, and prevented the man from shooting. But it was close, too close. A fist thumped into his head, again and again, and his vision started to go as the new pain threatened to overwhelm him. He moved his head away, another punch whistled past, and then the man hit him again, a jarring, bony strike to the chest. Then he remembered the knife, the guy had snatched it out and dropped it. He felt around the ground with his free hand, suffering more hard blows. The Afghan snarled something in triumph. He felt the hilt, hard and metallic, but another blow thumped into him, and his arm jerked away. He reached out again, knowing he had to take the punishment, and the blows kept coming. But he reached out and this time found the knife. Gripped the hilt, waited for another blow to hit him, and as the Afghan drew back his fist, he struck, sliding the blade into his chest. It struck a rib, and he altered the angle a fraction, keeping up the pressure. It went in, and he pushed harder. The blade hit something tough and leathery, and he twisted, keeping up the force until he felt the man go limp.

He'd struck the blade into his heart, a good aim, and if he'd missed, he'd have been in the shit. But he hadn't missed, and the Afghan was dying. He opened his mouth again, and bared dirty, stained teeth. Somehow, he summoned a last vestige of strength. He was about to shout aloud with his dying breath, and Stoner ripped out the blade, and jammed it all the way into his throat. He would not cry out, unless it was from beyond the grave.

Greg was close, where he'd been waiting for a give him a hand, the long, thin blade held ready. Stoner gave him a nod of thanks, and they continued walking into the village. When they neared the square, they found the two guards in the place Sara had described. They approached from behind, took one man each, and when they struck, it was in a sequenced move, almost worthy of a ballet. Two knives rose, and two came down together. He'd explained how to slash in from the front of the neck, to ruin the vocal chords and simultaneously cut off the air supply. Hold the man while he threshed and struggled to draw breath, and lower him gently to the ground. It went like clockwork, and as the bodies were cooling, he inspected the hatch.

The lock was formidable. There was no way they could open it without a key, not without making noise. He signaled to Greg and went on to the tent, stepping over the sleeping bodies. The guard was sitting outside, and he wasn't asleep. His eyes watchful, and getting to him would be difficult. Greg solved the problem, and he put his head close to Stoner's to whisper.

"I'll sneak to that broken wall close to where he's sitting and make a low noise. Someone groaning in pain should do it." He grinned, "I guess you know how to do the rest."

"I know. Do it. We don't have much time."

Greg slid away and disappeared behind a heap of broken stone. Stoner went the other way, as close to the guard as he could get, and waited. The moans came, and Greg was convincing. He even sounded like he was moaning with an Afghan accent, if that was possible. The guard looked up and glanced toward the noise. With a fluid motion, he climbed to his feet, and walked over to inspect the source. He didn't seem worried, and as he passed Stoner's hiding place, his eyes were looking ahead. Not to the side, and he didn't see the dark shadow detach itself from other dark shadows. Neither did he see the knife slash upward under his chin. Stoner pushed up hard, pushing the point all the way up through his mouth, soft tissue, and into his brain. Then he lowered the man and searched his clothing. His hand touched something hard, clipped to his belt. A key, a huge, iron key, and he had what he needed.

Greg came to him, and Stoner pointed to a dark corner, several meters away from the tent, where they could make the call. The time had come to call in Ivan and his men. They'd need help to get twenty women out from the underground prison. Men to soothe them, and besides, Akram and Daud were Afghan, so they spoke the same language. Otherwise, there'd be chaos and excitement when women condemned to a cruel death viewed the prospect of surviving, which meant noise.

The two men crouched in the corner of what had once been the walls of a stone cottage, and he pressed the button to call. Ivan answered at once. "Go ahead."

"We're clear. The three guards are dead."

"Roger that. We're on the way. You got the key?"

"Affirmative."

"We'll be there in ten."

The call ended, and both men waited in the shadows. At first, everything was silent, until something stirred. A dark shape, and it spoke a few words in Pashto. Too late, they realized a man had been sleeping in the place they'd assumed was empty, and their alien voices had intruded his sleep. Then the shape moved and resolved itself into a man. His eyes were wide open now, and his mouth opened to scream a warning.

Greg was nearest, and he made a hurried grab for his robe to drag him down. Too late, the darkness made it difficult. He twisted away and screamed a warning. Greg tried again, tripped, and fell. Stoner lunged at him and put an arm around his neck. He squeezed, and the second scream came as little more than a hoarse, choked cry. But the damage was done.

"Get to the women and free them," he murmured to Greg, "I'll cover you as best I can."

"On the way."

Both men were already running, and Stoner made a second call to Ivan. "We've got trouble."

"What kind?"

"The worse kind. Someone shouted a warning."

He murmured something about 'fucking amateurs,' but maybe it wasn't that. Then a new voice came on the phone. Carver, and she sounded breathless. They were running.

"What's happening? You know you have to get the women out. That's all that matters."

"I know. We're going there now."

"We'll be with you in a few minutes."

They reached the square, and Greg was already unlocking the hatch. He swung open the iron door, lifted the ladder into position, and called down softly, "We're getting you out of there. Hurry and come up."

A pause, the hubbub of startled women, and a voice replied, "You're American?"

"Some of us are, yeah. What matters is you're all going home, but only if you hurry. Get up here. We need to run before they all wake up."

A head appeared through the hatch, the woman who'd spoken. She stared at him for an age, a hard, bitter look, and then she appeared to be satisfied. She said something in Pashto and glanced back at Greg. "I told them you were genuine. They thought it might be a trap. Some men who wanted to rape us before the execution."

"It's the real thing, but we're short on time. The place is coming to life."

A moment later, Stoner opened fire. Three men were rushing toward them, and he blasted them with the .50 calibers. Two shots chewed up the ground close to him, and he looked for the shooters. Two men were standing in full view, bathed in moonlight, and the Desert Eagles spoke again. Two shots, and the men became bloodied bundles of rags on the debris-strewn ground. Some men had recovered enough to run, not enjoying the prospect of a firefight. They'd come for entertainment, to see women cruelly done to death. Their own suffering wasn't part of the deal, and it became a mass panic as women joined them, and they surged away into the darkness, leaving behind the true believers. The men who wanted to see the infidels die, to see anyone die. They'd come for blood, and they wouldn't leave until they'd tasted its heady flavor.

Stoner was doing his best to hold them off, but he was running out of bullets. The Desert Eagles emptied, and he unslung the AK and started to shoot. Walking forward, firing short bursts at the men who raced to intercept the fleeing women. All too soon the firing pin clicked on empty. They came for him then, a robed crowd of bearded sadists, closing for the kill. Savoring their prey, perhaps intending to capture him alive and give him a slow death. They'd reckoned without Ivan. The sound of a vehicle engine made them turn, and a Land Cruiser was boring in toward them.

The men looked around, assuming it was someone coming to help fight the infidels who'd ruined their fun. They turned back to Stoner, and he threw himself behind a wall as a dozen assault rifles opened up on him. Then stopped, and a louder noise intruded, the hammering, stuttering sound of a light machine gun firing on full auto. Moments later, Ivan appeared out of nowhere and hunkered down beside him.

"I got Akram to head in and Daud to use the 7.62mm from the Land Cruiser. He's pretty damn good with that thing," he said admiringly, watching the gunner stitch a line of bullets into a crowd of men making a desperate charge for the center of the square. They'd become aware the women were escaping the underground prison and moved in to stop the escape; to ensure Allah had his share of victims when the time came for the executions. They didn't make it. Daud was good with the machine gun, and when his shooting paused for him to reload, the line of running men had become a line of bodies.

But still more men came to stop them escaping. Greg was waving, calling for their attention, and the meaning was obvious. He'd got them all out, and now it was time to get out of Dodge. Ivan was still admiring his man's shooting, but Stoner grabbed him.

"They're all out. It's time to get them away."

They crawled part of the way after the firing became intense. When they reached Greg, he made the women lie flat, out of danger. He looked up as they came in.

"What's our next move? If we try to get them out while this is going on, they'll tear them apart. Tear all of us apart."

Stoner looked at Ivan, and they both looked toward the Land Cruiser as the machine gun fired again. But this time, it was short bursts. The crazies had had their day, made their charge in support of the values the Mullahs had taught them, and they'd died. Those who lived were the careful ones, the cautious fighters, the men who knew the importance of surviving to kill the enemy, rather than dying to kill the enemy. They were the dangerous ones, the ones who would kill them, if they let them.

Greg was still waiting for an answer, and the women were staring at him, also waiting. He had a single answer, the soldier's answer.

"We'll make a run for it, and I'll stay to give covering fire."

A head popped up from behind a heap of stones two meters away. Carver.

"I'll stay with you."

Before he could say no, one of the women spoke in clear, but accented English. "It won't work." She waved a hand at the women lying close, "They tortured some of them, and they can hardly walk, let alone run. We had to pull some of them up the ladder; they were that far gone. We need transport to get them away."

While Greg chatted to her, he glanced at the Land Cruiser. The machine gun had stopped firing.

We have the other Land Cruiser, but by the time we go back for it, the enemy will have counterattacked. Besides, how can we get these women out, some stretcher cases, in two SUVs? It's not going to happen. We'd go down under withering sheets of fire from enemy rifles and machine guns. There's a single alternative, take the fight to them.

He looked at Carver.

"I'll lead them away from here, and I want you to promise me to get them out."

"What about you? How will you get out?"

His reply was automatic. "I'll find a way. Don't worry about me."

"No, that won't work. We go out together."

"Then we die." He gave her the brutal reality, without softening his tone. She flinched away and turned back to look at the women, as if she was counting them, maybe working out how to cram them all into two Land Cruisers. That was when Greg dropped the bombshell.

"She's not here."

"Who's not here?"

"Shahay Pazira. They took her away earlier. I questioned them, and they said they've taken her to some place out in wastelands, somewhere off to the northeast."

"Taken her away, why?"

"To die."

* * *

He felt content riding in the Humvee, with the solid armor

protection of the Bradley leading the column. It had all gone to plan, until they reached the outskirts of Panjab and started to laager for the night. That's when a local woman had chanced across them and grabbed his arm, gabbled in Pashto. He'd called one of his men who understood the lingo. He listened to her and turned to the Colonel.

"Sir, there's something going on, some gathering of Islamists. Talibs, I guess. It's outside the city, in a ruined village not far from here. I don't get all that she says, but it's something about a great killing. It sounds to me like they're about to start something. Maybe they're on the way here, and think they can take over the city?"

Brewer rubbed his chin thoughtfully. It made sense. The Talibs periodically attacked larger towns and cities, to unsettle the combined government and Coalition presence. And this could be what he'd come for. To look for and monitor signs of insurgent activity, then act as the situation demanded. The situation demanded he make up for the foul-up at Tora Bora, when those two civilians had barged in and ruined everything.

Not this time. This time, I'm going in, and when the day's over, things will be different.

* * *

"I'm going after her."

They looked at Stoner as if he were crazy. Ivan shook his head. "You couldn't get a mouse out of this place. Look what we're facing."

Without thinking, he followed Ivan's gaze. More fighters were getting nearer, too many, and he was right. The Islamists had them outmanned and outgunned. In the next few minutes the bullets would strike flesh, and they'd start to die. The

221

nearest shooter was already only fifty meters away, and they were out of time.

Absently, Carver said, "We need more guns. More people. Otherwise these women will die sooner rather than later." She grimaced, "Maybe better to die quickly, but in the end it's all over. I just wish to Christ we had more people."

Stoner was staring around them, inspecting the carnage they'd already wrought on the initial suicidal charge. Bodies lay close by and weapons. Assault rifles, at least a score of AKs, and the detritus of battle. Magazines flung onto the earth, torn webbing, and even a limb, an arm detached from the body by a heavy burst. If they could reach the vehicles they might make it, but they were too far away.

We need more shooters, anyone who can handle a gun, spray bullets at the enemy. We owe it to the women to fulfill the promise that brought us here. Besides, Shahay is still in trouble. I have to reach her. We have to fight our way out of this trap.

"We have more people."

He stared at Sara. "Where?"

She waved a hand at the women, who lay prone, sheltering from the bullets. "There. Give each of them a rifle, and they'll shoot."

"Women? You're not serious?"

She glared at him. "What do you think I am, Stoner? Or have you forgotten already."

He blushed. "No, it's not that, but…"

She spun around and shouted at the woman who understood English. "Listen to me. We need you to shoot, to take a rifle, and kill the enemy. If you can't do it, we'll all die. It's our last hope."

The woman's face clouded, as she digested the information. She took less than ten seconds to work it through, and then she shouted at the women. They were sick, wounded, and terrified. But there wasn't a moment's hesitation once they'd made up their minds. As one, they jumped up and ran out to the bodies that lay scattered around. Picked up rifles, bandoliers, magazines, belts of cartridges, and as they ran back behind cover, left two of their number dead behind them. The Talibs had overcome their surprise and started targeting them.

They left it to Akram to explain how everything worked. Sara helped overcome their fears, by showing them how a female could kill Talibs just as easily as men with the right tools. The women chatted excitedly to each other as they examined and familiarized themselves with their new acquisitions. As if they'd got their hands on a new sewing machine, or a microwave oven. Stoner and Greg kept up a sporadic fire to keep the enemy from getting nearer. Ivan talked animatedly to Bukharin and Daud. In the end, out of frustration, he shouted at them to start shooting.

"I was just working out how to get back to my place at Bande," he said, "Problem is, we need transport for these women."

"One thing at a time, Ivan. We haven't beaten them yet."

He nodded thoughtfully. "Yeah, that's true. Thing is, I need those Land Cruisers to get home. One of them anyway."

"And I need one to go looking for Shahay."

"I can slip into Panjab to get transport. Find a truck or a bus, something they can fit into, and get them away from here."

"The fight's here, Ivan. Send one man. That's all we can spare."

Akram was busy, and he glanced at Daud. "How about it? If we give covering fire, one man should be able to get out. Can you source a large vehicle inside the city and bring it back here?"

"Of course. Leave it to me, Boss."

"Good man. Go." Minutes later he'd disappeared. The enemy renewed their offensive, starting with a vicious barrage of machine gun fire. The 7.62mm was out of bullets, and all they could do was hunker down and wait. Wait for the women to finish their five-minute lesson in how to shoot, and for Daud to return with transport. They crouched down, bullets roaring overhead, some tearing up chunks of stone from the rubble around them. It was bad, but he felt they'd come through the worst. They had hope.

Yet they still had to get away and find Shahay. The women had to learn fast, and so far, they were chattering to each other, as if they were shopping in the bazaar. It remained to be seen how they'd respond when ordered to actually pull the trigger. They also had to hope Daud made it through, and that was a big question mark.

There are too many things to go wrong. All it requires is for a single part of the plan to fail, and it all comes crashing down. What do they say? In war, no plan survives the first encounter with the enemy. Will we ever get out? Maybe, maybe not, shit!

CHAPTER TEN

Sara was staring into the distance, and he pulled her down below the low wall. "They'll blow your fool head off it you expose it like that."

"I think someone's coming. I'm not sure who it is, but I saw a cloud of dust."

He peered over the top, and sure enough, a convoy of vehicles was approaching. "Could be they've brought in reinforcements."

"Or it could be our people. That looks like heavy vehicles, too much dust for civilian SUVs."

They continued watching, and he sensed her stiffen with excitement. "They're ours. Americans."

She was right. The front of a Bradley AFV appeared through the dust cloud, followed by a Humvee. She grabbed his arm. "It's my outfit, the Big Red One. They've come to help us!"

He had a different perspective. "It's Brewer. God help us."

* * *

Khan needed a rest, but still he kept walking, with Mohammed Abdullah at his side. Behind them, fifteen new men walked, young men, chattering and excited. He'd recruited them as he went along. Shouted exhortations from the deck of the eight-wheeled BTR 90 they'd acquired, after he and Abdullah came across a group of smugglers ferrying it south to cross into Pakistan and sell it at a profit. When he expressed interest, they explained how the autocannon in the turret was in full working order. The sales pitch assured him it would make a useful vehicle for a man of his obvious status.

The immediate problem was the price. They wanted fifty thousand U.S. dollars. He paid them with lead, spraying them with bullets during an unguarded moment when they thought, wrongly, he was sincere. Big mistake. The vehicle ran well, the cabin designed to transport troops, so his new recruits were delighted at the prospect of riding into battle inside the armored hull; going to rid their sacred soil of foreigners and their puppets in Kabul, the politicians who allowed the enemy to roam freely across Afghanistan. To despoil the land that people believed Allah had made his own.

It was going well, and they were nearing the city of Panjab, when the BTR engine died. Not one of them could fix it, and so they started to walk toward their destination. They began to encounter other travelers, and Khan learned of something important about to happen in a place close to Panjab, where the faithful were gathering. Something he could use to his advantage. If they could find it, the detour would not take them out of their way, not by too much. It was also likely he'd pick up more men, the faithful, the young, the fanatics. They continued walking, looking for the village, and finding nothing, when they heard the shooting.

At first, he was alarmed, but then he exulted. It was probably no more than a small skirmish, a chance for his new men to see some action. To taste blood, and enjoy the pleasure of seeing the bodies of the infidels you'd just killed lying before you.

He'd looked aside at Abdullah and pointed. "We will head toward the gunfire and join the fight. Show them we are the warriors of Allah."

"You think that's wise? We don't know what we're getting into, and these boys are mere novices. We should be cautious, Rumi."

He snorted. "Caution will get us nowhere. Time is short, and we need to give these young men a taste of victory. More will join us if we go to the aid of our Muslim brothers. With enough fighters, we can move into Panjab and make it our new base of operations. Yes, everything is possible, my friend. Keep moving, and tell them to be ready."

He watched Abdullah shout orders at their men, and a fever of excitement swept over them. They would win this battle, and he would regain his tattered reputation. He felt tired, desperately tired, but the fatigue fell away as he considered what was to come. The name of Rumi Khan would once again be feted and admired, the length and breadth of Afghanistan. He was on his way back, and nothing could stop him, even Abdullah's panicked glance.

"Americans, heading into the other side of the village. Rumi, they have an armored vehicle and jeep-mounted cannon. We must pull back."

"We will not retreat! We must find a position where we can observe the battle, and when we feel it is safe to do so, we will come out and fall on our enemies." He grinned at his second-in-command, "Whoever is fighting in there, let them bear the brunt of the action. We will intervene when the Americans are falling back. Pursue them, harry them, and kill them. How does that appeal to your sense of caution?"

"It could work, provided they fall back."

Khan felt exasperated. "It will work. Tell our new men to keep moving, and no one is to fire a shot, not without my express order. We will watch, and we will wait. Until the right moment, and then we pounce."

They continued on, looking for a suitable site. One of the young men with better eyesight than most, raced up to him, as they were about to go behind cover.

"It's back, Sir. Our vehicle, I can see it coming in the distance. Look!"

There was a tiny speck, with a trailing dust cloud. "You are sure it is our vehicle?"

A grin. "I can see it clearly. It is our Russian armored car."

He looked at Abdullah. "God be praised. We have the means to destroy all who would oppose us."

He waited until the AFV drew alongside, and the turret hatch opened. He had a bad moment when a stranger appeared, but the man greeted him in the formal way.

"Salaam Alaikum. I came across this vehicle broken down when I was looking for you, and helped fix it."

"Who are you?"

"The man who can lead you to the men who caused you trouble at Tora Bora. I can show you how to kill them."

He didn't hesitate. "In that case, you are more than welcome. How far?"

"Not far, the village is named Sangdar. There you will find your enemies, and the killing can begin."

* * *

Colonel Brewer hunched rigid in the seat, staring ahead at the village they were closing. Bullets flew as both sides exchanged fire, and the strikes churned up little spits of earth and stone where they hit. Of more importance, the enemy was in sight.

Taliban, no question, and shooting at someone inside the village, a Coalition unit, probably Afghan Army trapped under fire. It makes sense. Maybe running out of ammo, fast running out of hope. That's no sweat, men. The Big Red One is on the way.

He looked up to make certain his command guidon flew from the radio aerial. It did, and the speed of the Humvee made it stream out in full view.

He looked aside at the driver, Corporal Taylor, as the tide of excitement took hold. "Overtake Captain Stevens' Bradley, Corporal. I'm leading us in, and I want the enemy to see who is about to give them a good whupping. Floor that pedal, man. We're going in fast."

The Corporal kept the speed the same. "Sir, we don't know what we're getting into. Shouldn't we leave the Bradley in front, and let them soak up the enemy fire first?"

"Not if you want to win a medal, son. I told you to put the pedal to the metal. Don't you want to win a medal?"

"Nossir, I don't. I want to get home in one piece."

"You will, I promise you. Now move it, or you're on a charge."

At last, the Humvee picked up speed and went past the Bradley. He used the internal comms to call the gunner in the cupola. "Fire when ready, Private, and cream those bastards."

"Yes, Sir."

The cannon chattered its slow, rhythmic message of death, and Brewer watched in satisfaction as robed and turbaned men fell, others scattered and ran. He grinned to himself. "Give 'em a taste of American lead."

Stevens' voice on the comms came through over the racket

of the gun. "Sir, there's another bunch of men approaching the village from the other side. Looks like more insurgents."

How many, Captain?"

"I make it around a dozen."

"Heavy weapons, any sign of RPGs?"

"No, Sir, I can't see any."

"That's good enough for me. Keep the advance moving. We'll roll over these bastards, straight through the village, and we'll finish them."

"Roger that, Sir."

Brewer smiled.

Even the normally uptight Stevens sounds like he's at last got some fire in his belly. War! You can't beat it.

* * *

He glanced around their position, careful to keep low. Their attackers hadn't yet become aware of what was coming in behind them, too intent on keeping up a steady stream of gunfire into Stoner's beleaguered position. It would have almost been comical, if he hadn't seen another two women mown down by the incessant gunfire. He had to leave them. Recovering the bodies was too much of a risk, and would lead to more deaths.

He shouted at Sara, who was still helping the Afghan woman named Azita to put the finishing touches to their instant lesson. Teaching the women how to aim, fire, and reload an assault rifle. "I hate to rush you, but we're gonna have more trouble in the next few minutes. When the soldiers hit them, they'll run in our direction, shooting at anything that moves. If we can't shoot back, we're done for."

"They'll be ready," she snapped, her voice grim, "They

know the theory. They'll take a minute to collect the magazines they need, and they're all yours."

"Okay, a minute is about all we have."

They were like black crows; all dressed alike. Religious black burqas, required garb for a medieval execution. An army of the damned, brought back from certain death. They would round on their accusers, and if things didn't go too awry, spit back some of what had been thrown at them. Fifteen women, and not one of them had fired a shot in anger before. Now they would be fighting for their lives.

He started to add something, but Carver was looking away from him to their rear, and her expression had tensed. "They're coming."

He didn't get it. "Yeah, I know they're coming, but I wouldn't turn your back on them."

"Not the men who've been shooting at us. More are coming in from behind, and they have some sort of a vehicle."

Greg popped his head up and muttered, "Jesus Christ, it's a BTR."

Ivan looked, too. "BTR-90, that's the newer version. You can see the automatic cannon mounted on the turret. That's a Shipunov 2A42, 30mm. We are talking heavy hardware. It could even punch holes in the Bradley if it hits in the right place. I wonder if they've seen it."

They hadn't. A Humvee was leading the charge, the Bradley close behind, and the other vehicles strung out in a long line. Guns roared, and the Taliban who'd been shooting at them ran. Straight toward where he waited. With Greg, Sara, Ivan, Gorgy, and Akram. And the Black Crows, fifteen women, rookies, each armed with a rifle and a few magazines.

Is it enough to turn the tide of battle? We'll soon know.

He barked an order to Sara. "Tell them to make ready."

"But they're…"

"Now!"

She spoke to Azita, who passed on the order to the Crows. Stoner felt encouraged. They flung themselves behind the rubble, rifles poking out toward the enemy. And not one opened fire. They were waiting for the order, and the Talibs were almost on them.

"Fire!"

The AKs spat out bullets in the short bursts he'd told them to use. Ivan and his men opened fire, and Greg joined in with Carver. He fired four rounds from his AK, and the magazine was empty. He dragged out the Desert Eagles and started shooting. The nearest enemy fighters were almost on them. Ignoring their losses, they were desperate to kill them. Anything to get past and escape the American infantry, and the mechanized death they brought with them. They either overran the position or they died, and they fought all the harder.

Some got through. Three Talibs leapt the low wall they used as cover, and he moved to meet the nearest man. A giant, with a beard to match, and he came at Stoner wielding a jammed PK machine gun in one hand, and a rusty bayonet in the other. He flattened on the breech of the PK. The big man let go the wrecked weapon as the impact of the heavy slug almost broken his wrist, and kept coming. The bayonet swept toward him, and he brought the gun around, but his opponent was too close to aim and shoot at again. He had to content himself with blocking the slashing blow intended to cut off his wrist, and he caught the blade on the barrel of the pistol. Tried to pull back to give himself room to shoot again, but the Afghan was no fool. He kept crowding in closer, and another slashing blow just missed Stoner's belly, as he feinted and came in again.

They were fighting all around him. Greg was side by side

with Sara, fighting off three Talibs who looked to be frantic to get past. If they got into their rear, they'd swing around and shoot them in the back. Ivan's men were boxed into a corner, and five Afghans had put aside their attempts to flee, realizing they had a chance to inflict a savage and brutal victory on their hated enemy. But they were holding, until a second wave came out of nowhere. They were those men less brave who'd been cowering in the rubble. Where the enemy numbers were dropping toward single figures, suddenly there were twenty, then thirty, then forty.

They sensed victory, knowing the American soldiers would not shoot at friendlies. As long as they stayed close, they could shoot and kill with impunity. They fought, and the bullets, screams, and slashing blades and bayonets were too much. Stoner made a last desperate move, kicking out with his boot to topple the big man. He went down. His head collided with a colossal 'bang' on the stones, and for a short time he'd be out of it. They needed reinforcement, and the Black Crows were puzzled, not knowing how to target, or what they should do.

There was one thing to do. He pointed at the Talibs. "Shoot the fuckers."

Azita wasn't certain. "But, they're all around us. We could hit our own people."

"I don't give a shit. Just shoot them. Wherever you see a hostile, kill him. Either that, or we all die."

She rapped out an order, and the swirling black robes were suddenly everywhere. Black-robed women plunged into battle, and they shrieked like avenging Valkyries. Some used the guns to shoot; others in their excitement used the weapons in a more primitive way, like clubs. He saw four women kneel to tear bodily at a man they'd clubbed to the ground, and in minutes, the fight was over. A few, a very lucky few had escaped, but the wrathful women had secured payback. It was all over within minutes, and the Crows were left searching for any they'd missed. Several attended to the wounded, and the women were not in a merciful mood. The screams ended, and they'd bought themselves a breathing space, although the huge Afghan had recovered.

Stoner sensed the danger rather than saw or heard anything. He shifted his stance a fraction and spun on his heel. The Desert Eagles were in his hands, both reloaded. He shot them both from the hip, two bullets from each muzzle. The tremendous kinetic force smashed into the big man and tossed him backward. He slammed into the ground, and little blood spilled from the terrible wounds in his chest and belly. The heavy bullets had killed him before he fell.

"Stoner!"

Carver was pointing toward the new force coming in from their rear, in the BTR. So far the autocannon hadn't started shooting, but it wouldn't be long. Then the lead Humvee coming from the other side swerved away, and for the first time, exposed the Bradley to the full view of the BTR. The gunfire started, as if the AFVs had spotted each other at the same time. Each crew instinctively knew there would be but one winner in the coming armored combat, the losers a heap of broken bodies lodged inside the smoking wreckage of their vehicle.

He heavy cannon fire hammered overhead and veered to one side, as the BTR worked toward the southern flank, and the tracked Bradley went to meet it. He surveyed the ground, and saw one chance to avoid the meat grinder swallowing them whole, a narrow fold in the ground, leading to the north. With Americans and Talibs to west and east, the two AFVs slugging it out to the south, they had a possible route out. He shouted to Carver and pointed.

"Get the women out now! Tell them we're going that way."

"You're sure?" She wore a worried expression, unwilling to forgo their fragile cover.

"I'm sure. Ivan, Greg, we're moving. Right now."

The pseudo Russian took a final look around the battlefield and acknowledged. "Good call. Akram, Gorgy, let's go."

The genuine Russian stared at him. "What about Daud? He went to get transport."

"He brought it," Ivan said grimly, "I wondered how they found us, when I saw a head poke out of that Russian tin can for a second. It was him."

"Daud?"

"Yes, and we'll be having words with friend Daud before long. Provided we live. Let's go!"

They ran. Stoner led the way, looking behind every few seconds to make sure no one was left behind. Carver led the Black Crows, with Azita. Greg ran with Ivan and his men as rearguard. The battle between the AFVs raged, and when they last saw the armored vehicles, the BTR was racing out into open country, pursued by the Bradley, its autocannon firing repeatedly. He pressed on for another kilometer, calling a halt beside a tiny stream flowing down from the mountain. A rare feature in Afghanistan, and he allowed them ten minutes to drink before they resumed walking. They stopped again after two further kilometers stumbling over the rubble-strewn landscape. It didn't look that different to the surface of the moon, and soon he had no choice but to call another halt.

Sara sat with him, and then Ivan came up to join them. "Me and the boys are leaving, now we're clear of Sangdar. My Land Cruisers are valuable, and I intend to go back for them."

"What about Daud?"

He grimaced. "A dead man walking. Bastard led them straight to us. You know it wasn't just him in that Russian tin can."

Stoner felt a chill. "Tell me."

"Rumi Khan. When it came close, I saw his face through the open vision slot."

"You're sure?"

"No question. How could anybody mistake that ugly bastard for anyone else?"

"Shit. He's like a ghost sent to haunt us."

"Yep. What about you, how you gonna get these women to safety?"

A good question, the exhilaration of freedom, of sudden action, and then revenge had put pep into the women, who a short time before were barely capable of walking. At least half the Black Crows looked ready to drop.

"I don't know. But first, we must find Shahay. That's what we came for."

Ivan frowned. "She could be anywhere, marooned in the middle of nowhere."

"We're not leaving without her."

He shrugged. "Suit yourself. We're going back. We'll skirt around the village and pick up our vehicles. So long, Stoner."

"Yeah, so long."

He grinned at Sara. "Hey, we helped you out some, Lieutenant. How about you put in a good word to Washington? Tell your daddy I saved your ass."

She glared at him. "And now you're walking out on us."

The grin didn't fade. "Operational necessity. I reckon you're safe now, and I'll report that fact to my people. Adios."

He walked away, whistling a Russian folk tune. No doubt he'd learned it at Langley, as part of his cover. Akram and

Gorgy gave him an apologetic look, and followed their boss. They soon disappeared into the nearby hills, and he felt overwhelmed by what they faced. To locate the woman he'd come to bring home to her family. Only to be trapped in the middle of nowhere with a bunch of women so tired they looked as if they couldn't walk more than another few meters before they dropped. Sara had gone to chat to the women.

Greg read his thoughts. "We're not finished, Stoner. Besides, we got them out, and that's a result."

"We didn't get Shahay."

"We tried, and we did everything we could."

"Try telling that to Faria."

He pulled a wry face. "Yeah, I'm not sure I can. How the hell do we find her out here? I mean; we believe they took her in this direction, but she could be anywhere. It's impossible."

"They know where she is."

Both men looked at Sara. Her face was caked with dirt, and her body covered in bruises and dried blood. Her clothes were little more than worn out rags, but she looked excited.

"Who knows where she is?"

"The women. The ones you call the Black Crows."

"Right. Er, that was a mistake. Tell them I didn't mean any insult."

"They thought it was funny, and they like it. Makes them sound more warrior-like. Azita talked to them after I explained about Shahay, and they think they know where they took her. It's about five klicks from here."

"Another village?"

"Nope, they decided on different punishment. It's a pit. The locals call it the Mouth of Zaqqum, and it's in the middle of nowhere, close to an old drover's trail. A deep, natural fault in the rock, and men used it when they decided a woman deserved a bad death for contravening Islamic law. They throw them down there and abandon them. It's at least twenty meters deep. The victims break their legs when they hit the bottom, and so lie there waiting to die of starvation and thirst. They like it because it's very remote and impossible to climb out of, which means they don't need to guard the place while they're dying, unless they want to listen to their cries of agony. They said that some do."

"Another gift from Allah. Why do they always want to bury prisoners, especially women, underground, in some deep, dark place?

"I guess it's to do with their deep, dark souls. They turn their societies into a living nightmare, and spend their lives making them worse. They're never too far from hell."

"Sounds about right. Do they think she could she still be alive?"

"They say it's possible."

"And they know where this place is?"

"One of them does, yes."

He felt a new energy surge through him, and he got to his feet. "Then what're we waiting for. Let's go."

* * *

Stevens pursued the BTR, using the M242 chain gun every time they got close. The enemy fired back, but the Bradley's frontal armor was more than a match for the 30mm Shipunov rounds. The problem was speed. The Russian AFV was almost twice as fast as the tracked Bradley, running on its eight huge wheels. The 25mm rounds slammed into the fleeing BTR, but none scored a lethal hit. Eventually, the enemy vehicle disappeared into the hills, and they had to give up the chase. Brewer, who'd kept the Bradley between him and the BTR, drew up alongside, leapt out, and waited for Stevens to join him.

"What happened? Why didn't you kill that bastard?"

"It's an armored vehicle, Colonel. The rounds bounced off the hull. Maybe if we'd got up close we'd have scored a worthwhile hit, but it didn't happen."

"Damn right it didn't happen. You let him get away."

Stevens winced with frustration, and something welled up inside. "Colonel, that Humvee of yours mounts an autocannon. Maybe you could have got close enough for a shot."

The eyes slitted; "What're you saying, Captain?" He put the accent on the word, 'Captain.'

"Nothing, Sir. Like I said, the Bradley can't catch a BTR. It's a pity we lost the Stryker."

The state-of-the-art AFV had succumbed to a missile during the Tora Bora skirmish, and Brewer's urgent call for a replacement had fallen on deaf ears. Pentagon cuts were hitting military procurement in what had become almost a forgotten war. The unfinished business was in Iraq and Syria. Besides, a resurgent Russia had given the military something else to think about, especially in Europe. Afghanistan was the poor relation where military equipment was concerned.

Brewer shuffled his feet. "Yeah, well, I did my best to sort that out. Bastards said they'd consider it."

"Yes, Sir."

"Right." He sighed.

"We have the equipment we have, Captain, and we worked with what we had." He looked into the distance, at the hills where the AFV had disappeared, "I'd still like to take that bastard on. I wonder where he's going. Panjab, maybe?"

"Could be, Sir. We could track him, follow at a distance."

"Track him, yes, we could. If we come up with him, we'd

have to hit him from a distance before he runs. Use a missile. How's your stock of TOWs?"

"We have three in the ammunition bin, Sir. We used a few at Tora Bora, and we're waiting for replacements."

"Three should do it. We'll follow their trail. Those eight big wheels should leave enough sign for a blind man to follow. Mount up, we're going hunting."

Captain Stevens felt encouraged by the Colonel's enthusiasm. He was an idiot, charging in without adequate reconnaissance, and losing men without good reason. But this time, his idea was sound. The BTR could be a menace if it got loose amongst unarmored troops, and following it at cautious distance, then standing off and killing it with TOWs, sounded like a good idea. He climbed into the Bradley and gave the order.

"Start her up and move out."

The Corporal turned to look at him, surprised by the new note in his voice. "Where
are we headed, Captain?"

"Hunting."

Corporal Wojinski looked down from the gunner's seat. "Hunting what, Cap'n?"

"Bear."

"Bear? With a 25mm cannon?"

"With TOWs."

The astonished look on Wojinski's face was something Stevens would remember for the rest of his life.

* * *

"Have we lost him?" Rumi Khan knew his voice betrayed a tremor that he couldn't hide. The Americans had surprised him, and for the second time, he'd come off worst in a duel with their Armored Fighting Vehicles. They'd done heavy damage at Tora Bora from prepared positions, although he'd lost most of his men. The battle at Sangdar had almost ended in defeat, and he knew his reputation hung by a slender thread.

"The crew is watching the rear, and we haven't sighted them in almost an hour. We've lost them."

"Allah be praised." Khan relaxed, thinking of his next move. He needed more men, as once again he'd suffered heavy casualties, for no gain.

Men are available in Panjab, the nearest city. But isn't that where the Americans will look for me first? If not Panjab, where can I lie low and rest while I plan my next move?

He spoke to Abdullah, who shrugged, and questioned the men sitting on the bench seats in the troop compartment. One man addressed Khan directly. His name was Hamza, and he looked very young. So young, his beard had scarcely sprouted on his chin.

"There is a place I know, several kilometers away. There is nothing there, just a deep pit they use for punishing women. They call it the Mouth of Zaqqum."

"What's so special about it?"

"It is a sacred place, according to the local Mullahs. Women who have sinned against Allah are thrown down there to suffer His mercy and die."

The place piqued his interest. "A sacred place, you say? You're sure?"

"I'm sure, yes."

Khan thought quickly. He needed something, some appeal to the mentality of these primitive fools to persuade men to join him. A sacred site in the middle of nowhere, it had the right feel to it. Even the Prophet himself had experienced a revelation in a lonely and isolated place. Mohammed used to retreat for a month every year to a mountain called Hira in Mecca. Gabriel appeared to Muhammad in his sleep, carrying a book. He commanded him to "read." Mohammed then recited the verses in his sleep. When he awoke, he felt as if the words had been engraved on his heart. On his way down from the mountain, the Prophet heard a voice from heaven saying: "O Muhammad! You are the messenger of Allah, and I am Gabriel."

The rest was history. Did he believe it? He smiled to himself. He'd believe what suited him, and what people expected from him. What mattered was what people believed. He would travel to this sacred place, riding in this armored monster with the few men he had left. There he would rest and send his men into the local towns and villages to spread the word. They'd tell the young men that Rumi Khan was waiting in a sacred place. Resting and building his strength, before he sallied forth to sweep the infidels from the land Allah had made his own. To succeed, he needed men, men with guns who would take the fight to the enemy. They would earn immortality and an assured place in Paradise.

He smiled at Hamza. "In that case, you may show us the way. Daud, follow the directions Hamza will give you. He knows the way to our destination."

"Where are we going?"

"To victory, my friend. And then to Paradise."

Daud nodded, but inside he was unsure. He'd abandoned Ivan because of his unease at the way the Westerners were rampaging through his country. Propping up the corrupt government in Kabul, killing the faithful fighting to establish a strict Islamic Republic run under the laws of Sharia. But this was more than he'd bargained for. Rumi Khan was a charismatic leader, without doubt. Victory was a word that had a good ring. But Paradise sounded too final, as if Khan had a plan to send them into some hopeless, glorious charge against a heavily armed enemy. Screaming the name of Allah as the machine gun bullets shredded them.

I want to live to see Sharia become a de facto part of Afghan life, not die for it. Did I make the right choice, joining Khan, or should I get out? It would be easy to drive away in the BTR when they're outside. Just fasten the hatches, and I'll be invulnerable to their gunfire.

It was a thought, and as he spun the wheel to change direction, the idea took shape.

Sharia law is worth fighting for, but not worth dying for.

* * *

They walked on across the harsh, desolate landscape. The Black Crows were finding it hard, and the fitter women half carried those unable to walk. He and Sara had a young woman supported between them, and Greg was helping Azita with an elderly lady who looked about to succumb. None abandoned their rifles. He felt it, a subtle thread that infused them with a determination to fight back against the Islamic cowards who'd wanted to kill them. So they walked on. And on, and the rasping, tortured breaths of the sick and injured became louder.

The woman who'd told them of the Mouth of Zaqqum showed them a source of water that had once been a swift running stream. Now reduced to a muddy trickle by years of neglect, they nevertheless slaked their thirst and filled what water bottles they'd brought with them. The journey was slow, but eventually their guide pointed to a pile of stones, less than half a kilometer ahead. They walked quicker with the destination in sight. Ten minutes later, they reached the place, a low, round, wall of stones, some tumbled with age and neglect.

The light was already fading, and Greg handed the old woman to Azita, ran the final few meters, and peered down into the depths. He was calling for Shahay to answer, when Stoner came up with him.

"Anything?"

He didn't turn his head but kept staring into the dark depths. "Nothing."

"She may be sleeping, or even unconscious. It doesn't mean she's dead, Greg."

"No." But the tone of his voice suggested he thought otherwise.

"I'll go down and look. If she's there, she'll need help to get out."

"You'll need a rope."

Stoner pointed to another, larger ruin. At first he thought it had been a dwelling. When he looked at the tumbled pile again, it was a platform, with a rotting wooden frame lying next to it. A gallows.

These people sure love their executions.

Lying on the ground next to the remains was a long rope, with an ominous noose at one end. It was thick and rotted, but it was all they had. He tied if off to part of the rotted timbers of the former gallows and tossed it down the deep hole. A sharp tug on the rope proved it wasn't about to part like thin cotton. He stepped over the wall and started to climb down.

The walls were rough stone, pitted with numerous cracks and niches, suggesting he might be able to climb out if the rope broke. Provided he was near enough to the bottom when it went, and he could fall without breaking something. His leg was still very painful, so it would not be easy if he were forced to climb.

Could I carry her up on my shoulder if it comes to it? An almost impossible climb, but then again, sometimes you have to make the impossible happen.

Halfway down, he was cut off from what little light came in from outside, and he continued his descent in pitch black. The rope parted when he figured he still had a third of the way to go. According to the woman who'd guided them there, that meant a fall of six or seven meters. He bent his legs at the knees and hit the bottom a second later. He rolled over, like making a parachute drop, and plummeted downward.

CHAPTER ELEVEN

Stoner almost landed on a body lying on the rock and sand floor of the shaft, feeling the softness when he flung out his arm to break his fall. He felt a moment of elation. After all they'd been through he'd found her, but she didn't move, and he stretched out his hands to ascertain the position of her body. Then he bent to listen for any sign of life.

At first, there was none, and he felt the terrible sorrow of knowing what she'd gone through. Then he felt a flicker. A faint pulse in the neck, and he brought out his water bottle and felt for her lips. Tipped it slightly, trying to trickle a small amount into her mouth. All the time he was talking to her.

"Shahay, we've come to free you. We're taking you home. You're going to live. Wake up, Shahay."

The lips moved, responding to the water, and then a cracked, almost inaudible voice said something. In Pashto, but she'd responded. He tried again.

"Shahay, Faria Blum sent me. You're alive. We're taking you home."

He waited an age, but the words came. Harsh, forced through

tortured vocal chords, but he understood. "Faria. She's here?"

"Greg is here. He's up on the surface. How bad are you?"

"One leg broken," she whispered.

He worried about gangrene, but if the flesh were bad, he'd have noticed the odor. "We'll get the leg set, but first we have to get out of here. Let me help you up."

She muttered, "How? Do you have a rope?"

"Not exactly, no. I'll carry you."

"Carry me?"

"Sure, piece of cake. Drink some more, and we'll get started."

He looked up, and night had fallen. First things first, he called up to Greg to give him the good news. Called twice, three times. No reply, and he felt an ominous foreboding. Something was wrong, and in Afghanistan, that meant men with guns. Hostiles. They could have their hands full fighting it out with Talibs, or they could be keeping their heads down, hiding from an enemy force. He didn't call again. He gently picked up the girl, slung her over his shoulder, and heard her sharp cry of pain as he touched the broken leg.

"Sorry."

"It's okay. I don't care if you break the other leg, as long as you get me away from this place."

The water had worked a miracle, and already her voice sounded firmer. Water and hope, the fastest healers.

"How about I get you out of here without breaking the other leg?"

"That would be nice. Who are you?"

"Stoner."

"Stoner? Is that it?"

"It's enough."

He reached up and searched for the handholds, the tiny

cracks and ledges in the rock. He found the first handhold, gripped it, and felt with his boot. Discovering a tiny ledge to help him up, he climbed.

There was not a solitary doubt in his mind this climb would figure in his nightmares for years to come. After the first five meters, he was drenched with sweat, and every muscle was on fire. His leg was in agony. The weight of the girl on his shoulders seemed as if he was carrying a small car, and his limbs were beginning to feel numb. At least that eased the pain a little for a short time. He kept going. Hand over hand, a boot wedged in a cleft, push up with one leg, and feel for the next handhold. Stoner lost track of time. He could have been an hour getting to what he estimated was the halfway point, or he could have taken twelve hours. The agony was all the same.

The climb was endless, and his brain went into autopilot, hand over hand, push up with the leg, shake his head to clear it, murmur a word of encouragement to Shahay, and on to the next handhold. Inside the pit was pitch-black, and when he looked up there were no stars, nothing to be seen. Just blackness. No noise, no people talking or calling out, not even any shooting. Nothing. Like he was climbing into a post-apocalyptic world, and when he reached it, he'd find everything and everyone had disappeared. He pulled up again, and his fingers touched a different kind of stone. Looser, less compacted, he'd reached the low wall that surrounded the edge of the pit. He heard voices, murmuring, speaking Pashto. Male voices, and his senses fired a stream of warning signals. He put his head close to hers.

"Shahay, we may have a problem. Stay quiet."

"Yes."

He hoisted himself up, his every muscle screaming in agony, and found a tiny ledge to hold most of her weight while he peered over the parapet. He saw six men, Taliban, and one was instantly recognizable. The man they'd tangled with since Tora Bora. A badly scarred face, ugly as the inside of a dumpster, big beard, and what skin showed in the lights was badly scarred and pockmarked. The light came from the headlights they were using as illumination. The lights were fitted to the familiar shape of the BTR-90. The man was Rumi Khan.

He cast his eyes around and saw a row of kneeling figures. Some wore voluminous robes, the Black Crows. Sara and Greg were together, and all of them had their hands fastened behind their backs. They were unguarded, but why would they bother with a guard? The prisoners were in full view of Khan and his men. Any attempt to escape or mount a rescue would be seen instantly. Between the prisoners and Khan's group their assault rifles lay in an untidy heap. As if to mock them, to remind them that arming mere women with guns was a waste of time. The black tide of Islam would find them, disarm them, and punish them.

He looked back at Shahay, and knowing she had a chance of getting out alive had worked wonders. She was balanced on the inside of the top of the pit. He held her with one hand to stop her toppling, his other hand hooked over the low wall. They had to get out of there soon, before the masonry crumbled and pitched them both back down to the bottom. If he broke a limb or two, there'd be no second chance at escape. He whispered to her where the water bottle was in his pocket, and she drank more. The fluid revived her, and she put her mouth close to his ear and murmured, "How can I help?"

"You can't. I'll work something out. Quiet."

Khan's voice was louder, and he harangued his men with a long speech. When it ended, Shahay translated.

"He's going to kill them all. The prisoners. He said his men are to share out the killings so each can enjoy the experience. They'll wait until morning, then film the whole thing and post it on the internet. A sign to the world that the infidels' time in Afghanistan is almost at an end."

He muttered "Bastard" under his breath. But at least it meant they had several hours until dawn. The problem was how to approach them. The area blazed with light from the headlamps. Any movement would be seen, and they'd open fire. He kept working out what was possible and discarded them all. He'd found no solution.

Shoot out the lights, no sweat, but they'll be alerted. It all comes down to doing it the hard way. I'll be exposed, and if anything goes wrong, I'll have no back up. Unless...

He whispered to Shahay again. "Can you shoot an automatic?"

"Yes."

He took out and handed her a Desert Eagle. Feeling a slight pang, it was the second time he'd parted with one of his guns, and he didn't like the feeling. As if he was wearing one boot and had lost the other.

"The recoil is a bastard. You'll need to climb outside the well and stay low, with your back to the wall. You have eight bullets, and if you need more, we're in more trouble than we can handle. Can you shoot straight?"

"Straight enough. My father taught me how it is done, just in case..."

He knew what she meant. Just in case some rampant Afghan male decided to take advantage. "Okay, here's how it works. I'll try sneaking up on them, but they'll probably see me before I reach them. I doubt I can make it all the way, so when you see them take aim, start shooting."

"I understand."

"Okay. I'll help you out, and settle you next to the wall. You ready?"

"Yes."

He made her hold on and climbed slowly over the wall. His body was recovering after the climb, and he could help her over. She sat with her legs stretched out, back to the wall, and the gun propped on a chunk of stone. She was as ready as she'd be, and he started crawling toward the group of armed men sitting in a circle, listening to Rumi Khan. Whatever he was saying, he had their rapt attention, which made getting nearer somewhat easier.

His muscles still shrieked with pain after the hard climb, but he ignored them and snaked across the ground; careful to move every object, every small stone that may have clinked and given him away. He made it to the halfway mark, and even though he was in full view, they hadn't noticed the man crawling toward them. He eased nearer and nearer. With around eight meters to go, one of the Afghans looked up, and his expression changed to puzzlement. Squinted hard, as if to confirm what his eyes had seen and his senses told him wasn't possible, and then he shouted a warning. A second later, they were all on their feet, reaching for their guns.

A shot rang out, the heavy 'boom' of Shahay's Desert Eagle, and a bullet smacked into the hull of the BTR. A second shot took out one headlight, and he realized she was a good shot, even with the heavy, unfamiliar gun. He had nothing to gain by crawling and leapt to his feet, running, his gun spitting bullets. Their assault rifles were clumsier to make ready, and he'd shot two men down before the first AK bullet sang over his head. Then he was in their midst, one man against four. A second shot rang out, and the area was plunged into darkness. She'd done the right thing, shooting out the lights, and now they'd lost some of their advantage.

The four survivors milled around in panic, shooting at random, and the muzzle flashes lit the night. They didn't hit him. When the bullets flew, he'd ducked low again. Now he was crawling at the nearest man, staying below his line of vision. When he reached him, he reached up, grabbed his rifle with one hand and the other arm with another, jerking him off his feet. He fell to the ground with a scream, and Stoner was on him, using his Desert Eagle as a club to hammer it into his neck. A single blow, and the guy was silent. The second blow left him dying with a ruined throat, unable to breathe, and as he choked his last, Stoner crawled on to the next man.

He tried to drag him down, but at the last moment he moved, saw Stoner, and stepped back to take aim. Stoner was quicker. He aimed from the hip, and the Desert Eagle spoke, a bellowing sound as a .50 caliber bullet slammed into the man's chest. The force of the bullet threw him back almost a meter, and his hand reached out to touch the big hole that had appeared in his chest. He didn't need a second shot, but Stoner ducked as a burst of 7.62mm bullets almost took his head off.

Muzzle flashes lit up the shooter for a few seconds, and he snapped off a quick shot that missed as the man jumped aside. He recognized Khan's second-in-command, and a man who'd be the most dangerous of his opponents. He went after him, searching for a shot, but the flashes of light had ruined his night vision, and almost reduced him to feeling his way like a blind man. Clouds had obscured the moon, but he couldn't wait until they cleared. He needed a target, and a moment later, Shahay's gun boomed. The bullets smacked into the ground, and a flash lit up the area as the Afghan reacted fast and returned fire.

This time, he'd marked his position, and he darted toward him and jumped. Rammed his gun into the man's belly and squeezed the trigger. Again, he was too fast, and he twisted to the side. The big slug missed the vital organs and tore a huge gash from the side of his body. He screamed in agony, but he wasn't done. He kicked out and connected with Stoner's gun hand. The pistol dropped out of his fingers as the blow caused his muscles and nerves to go numb, and the man kicked again.

Stoner had to move to avoid the blow, and he dropped down, feeling around for his gun with the other hand. The Talib found an opening and slammed the butt of his AK toward his head. The blow glanced off the side, almost taking his ear with it. At the same moment, Stoner found his gun. His fingers curled around the grip, he brought it up, and pulled the trigger. For several seconds, the shooting had stopped, and the explosion tore through the night. Incredibly, the man still didn't go down. The .50 caliber bullet had torn a hole in his belly, so big his intestines were spilling out down his legs and uncoiling to the ground. He still made a final, last, despairing effort to bring up his rifle and kill his tormentor.

Stoner took careful aim and fired a third time, and this shot hit the mark. He had been aiming at the center of his heart, and a sudden stumble meant it hit him as he was dropping. The bullet tore into his skull, through his head, and tore out the back of his head in a shower of blood and brains. His eyes looked surprised, just for a fleeting moment. They clouded as he fell for the last time. Two more shots boomed out, and he instinctively ducked, but they were the familiar sound of the Desert Eagle. Shahay. He moved nearer and asked if she was okay.

"I'm fine, but that last man was aiming at you, so I shot at him."

"The one with the big beard?"

"Yes, him. When I fired, he ran for the armored vehicle.

When he reached it, he seemed to argue with someone inside, I assume it was the driver. He shot him, dragged the body out onto the ground, and climbed aboard. He's there now."

Shit, Khan!

He ran toward the BTR, but he was too late. Halfway there, and the sound of the hatch clanging shut was the sound of their death knell. He couldn't get to him, not inside an armored fighting vehicle. Yet Khan suffered from a distinct disadvantage. He was almost blind after Shahay shot out the lights. He kept running, passing a dead man on the ground. He recognized the body of Ivan's deserter, Daud. He was wearing a wristwatch. Habiba's Rolex Submariner, which explained what happened to Ivan's other Afghan shooter.

Why did he desert? Did he covet the watch, or was it something else, the Afghan bugbear of perpetual vendetta, maybe, or Islam, the other bugbear? Too bad, you should have stayed with Ivan. He's tough to work for, but his people tend to stay alive. Okay, not always.

He leapt onto the armored steel of the hull. Searched for an opening, something he may have forgotten in his haste to escape, but the body was sealed as tight as a drum. And then the engine started.

Greg, Sara, and the Crows were still tied, although they'd struggled to their feet. The AFV was moving straight toward them. Khan would know his enemy was on the hull, and he'd be peering through the driver's periscope. Stoner wasn't aware if he intended to drive over the bound prisoners, or if he couldn't he see them. Probably he wanted to kill them, it would fit with his murderous psyche. But he'd have to see them to drive over them deliberately. The vehicle was crawling. He fumbled his way down to the front of the hull, found the periscope, and put a bullet into the glass lens. The BTR veered to the side as Khan recoiled from what his brain would have interpreted as a bullet fired directly at his eye, except it was a foot above his eye. He'd achieved his first objective; the second was to prevent him running over the prisoners. He leapt off the hull, shouting, "Greg, he can't see you. Get them clear before he runs them down."

"Some of them need help," he shouted back.

Stoner ran toward them, and two women lay sprawled on the ground. The others milled around, unable to assist with their hands tied. He grabbed an arm of each and ran. Dragging them across the rough ground, clear of the track of the BTR, which had picked up speed. The racing wheels missed them by inches, all except one of the Crows. She'd fallen in the path of the huge tires, and he didn't hesitate. He raced out into the open, scooped her into his arms, and dove, feeling the slipstream of the big body as it roared past. One of the monster tires actually touched his boot, nudging it aside instead of crushing it as if in a hydraulic press. Then it was gone.

It weaved a crazy path, veering from side to side, and Stoner guessed Khan had some limited vision. The vehicle steered a winding path until it stopped about a kilometer away. The clouds had cleared the moon, enough for them to see the top hatch clang open. A head appeared, a face staring back at them, and then the shoulders appeared when he was satisfied they were sufficiently far away. He shouted something, and the words were lost by distance and the noise of the engine. Then he shook his fist, and made another gesture lost in the gloom.

"I'm sorry, I can't hear him," Shahay said quietly, "But I think I get the meaning."

"We all get the meaning," he replied, "Unfinished business. That suits me just fine. Me and Mr. Khan are gonna have a reckoning one day."

"You'll kill him?"

He looked back at her. "Yes, like a rat catcher ridding the world of a particularly vicious, poisonous brand of the species. I'll use poison, like you would on a rat."

She looked surprised. "Poison?"

"Lead poison."

Beside him, Carver sighed with exasperation. "Knock it off, Stoner. We have more serious problems, like how to get these women away from here. Some of them are very ill, and this last thing has finished them."

He fished in his pocket and took out the satphone Ivan had given him. "You're the girl with connections in high places. I'd say it's time to give them a call. See if they'll call us a cab. A helicopter may be more useful, though. One with a medic on board."

She took the phone, punched in numbers, and spoke to whoever answered the other end. After that, she threaded her arm into his, pulling him close. He enjoyed the closeness and intimacy of that gesture.

They were still together when the roar of two General Electric T700 turboshaft engines announced the incoming aircraft. A Sikorsky UH-60 Black Hawk, and its searchlights came on to light up the area as the pilot looked for a suitable landing site. The helicopter landed in a whirlwind of dust, and as the skids settled on the ground, a man jumped out. He was wearing the uniform of an Army corporal, a corpsman.

He ran over to them and noticed Sara Carver, as she detached herself from Stoner. "Ma'am, I'm looking for a Second Lieutenant Carver. Would that be you?"

"It is, Corporal."

He saluted, and she returned it. "I'm here to triage and treat your wounded, Lieutenant. What do you have for me?"

She pointed to three black-clad women, lying prostrate.

"Start with them. After that, we have some minor injuries to take care of. You can attend to them when we're in the air."

He hesitated. "Civilians?"

"Did your Commander-in-Chief's Chief of Staff give you any instructions, Corporal?"

"Er, yeah. He said I was to follow your orders."

"Right. What are you waiting for?"

He threw her another salute. "Right away, Lieutenant."

He raced over to the women, and in less than a minute had prepared saline drips and painkilling injections. Sara shepherded the women to the Black Hawk, and after a nervous glance at Carver, the Crew Chief helped them aboard. Stoner and Blum lifted the injured women and placed them on the gurneys rigged inside. He nodded his approval. They'd sent a helo configured for medevac. But then again, she would have instructed her father to arrange it, so it shouldn't have come as a surprise.

He watched the last of them climb into the cabin. Sara helped him lift Shahay up to waiting hands, and then Greg climbed aboard. Stoner was the last, and as his foot left the ground, the engines roared, and the helicopter took off. The pilot set course for the southeast, taking them to safety, the military facilities, airfield, and antiseptic hospitals of Bagram, outside Kabul.

* * *

"They've been here, but now they're gone," Stevens called to Brewer, who had refused to alight from his command Humvee.

Chasing the BTR had been a long, dusty arduous trip, trailing in the wake of the faster vehicle. During the long night, they repeatedly lost the trail, and had to waste time quartering the area to pick it up again. They came to the end of the track and found nothing more than bodies and devastation.

"I guess we missed them," Stevens offered, knowing his Colonel would be seething with anger.

"I can see we fucking missed them. I'm not blind, Captain. The question is where have they gone. You can't hide a BTR in this place, yet the tire tracks are messed up." He looked past the bodies, at an area that looked as if a giant fan had blasted dust and chippings in a circle. He'd seen it before.

"Stevens, a helicopter landed here. Is it possible the Taliban have helicopters now?"

He gave a firm shake of his head. "Impossible, Sir. No way."

"I thought not, so it must have been one of ours. Contact Bagram, and find out who's been operating a helo in this region. What were they doing, and where did they go? Who was aboard? I want the whole works."

It took almost a half hour before they pieced it together, and he still didn't believe it.

"Second Lieutenant Carver was here? With two non-Afghans, one an American in a long, black leather coat, as well as a bunch of women? You know what I'm thinking, Captain?"

"I'm not sure, Sir."

"I'm sure. There's something going on between Carver and those two guys. Get back onto Bagram, and drag some more details out of them. There's something funny going on here, and I want to find out what it is."

Stevens nodded and talked to the radio operator. Then he turned back to Brewer. "Sir, about Lieutenant Carver, you know her relationship to the President. That would account for..."

"Yeah, I know, I know." He wouldn't voice it aloud, but inside he seethed at having to go soft on Carver, a woman, and with connections to the White House.

What have I done to deserve it?

"But those other people don't have connections. And just because she's the Chief of Staff's daughter, doesn't mean she's not up to something."

Steven's jaw dropped. "Colonel, for Christ's sake. You can't say that kind of thing. Not about her. She's untouchable. I'd be careful if you…"

"Cap'n, message from Kabul. It was a medevac flight ordered by the Pentagon, following instructions from the White House. After they landed, Lieutenant Carver went off with those two guys."

Before he could reply, Brewer walked up to the man, his face enthused with excitement. "Do they know where they went?"

"Yessir, a farm outside Jalalabad. And one of the guys has a business in Jalalabad." He paused, "They say it's a brothel."

His expression changed to astonishment. "You're kidding me."

"No, Colonel. That's what they said."

"They were heading for this farm outside the city?"

"Yes, Sir."

"Captain, mount up. We're moving out."

"What's the destination, Colonel?"

"Jalalabad. We're gonna find out what's going on and bust it wide open. President or no President, I knew I shouldn't have voted for him."

* * *

The flight was short, and the noise in the cabin made conversation impossible. Instead, he and Sara communicated with their eyes. Greg was not insensitive, and he left them to it, holding up drip bags, and helping the corpsman make the

Crows comfortable. And then they landed.

Ambulances were waiting next to the helipad. Men and women dressed in scrubs rushed forward when the whine of the engines faded. When the cabin had all but emptied, the pilot, an Army captain, walked aft to greet them, and Stoner thanked him for the ride.

He nodded. "It's no sweat, buddy, all part of the service. But I'll tell you, someone kicked up a shitstorm to get us moving. I was halfway to Kabul, about to spend a few days on leave with my girlfriend. She came over from the States specially, and she's gonna give me hell when I get back."

"She'll forgive you, Captain, so I wouldn't worry about it."

He didn't look convinced. "Maybe, maybe not. You don't know her. And when I got here, there was a real flap on. I mean, the aircraft, too, it's not my regular ship. She's the best we have on the base, the most reliable, and never lets us down. They say she's a lucky aircraft. I don't know who had the clout to order us to fly it for this mission."

"It's good to know we flew first class."

"Yeah, you did. Say, how high up the chain of command do you need to be to rope in an off-duty crew at a moment's notice? The most experienced crew on the base, and the best helo."

"Pretty high."

"Like what? I mean, the Coalition Commander inside Afghanistan? Something like that?"

"Something like that."

"Right. I just like to know, in case I'm flying VIPs. You a VIP?" He regarded Stoner's shabby black leather coat and frowned, "I guess not."

"Nope."

"Right."

She'd done more than sequester transport from the boonies back to Kabul. A Humvee was waiting for them, and they climbed inside. Without a word, the driver steered onto the road that would take him back to familiar territory, Jalalabad, little more than one hundred kilometers away. Two hours later, after a quick stop in Jbad to pick up his Jeep Wrangler, they arrived in Mehtar Lam. Minutes later, they were driving up to Greg's farm, and Faria appeared on the stoop with the children, and the important additional member of Greg's family, Archer, the Marine dog.

As Blum exited the Humvee, she rushed across and threw herself into his arms. "Greg, I thought you'd..."

"Gone off with another girl?" he grinned, "Not as long as I'm married to the prettiest girl in all Asia." He looked around as Stoner approached with Sara. "Isn't that so?"

He swallowed. It was still hard after all these years, seeing her in the arms of another man. Hard, but he'd moved on. "It sure is. How're things, Faria?"

Her smile acknowledged what had once gone between them, and then Ahmed raced up and grabbed his hand. He shook it violently, dropping it as Stoner winced, and the boy saw the dressing. "You're injured. I'm sorry. I didn't..."

"It's nothing. A mosquito bit me."

He looked back and smiled. "You mean a 7.62mm mosquito?"

"Hey, kid, you've been there, I nearly forgot. Yeah, it was something like that. Russian junk, couldn't hit a target if it stood a meter away."

They laughed at the lie, knowing of the millions who'd been wounded or died because of bullets fired from a Kalashnikov rifle. With over seventy-five million in circulation, no firearm had killed more people than the AK-47 Kalashnikov, Russia's gift to the world.

She looked at Sara, waiting for an introduction. Stoner did the honors.

"Faria, this is Sara. She's with the U.S. Army."

The two women hit it off automatically. Minutes later they went inside where they were chatting like old friends. Stoner left them to it, and he and Greg broke open two cigars. Ahmed brought out Greg's prized whisky, a very old malt made on a remote island somewhere off the wild coast of the Scottish Highlands. For a long time, they just smoked and drank, stroking Archer's coat. Ahmed wanted to know everything, and they told him next to nothing. He planned to be a medic, and his parents were eager to keep his mind on his ambitions. Not to paint a picture of war as other than what it was, bloody, gory, and the bringer of poverty and grief to non-combatants. A lesson the Taliban could do well to learn. And never would.

Finally, Ahmed left them to attend so some chore inside, and Greg looked across at him.

"What next?"

"Next?" He returned his gaze, "What makes you think there is a next?"

"Because there always is. There's unfinished business. Rumi Khan, for one. You said you were going to kill him."

"That's right, I am."

"So we're going looking for him?"

"We're going nowhere. I'm going home. I thought I'd show Sara how the other half lives."

"She won't be impressed with you living in a brothel."

"Nope. But that's the way it is. Besides, it's not like we're about to form a permanent relationship. She'll go back to the States, and I'll go back to doing what I do."

"Which is what?"

He stopped, thinking about the answer to that question.

What is the total of my life? I own a half share in a brothel. I contract to carry out certain jobs. Kill, provided it's a righteous kill, a kind of justice, rough justice, the target who deserves to die, not a settling of some old score. I run a surplus machinery business that loses money, but looks good on my tax return. Anything else? Well, yeah, there is. I'm alone. Maybe it's time to admit I've made a few wrong turns in my life. Is it too late? Should I look at a change of direction, sell my share in Ma Kelly's, and hang up my guns?

He didn't get to reply to Blum's question. Didn't get to think any more about whether he'd fucked up. The roar of engines coming out of Mehtar Lam announced they had visitors. In the lead, a Bradley, its tracks chewing up the driveway leading to Greg's farm. Behind it, several Humvees, and the lead jeep flew the familiar guidon of the Big Red One.

"It looks like Colonel Brewer," Greg remarked, "What does he want?"

Stoner gave a one-word reply, "Trouble."

CHAPTER TWELVE

He didn't look happy, and Stoner had to remind himself to keep his hands away from his guns. Brewer had no such reservations, and the cannons mounted in the turrets of the Bradley and the lead Humvee pointed at Greg's house. Both men deliberately avoided noticing the direction of their aim. Women and children were inside, and they had to defuse what looked like a potentially hostile confrontation.

Greg was the man in charge, and he walked to meet Brewer. "Colonel, what can I do for you?"

His expression was truculent. "For starters, release Lieutenant Carver. Where are you holding her?"

"I'm not holding her anywhere. She's inside the house, chatting to my wife."

"I want her out here."

As he spoke, the door opened, and Sara came out. Her look at Colonel Brewer was not pleasant, but she walked closer and saluted. "Colonel."

He didn't return the salute. "What're you doing with these people, Lieutenant?"

Her expression was cold as a deep freeze. "Thanking them for saving my life, Sir. It's fortunate they succeeded. Otherwise, you'd be reporting my death to my father. I doubt he'd be pleased."

The stiffness left him for a moment. "It wasn't my fault, you know. My men did everything possible to carry out their orders to find you."

"Yet they didn't find me. Did they, Sir? These men did," she indicated Stoner and Blum.

He cleared his throat. "They got lucky, is all."

Her eyebrows went up an inch. "Lucky, is that what you call it?"

He shrugged. "Yeah, well, you're free, and you're ordered to rejoin your unit."

"Sir, I haven't finished what I was doing here. I'll be back with you soon."

He shook his head. "Now, Lieutenant. That's an order."

She stared at him for several seconds, and then nodded. "Yes, Sir." She glanced at Stoner. "We have unfinished business."

He was reluctant to agree, but neither could he deny it. "Yes, we do."

"I still have that satphone from Ivan. You know the number?"

"Yes."

"Call me."

"Sure."

"And don't take too long about it."

"Count on it."

She shook his hand, did the same with Greg, and walked back down the column to a Humvee. Waved a final time and climbed inside.

Brewer frowned at Stoner. "I haven't finished with you,

Mister. I don't know what you're up to, but my people will be taking a long, hard look at your operations. Starting with this brothel you run. See if we can't get the government to close it down."

"It won't happen, Colonel."

He sneered. "No? Why is that?"

"Because most of the people you'll have to talk to are clients of the brothel. Regulars, know what I mean?"

He took a few seconds to get the meaning, but his face filled with rage. "You think that makes a difference you have another think coming. I'll be seeing you, Mr. Stoner."

Stoner nodded. "Yes, you will. Real soon."

They locked gazes for long moments. Then Brewer broke away and stormed back to his Humvee. He shouted an order, engines started, and they drove away. Greg looked troubled. "He's not going to forget, you know. He'll be coming back, and he'll bring a heap of trouble with him. What do you plan to do?"

"I'm going home."

"That's it? Forget about Khan, forget about Brewer?"

"Right now, I need a shower, a good meal, a good night's sleep, and…"

"Anahita?"

The whore from Ma Kelly's, who occasionally shared his bed, but she wasn't Sara Carver.

"I'll be seeing you, Greg. Let me know when Shahay gets out of hospital, and give her my regards."

He walked away, climbed into his Wrangler, and the engine started on the button. He drove away, and in the rear-view mirror, he saw them watching him. Greg, Faria, Ahmed with Archer, and the two girls, Kaawa and Rahima, his family. He'd acted like a spoiled brat. Left without saying goodbye, but he knew they'd forgive him. Knew they'd understand, but he didn't like it. He had a lot on his mind. That was the truth. He'd lied to Greg.

Khan is very much on my mind. Brewer, too, although he's an ass and just needs a sharp reminder he can't shove civilians around. But Khan, he's like a black, poisonous spider sitting in his web, waiting to suck in young fanatics and send them to their deaths.

As he drove, he focused on the Taliban leader, and his determination for vengeance grew. He'd almost killed Sara Carver, almost killed Greg and himself. Those women, the Black Crows, he recalled the BTR attempting to run them down. Rumi Khan.

You think you're the bringer of death, and that may be true. But here's the thing, pal, death is my business, too. You can run, but you can't hide. I'm coming for you, and when I find you, say your prayers to whomever it is you pray to. You'd better hope he's listening.

Something was different when he parked up at the rear of the brothel that was also his home. A man lay in the street, a body. He looked around, scenting an ambush, but there was none. He went over to the man, and he turned out to be a Westerner. Covered in blood, his first thought was he that he was dead. His second was one of startled surprise. The man should have been dead. Trapped inside Pakistan, and the soldiers would have ripped him apart in a brutal act of vengeance when they got their hands on him. Yet somehow, he'd made it here.

The third thought was one of astonishment. He wasn't dead. As Stoner touched his arm, ready to pull him off the street while he worked how to give him a send-off that would reflect the courageous man he was, he groaned. He was alive, and he called to him, "Wyatt, can you hear me?"

"I hear you."

"How bad is it?"

"I took five. Two in the legs, one in the arm, and two in the side, inches apart. One of 'em is still in there, the other four went straight through. I need water, if you can fix that for me."

"I'll fix whatever you need. Wait one minute."

He rushed into Ma Kelly's and emerged with Ma and one of her whores. Kelly knelt next to the wounded man and gasped. "How the hell did he get here in that condition?"

He had the only possible answer. "Willpower. The ornery bastard is too damn stubborn to just lie down and die. But he needs a hospital."

"No hospital," Evers croaked, "They'll find me, and the shit'll hit the fan."

He meant the military. After all those years, if he resurfaced, some asshole like Brewer could come after him, and they'd arrest him for desertion.

"We'll take care of him. Stoner, can you lift him inside? Put him on the sofa in my apartment."

"Sure."

The plan would work. She occupied rooms on the first floor, and he carried Wyatt inside the overblown living room, draped with plush wall hangings, paintings in ornate gilded frames, and the strong, cloying odor of expensive French perfumes. He lay him down, and she shooed him out. "Leave him to me. I'll take care of him from here on in."

They ignored him as the women bustled around the injured man, and Stoner left. He went to his apartment on the third floor, and spent a half hour under scalding hot water in the shower. Then heated up a microwave meal, too tired and uncaring to even send for a take out, and ate half before he pushed it aside. His thoughts were on other things. Khan. Brewer. Now Wyatt Evers, and he vowed to give him what help he needed. Last, there was Sara. He emptied a new bottle of

Bourbon and fell into a troubled sleep. The following day, he checked on Wyatt, who was recovering after Ma's ministrations and an emergency procedure on Ma's dining table to remove the bullet. She'd promised the Doc a three-month free pass.

His next move wasn't something he relished, but he didn't have a choice. He needed information, and one man in Afghanistan controlled that source. He called Ivan.

"I need to find Khan."

He sounded hurt. "After everything I've done for you, Stoner, how about a friendly greeting? No, 'Are you okay, Ivan? Not sick or anything? Business going well?' It wouldn't hurt to pretend, Stoner."

"Where is he?"

"How would I know? Last I heard, you got into a fight with him outside Panjab."

"He got away in a BTR-90."

He heard a low chuckle. "Yeah, his driving has already become the stuff of legend. He hit the main highway and collided with a truck. Then he ran into a convoy of Afghan Army jeeps. Wrote them all off and didn't scratch the paintwork."

"He's in Panjab now?"

Ivan sucked in a breath, a long, slow hiss. "Well, now, I couldn't say. I'm not aware of everything that goes on around here."

"How much?"

"Stoner!" His voice sounded even more hurt, "Would I do that to you?"

"I'm waiting, Ivan."

A pause. "I hear you. Look, pal, I can't tell you what you want know, not right now. But I'll ask around. As for the price, suppose we put it on the tab. You'll owe me."

"Agreed."

"Big time."

"Right."

"I'll call you tomorrow, or maybe the next day. Soon."

He ended the call, and Stoner knew he had no choice but to wait. He spent what remained of the day, and the next day, checking on Wyatt. Ma quickly tossed him out. She'd taken a proprietary interest in the former Special Forces operator who'd become a mountain hermit. He relaxed in the bar and spent a night with Anahita after she made herself irresistible. He thought about Sara a lot. And tried to forget her, a lot. She phoned on the third day.

"I thought you'd call."

He warmed to the sound of her voice. "Yeah, sorry, I've been busy." He told her about Wyatt, and she brightened.

"We owe a lot to that man."

"Yes, we do. And I'll make sure he gets everything he deserves. He's good people."

That he is. About Colonel Brewer…"

"Colonel Brewer is mine, Sara. Forget him, I'll handle him."

"You'll have to go a long way to do that. Thule, in Greenland. They transferred him, some liaison post with the Air Force."

"Thule?"

"Think of 'cold, remote military outpost' and you're thinking of Thule. It's the most northerly base in the world owned by the U.S. and about nine hundred and fifty miles from the North Pole, in Northern Greenland. Wall-to-wall ice and snow, and that's life at Thule. They built it to warn against incoming missiles, but there haven't been any. Not likely to be any either, so it's peaceful in those parts. Good time for a soldier to reflect on where his career went wrong while he's freezing his ass off. By the way, they gave his unit to newly promoted Major Stevens."

"So it's over."

"It's over. When will I see you?"

He thought of Madeleine, and then Sara, and how close they were in looks, in spirit, in personality, and in their personal bravery. Too many similarities, and he didn't want Sara going the same way.

"I'll call you. Take care."

He cut her off, feeling miserable, yet determined to keep her safe. Took a long shot of booze, and he still hadn't heard from Ivan. He looked in on Wyatt, who was already sitting up, drowning in Ma's mothering care. He didn't need to stay. The two were getting on well, so he went to the one place he could call home, his real home where his family lived and worked. Mehtar Lam. Ahmed and Archer rushed outside when they heard his Wrangler approaching, and he remembered how much they meant to him.

They're part of me, and I'd die for these kids, the clever, crazy dog, and Greg and Faria's warm friendship.

He fended off Archer's licks and barks, and Faria came out, a smile on her face. "Stoner, what a surprise. I was cooking dinner, will you stay?"

"I'd like nothing better."

He warmed to their lively chatter and cracked jokes with the kids, answered Ahmed's grave enquiries about what was going on in the world, and listened with solemn attention when the girls told him how they would save the world when they grew older. He felt exhausted by their energy, and after the meal, he and Greg went outside for another cigar. Each man carried a glass of Bourbon, courtesy of the small stock the Blums kept for his visit. When he was sure they weren't overheard, Greg asked him the question he didn't want to hear.

"Any word from Khan?"

"Nothing."

"Maybe he's dead."

"Not Khan, no. He's alive. Men like him don't just die. They have to exterminated."

He stopped, as the headlamps of a vehicle cut through the early evening twilight and swept into view. A Humvee, and he felt a mix of joy and misery. The vehicle parked close to them, and a soldier got out. An officer in camos, and she carried an M4 in one hand, with a pistol holster on her belt.

"Hello, Sara."

She nodded. "Stoner. I thought you might be here. I called to see Wyatt, and you weren't at home."

"He's doing well, recovering, thanks to Ma and her doctor friend."

"He is, yes. How about you?"

"I'm good."

There was an embarrassed silence, interrupted when the door flew open and Faria came out. "Sara, I didn't know you were here. Come in, I'll make some coffee."

"That would be nice." She gave a cold look to Stoner and followed her inside.

"You could have been friendlier," Greg admonished him.

"I know."

It was like a wound, a sharp pain in the belly. He wanted her so bad, and she wanted him.

So why don't I go for it? Because I want her to live!

They sat in silence as the darkness crept up on the farmhouse. The women left them alone, but at least Archer was inclined to want to share his company. He was about to say something about the dog, about how good he looked, when the German Shepherd gave a low growl; a warning from his in-built canine radar. Greg reached to ruffle his ears. "What is it, boy? There a wolf out there?"

The dog stopped growling, and then he cocked his head to one side. His ears went up straight, and this time, he gave out a small whine, a worried whine. Both men had heard it before, and Greg glanced at Stoner. "Trouble."

"Could be."

The headlamps appeared. Huge, glowing, like the eyes of a mythical monster. The vehicle made the turn at the end of the track that led to the farm. For a moment, the silhouette of a BTR-90 appeared in profile.

"Khan."

"Khan," Stoner agreed, "Pity, the vehicle must have been carrying spare headlamps. I'm going out there to face him."

"No!" Sara took hold of his arm to physically stop him, "You can't do that, one man against an AFV. Don't be so stupid."

Gently, he disengaged her arm. "You don't get it, and I don't have time to explain. Just that it's not as simple as you think. I know the kind of psycho he is. It's personal, and he'll want to see me face-to-face before he pulls the trigger. That means showing himself, and I'll be ready. Keep everyone on the floor, just in case."

He exited the house and slammed the door shut behind him, walking away at an oblique angle, so any shooting would not hit the house where they sheltered. The BTR came nearer, and then stopped around a hundred meters away. The engine note died as he switched off, and Stoner waited. Almost a minute elapsed before the hatch swung open, and a head appeared. First the turban, then the eyes, assessing the danger, and then the head and body; his eyes glaring, like hot, dark coals. The beard moved, and he spoke one word, "You!"

He kept his hands away from his guns. If he were going

to beat this guy, it would be by stealth and subterfuge. Khan had a thousand percent advantage in firepower, so it would be pointless trying to trade shots.

"Me. What do you want, Khan?"

The eyes widened. "What do I want? To kill you, of course! You, your friends, and your family. I want to clean your infidel filth from the Earth."

"It doesn't have to be this way, Khan. The people in the house, they're not my family, and they're not involved. Leave them. This is between you and me."

"No!" The single word crashed out, echoing around the hills. "You will all die. Only blood will wash away the insults you have reaped up on me."

He dropped lower in the turret, and Stoner knew he was going for the controls that would sight and trigger the autocannon. He still stared at him, his eyes burning with hate, "If you want to say your prayers, now would be a good time. I suggest you pray to Allah."

"This is you and me, Khan. Why don't you come down here and shoot it out, man-to-man?"

"Don't be a fool."

Then he played his last card, the final throw of the dice that might keep his friends safe. Keep them alive. "Okay, Khan, I get it. Here's my final offer. I can make you rich."

"Rich?"

A spark of interest, and his hopes rose. "I've got money, stashed away. You can have my share of my business. It's all yours. Just let them go."

He contemplated that information for a moment and returned a sneer. "No, I think not. With you out of the way, and this vehicle at my disposal, I can take everything I need. Men will flock to join me, so why should I grant you a concession for something I can have anyway? Goodbye, infidel."

The Afghan dropped down inside the turret, and the barrel of the cannon moved. So did Stoner. He dove to the side, hugging the ground, as the first stream of cannon shells smashed over his head. The shockwave of the heavy burst was awesome, an illustration of the power of the rapid firing weapon over mortal flesh. He was lying in a shallow fold of ground, and the gun couldn't depress far enough to kill him. How long before Khan realized he had only to move the vehicle closer, and he'd be able to chew him into little pieces? Not long, but for the first time since he'd walked out to face the steel monster, and the offer of money had failed, he felt hope.

Khan had made a mistake. The kind of mistake even the greenest soldier wouldn't have made. Standard doctrine with fighting an armored vehicle was to close the hatches before going into battle. For obvious reasons, an open hatch was an invitation to an enemy to lob a grenade inside. Maybe he thought fighting a single man meant he didn't need to take that elementary precaution, but it meant he had a tiny chance. A chink in his armor, and if he could stay alive for the next few moments, if the engine didn't burst to life, and Khan moved closer for the kill, he may get near enough to mount the hull and shoot through the hatch. If he could stay alive.

Too many ifs, and as he steeled himself to make his final run, the engine came to life, and the BTR was moving toward him. He still had a chance. His opponent couldn't drive and shoot simultaneously. He catapulted to his feet and ran, covering the first thirty meters when the vehicle lurched to a stop. He was still running when the barrel of the cannon swiveled toward him. There was no way he could outrun those deadly shells, but sheer, stubborn willpower kept his legs moving.

You can kill me, Khan, but if you think I'll turn away from the inevitable like a coward, you can forget it. It ends here. If you kill me, so be it. But you'd better make sure your aim is damn good, because if you miss, I'm coming for you. And this time, you won't be driving anywhere, except to hell!

The barrel stopped moving and then shifted in a different direction, toward the house. Someone had come outside and was running toward the BTR, firing an AK-47S from the hip, screaming a challenge. He recognized Sara's voice. He felt an icy chill grip him. It was happening again. Another girl he admired, a girl almost the clone of his dead fiancée, and now she was putting herself into the firing line to be torn apart by the deadly shells.

As he ran, he shouted to her, "No, Sara, I can do this. Go back. Hit the deck."

For Christ's sake, live!

He pulled both guns and sighted on the headlamps, but this time, firing on the run was inaccurate. He couldn't stop to take careful aim, and so fired repeatedly, hoping for a lucky shot. One that would once again blind the Afghan psycho and make it impossible for him to find a target. He missed with every bullet. Instead, they flattened themselves on the steel armor. From the corner of his eye, he could see Sara still running, reloading, and then she fired again. She was getting closer, but Khan had identified Stoner as the more dangerous target, and the barrel moved back to him.

No one saw the boy slip out the back door of the house with a dark, brown and black German Shepherd dog. They didn't see Ahmed murmur to the dog, and didn't see the canine start to run, picking up speed until he was sprinting like a thoroughbred racehorse. But he ran into the blaze of headlamps, and in that instant, Khan saw him. Sara saw him, and Stoner saw him. "No!!!"

The cannon roared, but by some uncanny instinct, Archer had swerved to one side, and then he doglegged back the other way. A dog, an almost black dog, the curse of Islam, the unclean creature from hell, and the devil came out to greet this creature. He realized he couldn't get in a good shot on the fast moving, swerving, and jinking target. Khan's head appeared out of the hatch, and then his arms as he brought out an AK-47. His intention was obvious, to kill the dog with a long, murderous burst of automatic fire from the assault rifle.

He lifted it to his shoulder, in full view now, and both Stoner and Sara desperately fired and fired again, missing with every shot. The first burst missed the dog. Archer swerved again, and he was closing. Great slavering jaws opened to tear and maul at the man Ahmed had told him to kill. Khan shifted his aim and paused for a fraction of a second. The dog was close, so close he couldn't miss, and his lips parted in a grim smile of satisfaction. A single shot rang out, and the lips opened wider. The head jerked back, and the bullet flung him back against the edge of the hatch, spraying blood over the hull. Stoner turned to look, and sure enough, Greg was walking out through the front door. He carried the 7.72mm Dragunov, the Russian sniper rifle with which he'd become expert.

Sara caught up with Stoner and flung herself into his arms. "Dammit, you fool, I thought we'd lost you."

He had to force himself back to life. Now he understood. When he started the final run, he'd committed his soul to the Grim Reaper. Hadn't expected to live, and by a miracle, he'd had an unexpected reprieve. He could feel his heart booming against his chest, even his eyesight was blurry, and his limbs felt like lead. But he answered her with a grin.

"A Russian BTR, it never stood a chance. I had him cold."

She stood back and glared. "You bastard." Her blow to

his chest was hard, but she was off balance and fell toward him. Clutched at him, and she looked up in surprise, "You're shivering."

"It's cold tonight."

Sara's eyes bored into him, and she understood. "Of course it is. We'll get you inside; you need a strong drink to warm you. Or something."

He murmured, "I'll take the or something."

She didn't reply, but her eyes sparkled as they met his. Greg still held the Dragunov, and Stoner nodded his thanks. "Not a bad shot. For a Russian gun, anyway."

The Russian half of Greg Blum shot him a scathing look. "This little piece of Russian technology just saved your life, pal. Admit it, Russian gear is the best."

"You're joking. That rifle must have come out of the factory on a good day. Maybe the vodka delivery truck broke down, so they were sober."

"That's crap, and you know it."

"Bullshit."

Faria came through the door with the two girls, her eyes shining. "I can't believe you did it. My God, the two men in my life, a pair of heroes, thank you."

Greg nodded. "He still doesn't get it; this rifle is the best in the business. Listen…"

"Shut up, Greg."

He shut up, and they went inside. Stoner came last, with Ahmed and Archer. He put his arm around the boy's shoulders and patted the dog. "You guys are the best, you know that?"

"Archer is the best," the boy corrected him, his face bursting with pride, "He made it all possible."

"He did that, pal, and no question. He deserves a medal."

"I could get him some fresh bones from the village butcher,"

Ahmed said hopefully.

Stoner dug into his pockets and handed him some bills. "Make it the best."

They went inside, Greg broke out a new bottle of Bourbon, and poured for them all. Even Ahmed had a small glass, suitably diluted. The girls had to make do with soda. When they'd taken the first drink, and he felt better, both men strolled to the BTR. Khan's body lay sprawled and bloody inside the turret. They dragged it out and dug a hole by the manure pile to bury it. The name of Rumi Khan would soon be forgotten. The BTR they drove into an empty barn. Greg said he'd turn it into scrap, rather than sell it on to another would be warlord who would terrorize his neighbors.

They returned to the farmhouse, and Sara took him to one side. "You know what we need when this is all over."

He had plenty of ideas, but he waited.

"A vacation."

It sounded like a plan. "Go on."

"Somewhere warm. Somewhere we could chill out, and put this behind us."

He liked the 'us' part of it. "Count me in."

She smiled then, and for the first time her face relaxed, and he realized how beautiful she was. They swayed together, their lips met and locked, and he felt like an electric current had passed through him. When they parted, she murmured, "Stay alive until then, Stoner. That's an order."

"I wouldn't dream of dying, Lieutenant Carver."

"That's okay, then. We have much to discuss."

Discuss, is that what they call it these days?

"Right."

Eventually, they left to go home, her to report back to her unit. She climbed into the Humvee and drove away. He took longer, saying his farewells to the family, and discussing with Ahmed whether beef or goat would make the tastier bones for Archer. But he was American, and he insisted on beef. He drove back to Jbad, to his home, and felt like a ten-ton weight had lifted off his shoulders. He was alive, he had a date with the prettiest young Lieutenant in all of Asia, and Khan was dead. When he parked outside Ma Kelly's, he felt he'd broken free of the violence that had nearly eaten him up over the years.

He whistled as he sauntered toward his door, the rear entrance to the brothel. When he looked up, the stars shone brightly overhead. Like they were conveying a message, which is why the bullet nearly had him. He almost lost his balance as the events of that night rushed back into his brain, like a tidal wave. He felt dizzy and was close to blacking out, but he stumbled and floundered to keep his balance. The bullet hissed past him and buried itself in the wooden fabric of the building. For precious seconds, he was stunned, too stunned to react. He'd cheated death, for himself and his friends. The sudden attack was an eerie echo of the events of the night.

His brain couldn't process the data, and he did everything wrong. Instead of diving for cover, he stayed in place and searched for the shooter. Didn't draw his guns, didn't find somewhere to shelter from the next bullet, but stood there like a zombie. He was vulnerable. Perhaps for the first time in his life, he was a target, waiting for a bullet to cut him down as surely as if he were standing in front of a firing squad. Then he saw him, standing in the open window of the building opposite. He'd put his head through the opening, into plain view, and was staring down at Stoner. Safe in the knowledge he could do nothing about it. Couldn't draw his guns and return fire, or find somewhere to shelter from the next bullets. Soon he'd be dead.

He recognized him, in the spill of light from an unshaded window coming from the brothel, an old man, too old to be an insurgent. The janitor, the man he'd encountered when he searched for the source of the previous bullet that came from the same place. Last time, he'd wielded nothing more lethal than a broom. This time, it was a rifle. Too far and too dark to identify it, but he'd come close with the first shot, and he could safely assume he'd hit him with the second, or the third.

For long seconds they stared at each other. He willed his thoughts toward the other man, to tell him he was no threat to him. He didn't go around killing old men, and whatever grouse he had, they could thrash it out. But this was Afghanistan, where grudges festered over years, sometimes centuries, and he knew whatever this guy wanted, there'd be no stopping him. In desperation, his mind snapped into focus, and he searched for a way out, but there was none. All he could do was try a rolling dive, and attempt to keep one step ahead of the bullets. The guy was in a commanding position, looking down on him, and the angles were all in his favor.

Face it, Stoner. You've had a good run. All for it to end like this, for a fucking Janitor filling me full of lead outside my own place. No glorious battlefield, the rattle of machine guns, the explosions of grenades, and the war cries of brave men. No salutes for the fallen, just a lonely, squalid death at the hands of Mr. Mop. Floor polisher, garbage disposal man, and assassin.

Their eyes stayed locked for what seemed like an age. As if the shooter wanted to savor his kill. To enjoy watching his final moments, until he, and he alone, decided on the exact moments of Stoner's death. He was still, watching, and then at last, as if he'd sipped at the cup of sadistic enjoyment for long enough, the rifle moved a fraction as he took aim.

The sound of the bullet was loud in the night, louder than

the previous one, for good reason. The rifle was different, the shooter was different, and it came from behind him. The bullet slammed into the janitor, and he slumped to one side. The body contorted in his final death throes, and then he tipped out to plunge to the street. He looked around, and Wyatt Evers was leaning in the doorway to the brothel, a rifle in his hands, Stoner's rifle, the spare M4A1. He'd kept it beside the sofa where he was supposedly resting. Wyatt was that kind of guy, couldn't relax without a rifle close at hand. He was shivering and swaying with exhaustion and fatigue. The man should have been inside an intensive care unit. Instead, he'd become aware of the problem and walked outside, or maybe crawled outside, to help him.

"Wyatt."

"Stoner."

"You got him."

"I did, but how about we take a look and make sure."

Evers made three steps before he almost fell. Stoner caught him, hooked an arm over his shoulder, and helped him on. The man was his kill, so he was entitled to inspect it. Incredibly, he was still alive. The old Afghan stared up at Stoner through hate-filled eyes. "You."

"Yeah. Why did you do it, Grandpa?"

The words were a pain-filled murmur, but he made them out. "My daughter."

"Your daughter? What did I do to hurt her?"

"You made her a whore."

"I'm sorry," he said gently, "That's not the way I operate. You got it wrong. This is all for nothing. When they work in Ma Kelly's, they choose to do it for the money."

"You…took…my…daughter."

Whoever she was, it wasn't the time to argue the point. He

glanced at Wyatt. "We should call an ambulance."

"He'll be dead before it gets here."

"We still have to do the right thing."

He stopped as the man mumbled something else. "What was that?"

"Anahita."

His blood chilled as he began to understand. "What about her?"

"My daughter."

Those two words were the last he'd ever utter. His final breath sighed out of his lips, and his body went still. Anahita, Stoner's favorite whore, was his daughter. It seemed impossible, and yet he'd stated it as a fact with his dying words.

How can I face her, and tell her what happened? Yet I have to tell her the truth.

She meant a lot to him, and they'd become good friends, often sharing a bed. She'd wanted to marry him, settle down, and live a normal life. Now her father was dead.

He'd almost died. After everything he'd said less than an hour ago to Sara Carver, he'd almost stopped a bullet. He should be dead. The curse was still a burden weighing him down, and he'd never be free. Every girl he knew ran the gauntlet of death. And if they didn't die, their families died. In that moment, he knew he'd never make it with Sara. Not if he wanted her to live, and he wanted her to live more than anything else in the world.

I'm sorry, Sara. I'll make up a story, and you'll go home to the U.S and get over it. I'll carry on. Dodging bullets, and living out my penance in this shithole they call Afghanistan. Why do I stay? I don't know. It's my home, I guess. My family is here, Greg, Faria, and the kids. Even Archer. One day, they'll need me again to step between them and a bullet.

He dragged the body off the street and hid it in the alleyway, just another victim of a random shooting.

I won't tell Anahita how it happened. How can I? If I talk to her, it will ruin her life. But I'll never sleep with her, not again. Not after tonight. Nor will I sleep with Sara Carver. I'm death, a dark shadow walking the Earth.

His mind cleared. He fastened his arms around Wyatt and helped him up. "How about we go inside? I reckon I owe you a few drinks. That was good shooting."

"You got it."

They went through the door, and Stoner almost carried him up the stairs. They were two men. One who'd come back to life after many years of living on a bleak mountainside like a crazed hermit.

The other had looked at life, considered it for a good, long while, and waved farewell. He was death.